Promises to Keep

Tales from Grace Chapel Inn

Promises to Keep

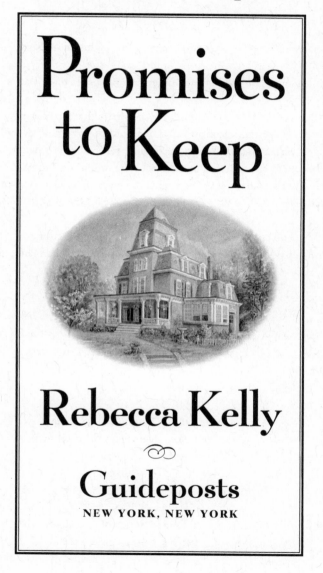

Rebecca Kelly

Guideposts

NEW YORK, NEW YORK

Acknowledgments

All Scripture quotations are taken from *The Holy Bible, New International
Version.* Copyright © 1973, 1978, 1984 International Bible Society.
Used by permission of Zondervan Bible Publishers.

Guideposts.org
(800) 932-2145
Guideposts Books & Inspirational Media
Series Editors: Regina Hersey and Leo Grant
Cover art by Edgar Jerins
Cover design by Wendy Bass
Interior design by Cindy LaBreacht
Typeset by Planet Patti, Inc.
Printed in the United States of America
10 9 8 7 6 5 4

Chapter One

A spring storm swept across the grassy knolls and buttercup-speckled fields of southeastern Pennsylvania to shower over the little town of Acorn Hill. It brought the softest of rains, a gentle cascade that pattered merrily on wood-shingled rooftops and bejeweled every windowpane with crystalline beads. The melancholy clouds that ushered in the storm moped around long enough to wash the air with a crisp, new freshness before they drifted past a graceful old house near the outskirts of town.

Louise Howard Smith shook the heaviest droplets from her umbrella and closed it neatly before she entered the front door of the old house. Her childhood home, now a thriving bed and breakfast that she and her sisters had named Grace Chapel Inn, bore the rain with the same calm dignity that had witnessed the passage of many such storms. Today the inn reminded her of a grand old lady, her shoulders artfully draped in a diamanté cape as she looked with approval and satisfaction over a well-tended garden.

"I know April showers bring May flowers," Louise's sister, Jane Howard, said from the reception desk. She had a large, heavy book open before her and was idly turning pages as she rested her cheek against her palm. "But are we getting too much of a good thing?"

"Are you referring to the mudslide in your garden?" Louise hung the umbrella by its loop to dry on the beech coatrack near the front door.

"Don't even kid about my garden, if you please." Jane wagged a finger, making the copper and agate-beaded bracelet on her wrist jingle. The beads matched the vivid colors of the cerulean-and-bronze paisley dress she wore, and suited the most adventurous Howard sister perfectly. "Good thing you remembered to take an umbrella or you would have been soaked. How is Aunt Ethel?"

Just before the storm struck, Louise had walked over to the inn's carriage house, in which their late father's widowed sister, Ethel Buckley, resided.

"She was very grateful for the loaf of potato-herb bread you sent over. She plans to make Irish stew this afternoon and said it will go perfectly with it." Louise removed a pale green, cotton knit sweater from the coat closet. The weather had been on the cool side for spring and combined with the rain-washed air to make her feel momentarily chilled. "I hope she has the time to cook. She received five phone calls while I was there."

"Really?" Jane closed the book on the desk. "Did something happen in town?"

Ethel Buckley was inordinately fond of gossip, and collected it from her various and sometimes mysterious sources whenever she could. She prided herself on her long-standing reputation for being the first to know anything that happened to anyone in town, and she regularly passed along her gleanings to her nieces.

Louise smiled. "It seems that Roland Jones has proposed marriage to Edna Grassnickle, and Edna has accepted."

Jane's eyes widened. "Roland and Edna, getting *married*?" Her voice rose comically on the last word.

The news had also startled Louise at first, until she recalled the number of times she had seen the widowed Edna seated beside Roland during services at Grace Chapel. They were both quiet, reserved people, and thus their friendship had seemed only natural. Now, to the astonishment of the entire congregation, it was apparent that the couple had been enjoying a private courtship.

Ethel, on the other hand, had claimed not to be surprised at all at the news.

"I knew something was brewing between those two at the last meeting of the Seniors Social Circle," she told Louise during her visit to the carriage house. "Roland insisted on driving Edna home."

"How does offering a ride equal a marriage proposal, Aunt?" Louise wanted to know.

Ethel chuckled. "Edna accepted the ride. I had to stop and remind her that her grandniece had driven her to the meeting and was coming to pick her up."

"Good point," said Louise.

"Roland and Edna," Jane repeated, shaking her head and making the long ponytail of her dark hair sway. "Aren't they both in their early eighties?"

Louise smiled a little. To Jane, the newly engaged couple seemed ancient. "Indeed, they are."

"That's simply outrageous."

"That is life, which does not end at sixty, I assure you," she corrected dryly. Louise checked her ecru skirt and the shoulders of the matching sleeveless shell for damp spots. Unlike the audacious Jane, she preferred to wear subtle, gentle colors that complemented her fair skin and neatly cropped silver hair. "Aunt Ethel will doubtless have all the details by tomorrow."

"Maybe I should invite her for tea today. That would give me an excuse to stop hunting through these books and go whip up something special." Jane closed the book before her with a decided thump and placed it on top of a stack of five others. "How do you feel about having some toasted buttermilk crumpets with cream and apricot jam?"

"Very enthusiastic, as long as I do not think what they will do to the width of my hips." Louise walked over and examined the titles embossed on the spines of the stacked books. *"The Complete Works of John Keats,"* she read out loud. *"The Age of the Romantics. The Pastoral Tennyson."* She knew Jane liked FBI thrillers and the occasional romance novel, but she had never once observed her reading verses from anything but the Bible. "What brought about this sudden interest in poetry?"

"I wanted to use a line from a poem on our Web site, to caption the photo gallery page for our gardens," Jane explained. One of her pet projects was maintaining Grace Chapel Inn's Web site, which had drawn a considerable amount of business for the sisters. "The only problem is that I can't remember the title, the poet or the exact wording."

"That would certainly make finding it difficult. What *do* you remember about the poem?"

"It went something like, 'To see eternity like a grain of sand, hold a flower in the palm of your hand.'" Jane gave her a hopeful look. "You read a lot of poetry, Louise. Does any of that sound familiar?"

"It does, vaguely." Louise searched her memory, but the identity of the verse proved to be just as elusive for her. "How long ago did you read this?"

"In high school, I think. I tried searching for it on the Internet, but nothing came up. I think I have the wording wrong. Maybe it was, 'To see eternity with a grain of salt'?" Jane grimaced. "I knew I should have paid more attention in English class."

"Are we reminiscing about our school days?" Alice Howard, Jane and Louise's middle sister, came out of the kitchen. She wore her white nurse's uniform, since she was scheduled to work a shift at Potterston Hospital that afternoon. Two gold slides kept her bobbed, brown hair back from her pleasant face and brought out the warmth of her golden brown eyes.

"Sort of. I'm trying to remember a line from a poem I read in school." Jane repeated what she had told Louise, and added, "It was lovely and simple, but very profound. Something about finding eternity in a grain of sand or salt, or maybe flowers. Does any of that ring a bell?"

"No, I'm afraid it doesn't, but I was never one for reading much poetry." Alice gave her a sympathetic look. "Why don't you use something from the Bible instead? There are several wonderful verses about gardens, such as Genesis 2:9. 'And the Lord God made all kinds of trees grow out of the ground—trees that were pleasing to the eye and good for food.'"

"That really makes me think more of orchards than gardens," Jane said.

"All right, what about Job 8:16? 'He is like a well-watered plant in the sunshine, spreading its shoots over the garden,'" Alice quoted.

"Shoots?" Jane's dark eyebrows arched. "You mean, like kudzu, strangler figs and poison ivy?"

Louise suppressed an involuntary chuckle. "*Jane.*"

Alice tapped a finger against her lips as she thought. "Well, then Luke 13:19 might do. 'It is like a mustard seed, which a man took and planted in his garden. It grew, became a tree, and the birds of the air perched in its branches.'"

"I believe that was Jesus' description of the kingdom of God," Louise put in. "While our gardens are delightful, I would rather we not make such a presumptuous comparison."

"That's a good point, Louise," Alice said. "I'm sorry, Jane, but I can't think of anything else that would be appropriate. I'd ask Pastor Thompson, but he's out of town until Sunday morning."

"See? This is hopeless." Jane sighed. "Never mind. I'll just put 'The Gardens at Grace Chapel Inn' on the page and be done with it."

Louise was too intrigued now to allow her sister to give up the hunt. She also knew the perfect person to ask. "I have to go to town to pick up something that I ordered from the bookshop," she told Jane. "Let me consult with Viola and see if she recognizes the verse."

Viola Reed, the owner of the Nine Lives Bookstore, was one of Louise's closest friends. A single woman in her sixties who lived with fourteen cats in a grand old Victorian house in town, Viola was considered both eccentric and stubbornly opinionated, particularly when it came to the reading habits of the local residents.

As if responding to the sound of Viola's name, Wendell, the family tabby cat, wandered out from the study and rubbed his head against Louise's ankle. Absently she scooped him up and scratched the small, furry space between his ears.

The pampered pet began to purr as his paws curled with feline bliss.

"Does Viola read poetry?" Alice asked.

"She does indeed. Viola is one of the best-read women I know, and her memory is formidable. It often makes mine resemble a sieve." Louise placed Wendell back on the floor. "If you do not mind managing things here for an hour, Jane, I will go now."

Jane had no objections, so Louise retrieved her purse and car keys from behind the desk.

"Oh dear, I'm going to be late for work if I don't hurry," Alice said as she checked her watch. "Louise, would you mind dropping off something at the hardware store? Just give this to Fred." She removed a sealed envelope from the pocket of her skirt. "I promised Vera I'd get this recipe to her today."

Hardware store owner and town handyman Fred Humbert's wife Vera was one of Alice's dearest friends.

"It should be no trouble." Louise put down Wendell, accepted it and tucked it into her purse. "Shall I give Fred any message to pass along to Vera?"

Wendell yawned and wandered off to investigate a new patch of sun on the floor.

"No, she's made it before, she just needed a list of the ingredients. I'll eat at the hospital, so don't worry about me for dinner. See you tonight." With that Alice hurried out of the inn.

∽

Louise waited a few minutes to be sure that the storm was not going to make a return visit, and then drove off to town. She enjoyed driving her old white Cadillac. It was one of the few luxuries she allowed herself. Taking little trips in it now and then made her feel young at heart.

When she arrived at the bookshop, she saw a small package and bound stack of envelopes sitting outside the entrance. Louise paused to pick them up, and noticed a trio of small, furry faces watching her.

Three cats sat in a row just inside the beveled glass door of the shop. The smallest, Kane, a tiny black-and-white feline that was marked as if wearing a formal tuxedo, darted off as soon as Louise placed her hand on the doorknob. The other two, Diver, a huge tabby with a completely white underside, and Ahab, a sleeker, ghostly gray tom with a crooked hind leg, regarded her with faintly indignant expressions as she stepped inside.

"Too wet for you and your pal to sun yourselves outside today, is it?" Louise asked the two remaining cats. She had often encountered the pair napping beside Viola while she sat reading on the bench just in front of her shop. "No wonder you look so disgusted with the world."

Diver sprawled on the floor in front of her shoes and rolled over like a playful puppy. He was one of those cats who enjoyed having his belly scratched, and he begged for attention from anyone who entered the shop. The more dignified Ahab stalked off with his usual stiff-legged hobble, his long tail standing straight up.

"Hi, Louise." Viola Reed emerged from the bookcases with one hand smoothing her short, steel-gray hair.

Louise always admired her friend's tastes in color and style, however eccentric they could sometimes be. Wherever Viola went, she usually made a statement without saying a single word.

Today the bookshop owner had donned comfortable, jade-colored slacks, paired with a long-sleeved ivory blouse with ribbon-embroidered flowers on the collar tips and breast pocket. A bright, floral silk scarf lay draped artfully around her neck. The ends of the scarf were tied in such a way as to resemble a large flower.

"Hello." Louise held up the package and bundle of mail she had found outside the door. "This was left outside."

"Oh, drat that postman." Viola's brown eyes showed her annoyance. "My regular carrier, Norbert Meinhard, is on vacation, and this substitute fellow has yet to step one foot inside the shop." Viola peered through the bottom of her bifocals to read the label.

"Perhaps he thinks if he opens the door, the cats will run out into the street." Louise had assumed the same the first time that she had come to the shop.

"Silly man. They're cats, not dogs." Viola placed the package on her desk. "You're here to pick up your order, aren't you?" Without waiting for an answer, she went around the desk and opened a drawer. "I have it right here."

"That, and to ask for your help with something." Louise took out the scrap of paper on which Jane had written what she could remember of the hard-to-pin-down verse.

"Are you looking for a book recommendation? All you seem to read lately are biographies," Viola commented as she bagged the large book Louise had ordered about the life and times of famous composers. "That will be nineteen ninety-five, by the way."

She handed her friend a twenty-dollar bill. "Are you sure about the price? I thought that book listed at twenty-six dollars."

"I found it on a remainder list for less," Viola told her. "Now, what are you interested in reading? I don't think you've given John Steinbeck a proper chance, and as it happens, I just got in a beautiful edition of *Cannery Row*."

Ever since Viola had opened the Nine Lives Bookstore, she made it her personal crusade to improve the reading habits of her customers. As her friend, Louise was not exempt from well-intentioned advice.

"I believe I have enough to read with this, but I will consider it on my next visit," she said with as much tact as she could muster. "The reason I need your expertise today is to identify a mysterious verse my sister Jane would like to quote on our Grace Chapel Inn Web site." She turned as the entrance doorbell jingled and Vera Humbert came into the shop and exchanged greetings with Viola and Louise.

"Is school out early today?" Viola asked.

"It's a teacher planning day, so the kids are off, and I only had to be at school a half-day." Vera smiled at Louise. "Don't let me interrupt you two. I'm just going to look for the latest military thriller for Fred."

Louise took the envelope Alice had given her out of her purse, but by then Fred's wife had wandered to the back of the store. "I have a recipe to give you before you leave, Vera," she called out to her. "It is from Alice."

"Military thrillers." Viola made a dismissive sound.

Although Louise herself didn't care much for that particular type of book, she did not share Viola's contempt for most modern best sellers. "I have not read any, but my sisters certainly enjoy them. I believe Jane is presently working her way through a series about spies and submarines."

"Your sisters need to hunt for better ways to occupy their free time." Viola eyed the scrap of paper Louise held. "What is this verse Jane wants?"

"It is apparently from a famous poem, but neither she nor I can recall the author, title or exact words." She read what Jane had written on the paper.

"Ah. That was written by William Blake, and is the opening verse to 'Auguries of Innocence,'" Viola told her. "The precise wording is

"To see a world in a grain of sand
And a heaven in a wild flower,
Hold infinity in the palm of your hand,
And eternity in an hour."

Her friend's flawless memory astonished Louise. She quickly jotted down the information for Jane, and then asked, "Is this one of your favorite poems?"

"One of many. I especially like the ending," Viola said, and then recited,

"God appears, and God is light,
To those poor souls who dwell in night;
But does a human form display
To those who dwell in realms of day."

"What a fascinating notion," Louise responded. *One that I hope we will not have to discuss.* When it came to faith, Viola could be quite caustic, and her unorthodox viewpoints often directly challenged Louise to defend her own beliefs.

Today her friend didn't seem interested in debating God or religion, however. "Blake was a complicated soul." Viola went to one of the front bookcases and selected a slim volume. "There is a copy of it in this edition of his selected works if you'd like to read the entire poem. It was one of his longer works."

Vera, who had come out of the back of the shop and had apparently overheard their conversation, tucked the paperback book she carried under her arm and applauded.

"Amazing! How in the world did you remember all that, Viola?"

"I have a soft spot in my heart for verse," the bookshop owner confessed. "Particularly works by great poets like Blake. His work sounds simple, but the meanings behind the verses are very deep."

Vera, who was a grammar school teacher, seemed intrigued. "How so?"

"Blake was unhappy with the church and government of his time, as they were often corrupt," Viola replied. "He brought out his feelings in his poems. His vivid images and simple words were easy for the reader to understand, but they were very profound, too. Although they had different styles, I've often thought that Blake's talent rivaled Wordsworth's."

"Now I'm utterly impressed." Vera held out her hand. "And I must have this Blake book." She glanced at Louise. "That is, if it has not already been spoken for."

Louise made a casual gesture. "I believe my father's library has Blake's complete works, so please, go right ahead."

"My favorite of Blake's work has always been 'The Tyger,'" Viola told Vera as she wrapped up the paperback novel and the poetry collection. "If there was ever a poem that shows how two-sided man's nature is, it's that one."

"Blake asks questions that stay with you," Louise added. "Some of the lines from 'The Tyger' are extraordinarily thought-provoking."

Viola gave her a shrewd look. "I imagine two of them were 'Did he smile his work to see? / Did he who made the Lamb make thee?'"

That startled Louise. "How did you know?"

"I know *you*, Louise." The bookshop owner smiled. "But you shouldn't let those lines scare you. Blake was only saying that life is a personal journey. We all start out as innocent and helpless as lambs. As we grow older, we have to be more self-sufficient, like the tiger. He believed that to live fully, we have to see life both through the eyes of innocence and experience. They balance us."

"Oh, Viola." Awe replaced the surprise in Vera's expression. "That was so eloquent. You should give a talk about poetry."

The bookshop owner shrugged. "Who wants to listen to an old woman natter on about poetry these days?" She held out Vera's bag and added slyly, "Certainly not your husband."

Vera chuckled. "No, Fred likes poetry about as much as he likes attending the opera or the ballet, which is to say only when the girls and I make him. What I meant was, I'd love to see you give a talk to the poetry club over at Franklin High School."

"Do you have a new assignment?" Louise knew Vera had been teaching for several years at the local grammar school.

"No, but I have a friend, Eleanor Renda, who works at Franklin as a P.E. teacher. She's also supervising the poetry club this year. Since her expertise is more in exercise and sports, she's been looking for someone to talk to her kids. The club is working to publish a magazine with poems written by the students this year, but they've never done it before."

"A physical education teacher supervising a poetry club?" Viola's eyebrows arched. "That seems an unlikely match."

"The English teacher who usually serves as moderator of the club had other commitments this year and was unable to do it." Vera grimaced. "Eleanor volunteered—under some pressure—to take her place."

Viola shook her head. "I can't see myself talking to a bunch of teenagers."

"Most of the work—the heavy lifting—has been completed. Eleanor is just looking for someone to provide some advice and inspiration," Vera assured her as she paid for the books. "These kids are having a tough time finding the right direction to take in finishing this magazine project, and apparently the poets they've studied aren't providing much inspiration."

"Poetry can be quite difficult for young people to comprehend," Louise agreed, thinking of her own youthful struggles to fathom epic poems like *Beowulf*. "The language alone can seem like a secret code."

"Great poetry has the right to demand certain efforts by its readers," Viola said. "It takes careful thought and reflection, as well as guidance, to find the meaning behind the verses."

"According to Eleanor, the kids in this club need that sort of thing," Vera said. "Viola, you know so much about books and poetry. I really believe that you'd be an ideal speaker, and they'd jump at the chance to have you."

"I just bet they would." Viola gave Louise an ironic look. "Oh, I would just *love* to help the little dears." A faint rattle made her turn toward the front window, and her expression changed. "Aha! There you are, you little sneak."

Louise followed her friend's gaze to the bench outside. On it, a straggly looking cat with white, orange and black calico fur was climbing up on the seat, attracted to the dish of dry cat food Viola had left there. A dingy-colored flea collar encircled its neck, and the poor creature was unkempt, with visibly dirty fur and with a sore festering on the rim of its right ear. It looked from side to side before it began feasting from the dish. Its neck and legs resembled matchsticks, while its belly appeared quite swollen.

"Excuse me, ladies." Viola came around the desk and, never taking her eyes off the small cat, eased the door open an inch. "Here, now, Tess," she murmured, using a soft voice to catch the little feline's attention. "I was hoping you'd show up again."

"Tess" gave Viola a wary look from her large, golden eyes and, despite her evident hunger, took a step back away from the dish.

"It's all right, little darling. I put that dish out there for you." Viola began to push the door open.

Louise glanced up. "Viola, the b—"

Before she could complete the warning, the bell above Viola's head jingled. The sound made the calico cat leap from the bench and dart around the side of the building.

"Wait, Tess, don't run away again." Viola hurried out after it.

Vera and Louise watched Viola give chase, but Tess was faster than her heavyset pursuer. Both disappeared behind the bookshop, but Louise doubted her friend would catch the stray.

"I think it's marvelous how Viola always looks out for the stray cats in town," Vera murmured as she tucked the two books she had purchased into her purse. "Did you say you had something for me, Louise?"

"Yes. Alice asked me to drop off this with Fred so that he could give it to you." She handed over the unmarked envelope. "Are you quite certain you want to cook one of Alice's recipes?"

Alice Howard rarely prepared meals, and when she did, she made easy things like salads, soups and sandwiches. Anything else had to be approached with extreme caution.

Vera laughed. "This is one of your Aunt Ethel's recipes, actually. Alice just copied it out of her cookbook for me."

Before Louise could ask which recipe her sister had copied—Aunt Ethel was very possessive with recipes for things like her prize-winning peach tarts—two elderly lady tourists, both wearing straw hats and carrying shopping bags, entered the bookstore.

"Does this shop sell used as well as new books?" one of them asked Louise.

Vera touched her arm. "I should go and call Eleanor and tell her the good news. I know the poetry club will really like having Viola as a guest speaker. Have a great day, Louise." She smiled at the two older women and went toward the door.

"Oh, but Vera—" Before Louise could correct Vera's assumption, the second lady tourist asked if there was a restroom available. By the time Louise had given the two women answers, Vera was gone.

Chapter  Two

Viola returned to the shop a few minutes later, flushed and out of breath. Diver, the chubby attention-seeker, yowled as he met her at the door. With absent-minded movements of long familiarity, Viola stepped over him and reached down to pet him at the same time, an action that caused her to trip.

"Are you all right?" Louise inspected her friend closely. Viola had the unhappy trait of being accident-prone—often quite serious accidents at that—and yet she somehow miraculously escaped permanent injury each time. She had named her store "Nine Lives" to reflect her self-deprecating attitude about her brushes with disaster.

"Fine, although I should have named that little sneak Wonder Woman instead of Tess." Viola took a tissue from the box on her desk and blotted her damp brow. "I think she runs the hundred yard dash in four seconds."

"You should not have tried to do the same," Louise scolded her.

One of the elderly ladies reappeared. "Excuse me, but could you help me find a book? I can remember the title, but not the name of the author."

"That appears to be my specialty today, ma'am." Viola gave Louise a wry smile and went to assist her customers. It was several minutes before she returned to her desk.

"I wish I knew how to lure Tess back here." Viola regarded the bench in front of the shop. "Maybe I'll set out some flaked tuna fish in oil. I've never known one of mine to pass up that sort of treat."

"Are you going to place her in the shelter?" Louise asked, referring to Acorn Hill's no-kill cat shelter, which Viola had founded and funded with her own money.

"Not until after Tess has her litter, and her kittens are old enough to be weaned." Viola sat down in the chair behind her desk. "I saw her skulking around the garbage bins six weeks ago, and she had a little tummy then. I haven't been able to get within ten feet of her, but the normal gestation period for a domestic cat is fifty-eight to sixty-five days. That means she'll be having her babies any day now."

Louise recalled the stray's oddly swollen belly. Some of the stray dogs her sister had taken to the no-kill shelter in Potterston had carried a horde of internal parasites and had been in similar shape. "If you could not get close to her, how can you be so certain that she is pregnant, or even a female?"

"Besides the fact that I've delivered hundreds of kittens, and know exactly what a breeding female looks like?" Her friend gave her an ironic glance. "The fact is, some coat colors in cats are linked to the chromosome that determines gender. Calicoes, for that reason, are almost always born female. There are genetic glitches now and then that turn out to be male, but they're usually unable to provide kittens."

"It always astounds me, how much you know about felines." Louise smiled. "Where did you come up with the name Tess for your latest friend?"

"After the heroine of Thomas Hardy's *Tess of the D'Urbervilles*." Viola sighed. "I'd like to see my Tess enjoy a happier fate than that of her namesake. If I can catch her, I'll bring her home and look after her until she has her litter. Once they're weaned, I know I can find good homes for the kittens."

Louise had no doubt she would succeed. A quarter of the pet cats in town had been given by Viola to their current owners. "Do you think Tess once belonged to someone in Acorn Hill?"

The bookshop owner shook her head. "There's no license on her collar, and I've already asked around town, but no one has claimed her. I think she may have strayed over from Potterston or jumped ship from one of the RVs the tourists regularly drive through town."

Louise knew that Alice had found homes for several abandoned dogs over the years. "It is a shame that her original owners did not have her spayed."

Viola nodded. "Most people don't bother, which is why up to three-quarters of all female stray cats are found either pregnant, lactating or in heat."

Louise had no idea that the problem was so prevalent. "That is terrible."

"Her former owners weren't just irresponsible. The way Tess behaves—so terrified just at the sight of people—makes me think that she's been kicked around." She thumped an angry hand against the desk top. "Why can't people treat animals with common decency?"

"Most do," Louise reminded her. Like Viola and the Howard sisters, many people in Acorn Hill were animal lovers who looked after their pets with loving attention. Her own sister Alice was a staunch defender of animal rights. "It could be that she has lived as a stray for so long that she has turned wild, Viola."

"I can teach her to be gentle again," her friend insisted. "All she needs is a little time and TLC."

"Speaking of *teaching*, I believe that Vera Humbert took you seriously, by the way."

Viola seemed puzzled. "Seriously about what?"

"Your giving a talk to those high school students in Franklin's poetry club. You told her that you would do it, and she said just before she left that she would call her teacher friend right away so that she could arrange it."

The redness returned to Viola's face. "Good grief, Louise. Couldn't you have told her that I was only kidding?"

"I intended to, but unfortunately your customers distracted me, and Vera left in the interim." Louise stepped to one side as the two lady tourists reappeared with their arms filled with paperback novels. She waited until Viola rang up their purchases and they left the shop before she asked, "What are you going to do?"

"I'm going to call Vera and tell her it was all just a bad joke." Viola reached to pick up the phone.

Louise forestalled her by placing a hand on the receiver. "Before you talk to her, you and I should go and have a cup of tea."

Viola gave her a brooding look. "You're stalling me."

"I am thirsty," Louise fibbed without a shred of guilt. "So are you."

Viola checked the time and released a sigh. "Well, I haven't taken my afternoon break yet, and Tess might have strayed over toward Clarissa's."

Louise waited as her friend put up her out-to-lunch sign and locked up the bookshop, and then escorted her over to the Good Apple Bakery. Clarissa Cottrell, the owner, hailed them as they came in.

"Good afternoon, ladies." Clarissa put down clean napkins and utensils for them. "I just finished frosting an eight-layer, mint chocolate torte, if you're interested."

"You won't be happy until I weigh three hundred pounds," Viola grumbled.

"If you're worried about your figure, come on in the back and work with me for a couple of hours," the baker joked. "That'll melt off any extra pounds."

"In all that heat?" Viola was incredulous. "Take my money instead. Please."

Clarissa grinned. "Can't make cake without heating up some ovens."

"I don't know how you stand it, but it does explain why you're so slender." The bookshop owner gave Clarissa a faintly envious glance.

"I think we will have a pot of Earl Grey, Clarissa, and two of your apple turnovers," Louise said wisely, nodding toward the luscious assortment of pastries in the glass display case.

Clarissa nodded. "Coming right up. Yell if you change your mind, Viola. I have a big order of sandwich bread to bake for the Coffee Shop, and with one of my girls out sick I could sure use the help."

"I'll give it some serious consideration."

Once the baker had served their tea and pastries, Louise casually returned to the matter of the poetry club talk. "Before you run off to call Vera Humbert, I think you should reconsider. You have a great deal to offer these students."

Viola dropped two cubes of sugar into her cup and stirred it. The delicate scent of bergamot, which Louise had always thought made Earl Grey tea taste the way violets smell, filled the air.

"I told you before, teenagers aren't interested in listening to an old bookworm like me."

Naturally Viola would think that. Although she wasn't in the least bit shy, she had distinct and long-standing reservations about younger people. "In the Bible, Proverbs 8:1–2 says, 'Does not wisdom call out? Does not understanding raise her voice? On the heights along the way, where the paths meet, she takes her stand.'"

"I'd rather sit, thank you very much," Viola snapped, and forked off a bite of turnover.

Louise smiled a little. "It is not like you to back down from a challenge."

"I'm not backing down." She jabbed her fork in the air with no small amount of indignation. "I have nothing to offer those children. Nothing that they'd find of use, anyway."

"You might surprise them and yourself, Viola. Proverbs 8:10–11 tells us, 'Choose my instruction instead of silver, knowledge rather than choice gold, for wisdom is more precious than rubies, and nothing you desire can compare with her.'"

The bookshop owner snorted. "Offer them silver, gold and rubies, and watch what happens."

A young mother with two small boys entered the bakery. Louise had to smile as she watched the brothers eagerly rush to the glass front of the display case, in which chocolate, fruit, and golden-brown Snickerdoodles were arranged in pyramid-shaped stacks. Although the mother was only there to purchase some bread and rolls, Clarissa kindly handed over two free cookies to her young patrons, for which they repaid her with big grins.

"There are more important things than material wealth," Louise chided, drawing inspiration from the boys' delight. "Young people need the wealth of knowledge and wisdom that you possess. Some obviously love poetry or they wouldn't have formed a club. Would you begrudge sharing what you know with them, simply because they are not our age?" Before her friend could answer, she added, "Would you deny Tess what she needs, simply because she is young and runs wild?"

Viola frowned, but a glimmer of indecision entered her gaze, and she sipped her tea. Finally she shook her head. "It's not the same thing."

"I believe it is." Louise sat back. "You freely discuss books and give advice here to anyone who comes to Nine Lives. All Vera is really asking is that you do the same at the school."

"If I bore them, or they laugh at me, I'll feel like a ninny for trying." Viola's voice dropped to a murmur. "To be honest, Louise, it's simply the idea of going to a high school that puts me on edge."

Louise frowned. "Heavens, why?"

"I hated my high school. The classrooms were so small they almost made me claustrophobic, and the other kids teased me unmercifully. I think I spent every spare minute I could hiding out in the library."

There was the crux of the matter. "We could arrange to have the talk at the library, or perhaps somewhere outside the school itself."

Viola thought it over. "I'd rather talk anywhere than in a classroom. Even the school cafeteria." She glared across the table. "I should have known you'd coax me into this. You're always doing that."

"Do not discount your own efforts." Louise smiled. "C. S. Lewis said, 'The very man who has argued you down, will sometimes be found, years later, to have been influenced by what you said.'"

"I should live so long." The bookseller's expression softened a degree. "Very well, I'll give it a try."

"Marvelous."

Viola held up a hand. "There's one condition. You have to come with me." Before Louise could react, she added gruffly, "You're better with children than I am, and I could use the moral support."

The vulnerability in Viola's eyes touched her heart. "I would be glad to, but I would have to check with my sisters to be sure they don't need me at the inn. You know that you really do not need me there, my dear."

"Two are better than one," the bookseller insisted. "Whoever said that knew what he was talking about."

"That comes from the Bible, Ecclesiastes 4:9–10. 'Two are better than one, because they have a good return for their work: If one falls down, his friend can help him up. But pity the man who falls and has no one to help him up!'"

Viola smiled. "See? Even God thinks you should come with me."

"I could bring some of my own favorite literary magazines to show as examples to the students." Louise thought of several that might interest the aspiring writers.

"Good idea. If they hate my talk, then you can distract them with the pretty pictures."

"Give yourself, and them, a chance." Louise refilled their cups, and then lifted hers in a toast. "To great poets, brave booksellers and the children whom they will inspire."

Viola touched the rim of her cup to Louise's. "To crazy ideas, nagging innkeepers and not making complete fools of ourselves."

∽

Over dinner that evening, Louise told her sisters about her visit to town and what had happened at Viola Reed's shop.

"How pretty that sounds," Jane said after Louise recited the correct wording of the Blake poem that Viola had identified. "I'll post it to the Web site tonight." She filled each of their glasses with a sparkling, lemon-flavored mineral water. "What's the matter, Alice? Would you rather have something else to drink?"

"Oh no, this is fine," Alice said, her frown vanishing. "I was just thinking of poor Tess."

Louise had related the plight of the elusive, soon-to-be mother calico, and had expected that the story would immediately capture animal lover Alice's interest. "It is a shame that her owner abandoned her so cruelly. As skittish as Tess appears to be, I think Viola will have a difficult time catching her."

"It's not Tess's fault. Cats revert very quickly to the feral side of their nature when they're abandoned. They have to in order to survive." Alice frowned again. "She'll have it so much harder when her litter is born and she has to feed her kittens. If any of them survive."

"Won't she hide them away, to keep them safe?" Jane asked.

"She'll seek the most secure spot she can to birth them, but a day or two after she'll have to leave them unguarded while she hunts for food. They won't have her to drive off any predators that come along." Alice's expression turned gloomy. "Last week I read a Humane Society article about the problem of stray cats. Did you know that half of the kittens born in the wild don't make it?"

"That's not fair." Now Jane sounded upset. "They're just defenseless little babies."

"However much we dislike it, that is the natural way of things," Louise advised her sadly. "If predators did not provide population control, we would be virtually overrun with feral cats."

"But Tess wasn't born feral, and nature doesn't always have to win, does it?" A light of battle glowed in Alice's gentle eyes. "I'm sure I can do something to help Viola."

"As long as your help does not entail bringing this cat or any of her kittens here," Louise said firmly. "Please remember that our Wendell is used to having the inn to himself, and I doubt he would take kindly to having his kingdom invaded."

"It might be dangerous to Tess and her babies, too," Alice said, surprising her with the agreement. "Wendell is an old darling, but he's also an adult male cat, and they don't always take kindly to new kittens."

A chuckle escaped Jane.

"Do you find that amusing?" Louise asked.

"Not at all. It only made me imagine Viola talking poetry to a bunch of high school teenagers." Jane shook her head. "Kind of the same thing, minus the mews and the fur."

"She should do very well," Louise said.

Jane gave her a skeptical look. "You'd better hold this thing close to the parking lot anyway, in case you two need to beat a hasty retreat."

"Nonsense." Louise helped herself to the steamed broccoli and added a thin drizzle of Jane's sesame-honey sauce.

"Viola's book readings at the shop are always enjoyable and well attended. She has a marvelous speaking voice and remarkable knowledge of the subject. I think she will rise beautifully to the occasion."

"If it were a group of adults, I would agree. But with youngsters, Viola might be . . . well . . ." Alice made an uncertain gesture.

Jane was not so tentative or diplomatic. "Stuffy."

Louise set down her fork and regarded her sisters. "Children do come into Nine Lives Bookstore on occasion, you know, and Viola deals admirably with them. She neither patronizes them nor chases them out."

Jane snorted. "No, she's usually too busy lecturing them about the books they *should* be reading."

"She can be a little set in her ways," Alice agreed.

"Like they were quick-drying cement," Jane joked. "Louise, the best thing you could do for Viola is to talk her out of this."

"Indeed? After the effort I put into persuading her to agree to it? I think not." Feeling distinctly annoyed now, Louise lost her appetite and pushed aside her plate. "Viola and I are not that different, you know. We are nearly the same age, have the same type of interests, and share many of the same opinions. Does that also make me stuffy and set in my ways?"

Jane rolled her eyes. "Well, now that you mention it . . ."

"Not at all, Louise," Alice said, giving Jane a reproachful look. Alice often derailed brewing arguments between her older and younger sisters. "You're very patient with kids, but then, you teach them all the time."

"While Viola isn't, and doesn't," Jane tagged on. She passed the platter of London broil to Alice. "I'm not trying to insult your pal, Louise, but really, think about it. High school kids can be a pretty tough crowd. They're more into rap and rebellion than into Percy Shelley. How is Viola going to handle it if one of them challenges her, or makes fun of what she thinks?"

That made Louise fall silent. Viola was already nervous about giving the talk, and she likely felt a little defensive too. What if the members of the poetry club goaded her into losing her temper?

"Viola isn't always as tactful as she could be, in certain situations," Alice said, very tentatively. "We've all seen how she gets when someone disagrees with her about literature."

"We all have strong convictions about subjects close to our hearts," Louise reminded her. "But I do see your point, and I will speak to her about it." *But what shall I say? Viola, would you mind bringing up some modern poets, and leaving your temperament at home?*

"I'm sure Viola will listen to you, Louise," Alice said.

At that moment, the door leading from the kitchen to the garden opened and Ethel Buckley came in. The short, plump woman was wearing a comfortable housedress in a pretty shade of mint green. Right then her expression was harried, and her frosted red hair was practically standing on end, as if she had been running her hands through it.

"I made more stew than I can eat, girls, so I thought you'd like it for—oh, fiddlesticks, you're already eating dinner. I should have looked at the clock before I left the house. I had to get away from the phone for a few minutes, though. It's been ringing off the hook all afternoon." She paused to take a breath and scan her nieces' expressions. "Now what's this you were saying about Viola?"

Louise politely rose and took the covered pot from their

aunt and placed it on the stove's back burner. Ethel had a habit of popping over to the inn without warning and immediately taking part in any conversation that she happened to overhear. She meant no harm, but the sisters sometimes found her unexpected appearances a little exasperating.

"Sit down, Auntie," Jane urged, as if trying to distract her, and made a place at the table. "We'll be finished with our dinner in a few minutes, and I made banana pudding for dessert."

"What sort of banana pudding?" Their aunt looked suspicious. "I know that you wouldn't make that chalky-tasting instant from the box, but is it some new-fangled concoction of yours with God knows what-all in it?"

"Neither, Auntie." Jane patted her cheek. "It's good old-fangled, old-fashioned banana pudding, slow-cooked and garnished with sliced fresh bananas and vanilla wafers. Straight out of Mother's cookbook."

"Madeleine's recipe? Heaven's sake, girl, why didn't you say so?" Ethel sat down at once.

"We're all grateful to Jane for bringing back a lot of happy memories from Mother's cookbook," Alice said.

"What's the latest on Roland and Edna?" Jane wanted to know. "Are they going to elope to Las Vegas? Are they spending their honeymoon in Fiji?"

"They're going to be married at Grace Chapel, silly girl," their aunt said, "and why on earth would anyone want to travel to Las Vegas or the other side of the world for their honeymoon? Now what's all this about Viola listening to Louise?"

"Viola agreed—in a roundabout way—to talk to some students over at Franklin High School," Louise said slowly. "They are members of the school's poetry club, and are publishing the school's first student-written poetry magazine." She braced herself for a new wave of criticism.

"That's a fine idea," her aunt said. "I can't think of a soul in this town who knows more about books and such than Viola Reed. Except maybe you, dear."

Would the sisters ever be able to predict what their aunt would say, or think? Probably not.

"Thank you, Aunt."

"Come on, Auntie. Don't you think Viola's far too curmudgeonly for this sort of thing?" Jane demanded.

Ethel shook her head. "She's a strong-minded woman, is all. When I was a girl, I had a Sunday school teacher just like her."

"You did?" Alice looked interested. "Who was she? What was she like?"

"Her name was Mrs. Briggs, and she was the terror of our church," Ethel said bluntly. "She expected the very best from her students. Hadn't the least bit of patience with sassy mouths or lazy dispositions. We all respected her, and so did our parents."

"Or else," Jane quipped.

"No, Jane, Mrs. Briggs wasn't only an authority figure," their aunt continued. "Certain portions of the Bible confused me, and the first time I told Mrs. Briggs I didn't know something, she made me stay after class. She didn't punish me, as I thought she might. She explained the verses to me in words I could understand. She did the same for the other kids, too. She really was the kindest, gentlest teacher I ever had."

"She must have cared for her students very much," Alice said, sounding thoughtful.

Ethel nodded. "Viola is just like her. She puts on that gruff front to hide her kind heart."

"I'm sorry, but I can't see Viola Reed getting so involved with some kids," Jane said, "even if they do belong to a poetry club."

"I will talk to Viola," Louise added. She thought of her friend's comments about speaking in a classroom setting. "I only wish we could meet somewhere outside the classroom." She was tempted to explain Viola's aversion to meeting in the school's interior, but it was better to keep that in confidence, especially with Ethel present.

"Craig Tracy did the landscaping over at Franklin," Jane said. Craig was Acorn Hill's resident florist and garden expert. He also worked as a landscaping consultant, and all over the area there were fine examples of his gift for growing things. "I've driven past there, too, and the school grounds are beautiful. So why don't you have it outside?"

Louise sighed. "Everything cannot be made into a picnic, my dear."

Jane wrinkled her nose. "It's a talk, Louie, not a funeral."

"Nature and poetry do seem to go together," Alice added, "and the informal setting might help."

"I have to call Vera Humbert in the morning," Jane said. "I'll suggest it to her, and she can pass the idea along to her teacher friend."

Chapter  Three

Vera Humbert passed along Jane's suggestion about having the poetry talk outside the school building, and Eleanor Renda sent back approval for the idea. The talk for the poetry club was scheduled for Wednesday afternoon.

"Eleanor says that there is a lovely little grove of elms on the west side of the school grounds," Vera told Louise. "The school keeps a few picnic tables there for outdoor classes and teachers' breaks, and the trees provide plenty of shade."

Louise collected the magazines that she thought showed the best examples of different layouts. She thought she might plan a few remarks about her own love of poetry, and then decided against it. She did not have Viola's photographic memory when it came to literature, and while she could recite a number of poems that were special to her, she had never tried to analyze why they were favorites.

When Louise went downstairs, Jane was waiting with a white baker's box for her at the front desk.

"Some goodies to take with you," Jane said as she handed over the box.

Louise smiled. Her youngest sister sometimes baked more than the Howards and their guests could consume, and shared the surplus with their friends and neighbors. "Is this for Viola? I believe she is watching her weight."

"No, they're for the poetry club," Jane told her. "Teenagers are like baby tigers. Feed them and they probably won't snarl at you as much."

"What a good idea." *And a canny one, too*, Louise thought as she leaned over to kiss Jane's cheek. Trust a former chef to know that the way to a teenager's heart is through the stomach. "Thank you, dear."

Jane's goodies would serve as a nice ice-breaker, Louise thought, and her magazines might stir some imaginations, but the main burden fell on Viola's shoulders. When Louise arrived at the bookshop, her friend appeared to be feeling the weight already.

"You're too early. I'm not ready," Viola snapped from behind her desk. She was sitting and fumbling with the knot of the scarf around her neck. The summer linen suit the bookseller wore was a subdued shade of lavender, and tailored plainly, which flattered Viola's fair complexion and ample figure.

"That is a lovely ensemble," Louise assured her. She noticed that none of the bookseller's pets had come out to greet her as they usually did. "Where are the cats hiding today?"

"Tess hasn't come near the shop, so I took all of the boys home last night. Sometimes being close to males frightens breeding females." Viola finished adjusting the knot, but then stood and began fussing with her lapels before she stopped and peered at Louise. "How do I really look? Tell me the truth."

"You are the picture of a professional businesswoman." She nodded at the tote bag of books Viola had set to one side. "Shall I put that in the car?"

"No. I knew this suit was too formal." With nervous fingers, Viola tugged at the drape of her scarf and made its beaded fringe rattle. "I'll have to go home and find something else to wear."

Louise shook her head. "There is no time for that, Viola. We are expected at the school in twenty minutes."

Her friend's expression turned to one of alarm. "I'll call and cancel."

Louise was tempted to tell her she would do no such thing, but giving orders to Viola for anything but books was always an unwise move. *Why is she so nervous?* "I have always liked that suit. You were wearing it on the day we met, when I moved back to Acorn Hill."

"Was I? I can't recall what you were wearing. I just remember how glad I was that someone who had actually read Emerson and Melville for pleasure had moved to town." Viola's expression softened for a moment. "I was impressed right up until the moment you picked up that ridiculous Nash book."

Ogden Nash's worth as a writer and poet had been their first—and oldest—debate. As a distraction, it was perfect.

"Nash was a master of light verse and whimsy," Louise said, deliberately casual. "I still read from that book now and then when I need a pick-me-up."

"How can you say that? The man was a buffoon," Viola countered at once. "'Hark to the whimper of the sea-gull / He weeps because he's not an ea-gull.' Stuff and nonsense! His work shouldn't be mentioned in the same breath with true poetry. Why, if he'd tried publishing his drivel in England, they'd have deported him in a heartbeat."

That was more like the friend Louise knew and loved. "All the better that he was born here in America." She kept a straight face as she added, "English literary stodginess might have smothered his genius."

"Someone should have smothered him with a pillow, and watch what you say about the English." Her friend glared at her. Viola's family had emigrated to America from England, and she always defended her ancestry with predictable zeal. "If not for the English, we'd have no literature."

"If not for writers like Nash, we might forget to laugh at ourselves," Louise pointed out. "Poet Archibald MacLeish said that Nash 'altered the sensibility of his time.' Considering that he wrote from the era of the Great Depression through the Vietnam War, I imagine it was often quite a welcome change."

"It's incredible that someone as educated and intelligent as you could take that position." Viola threw up her hands. "For Heaven's sake, Louise, Ogden Nash thought creating poetry meant writing inane absurdities like 'Parsley / Is gharsley' and 'You never get any fun / Out of the things you haven't done.'"

"Yet like so many great humorists, he revealed truths through his verse, and still made us laugh," Louise said. "And is not enlightenment the ultimate duty of the poet?"

Viola quoted Wordsworth to Louise,

"O Duty! if that name thou love,
Who are a light to guide, a rod
To check the erring, and reprove—"

"'O Duty,'" Louise interrupted, quoting Nash back at her, "'Why hast thou not the visage of a sweetie or a cutie?'"

Viola's lips twitched for a moment. "You are shameless."

"If I am, you are my match." Louise pretended to think

for a moment. "The Franklin students would likely appreciate Nash's wit, and I am familiar enough with his work to
quote some of it from memory. If you are certain that you do
not want to go—"

"Over my dead body, Louise Smith." Viola seized her
tote bag and keys, and marched out from behind the desk.
"Come on. We're going to be late."

∞

Franklin High had been planned and built to serve as a
regional school, and was attended by children from families
living in Acorn Hill, Potterston and Riverton. Situated in the
middle of some of the region's prettiest farmland, Franklin's
grounds covered more than twenty acres, which included a
football field and baseball diamond.

As they turned the corner to enter the visitor's parking
lot, Louise saw a number of teenagers jogging around a track
behind the school's building complex. The students wore
bright, white T-shirts marked with an oversize capital F in
navy blue, which matched their white-striped gym shorts.

Shadowing the track was a tall, square building, the
doors to which were marked with a large sign that read
PATRIOTS GYMNASIUM. On each door was painted a
Revolutionary War era soldier, also uniformed in navy and
white, which Louise surmised to be Franklin's school colors.

"The school must have an extensive physical education
program," she commented to Viola as she parked in one of
the visitor's spaces. "That track over there looks like something from the Olympics."

"I never played sports when I was in school," Viola said.
"It took too much time away from my studies. Of course, in
those days the teachers didn't make the girls run themselves
silly." She nodded toward the track, where a group of female

students were poised to begin a race. Their coach, a slim, ath-
letic-looking woman with short, sun-bleached blond hair,
blew a whistle hanging from a strap around her neck to start
the next race.

"Neither did my school, but some friends and I formed
the first girls' tennis team." Louise smiled a little. "We were
not allowed to compete with other schools, but we played—
and often trounced, I might add—the boys' team in doubles
matches."

When Louise had parked, she reached for her purse and
went to open her door, until she saw that Viola hadn't
released her seatbelt. "Is something wrong?"

The bookseller stared at the school's main building. "You
wouldn't have talked to them about Nash, would you? You
only said that to get me here."

Rather than confirm or deny the accusation, Louise only
smiled.

"That's what I thought. You know, for an honest, God-
fearing woman, you can be incredibly devious and under-
handed." Viola removed her seatbelt and picked up her tote
bag. "It's one of the things I like most about you."

As they walked to the pre-arranged meeting place,
Louise admired the landscaping around the school. Along
with a neatly cut, dense green lawn, many different types of
shade trees and small, oval flowerbeds adorned the grounds.
On the west side of the school stood a double row of tall elms
with bright, sawtooth-edged green leaves and thick trunks
wrapped in ridged silvery bark. The dense treetops formed a
natural canopy over a quarried stone walkway and the rows
of tri-colored impatiens that had been planted on either side
of it. Here things were not so manicured: Wildflowers sprang
up here and there in unexpected bunches, and rambling ivy
draped itself wherever it fancied to grow. In the center of the

trees the walkway ended in a circle, around which picnic tables had been set.

Louise spotted the coach with the whistle walking toward them. At the same time, a cluster of six students carrying backpacks and notebooks emerged from a side door to the main school building.

"I believe that is our group over there." Louise waved to catch the teacher's and students' attention.

The coach nodded to her, but instead of walking toward her guests, she changed direction and intercepted the group. She drew one of the boys off to the side, as if intending to have a private word with him. Louise recognized the young man with the coach as Conor Byrne, a renowned local athlete and the son of William and Isabel Byrne, prominent members of Grace Chapel's congregation. She also saw Conor's sister Sherrilyn among the other five students.

The Byrnes attended services every week, but it had been some time since Louise had seen Conor at Grace Chapel. It wasn't unusual for some of the young men involved in sports to miss services occasionally, but Louise couldn't remember the last time she had seen William and Isabel's son at church.

Whatever the coach had said to Conor, it didn't make the boy happy. He uttered a few words, shook his head and rejoined the other five students waiting for him. The coach gave him an oddly frustrated look before starting toward Louise and Viola.

"They look older than I thought they would," Viola said under her breath as coach and students drew near. "Why is it that so many teens these days dress down the way they do?"

Louise noted a few scowls among the students' faces. "Adolescence is the rite of passage from childhood to maturity. We were just as eager to dress up at that age."

"The difference is that we girls weren't allowed to dress like anything other than ladies." The bookseller gave the coach's unisex sports attire a slightly derisive glance. "My grandmother wouldn't even hear of me wearing trousers or jeans. She said they were for people too poor to afford proper attire."

Both the boys and the girls wore jeans, Louise noted, which she knew were sold already artfully faded by the manufacturer. "What I cannot understand is why they want to wear clothing that is made to appear preworn."

Viola snorted softly. "At least they seem to have abandoned that awful fashion they had of fraying the hems and ripping holes in the knees."

"Hello, ladies," the coach said, striding up and offering her hand first to Viola, and then to Louise. She gave them each a strong, brisk handshake. "I'm Eleanor Renda. Welcome to Franklin High School."

"How do you do." Viola paused and cleared her throat. "I'm Viola Reed, and this is my friend, Louise Smith."

Louise returned the coach's nod and smile. Dark sunglasses hid Eleanor Renda's eyes, but the light streaks in her hair and the tiny freckles spattering her unlined, tanned face gave her a youthful, friendly look. The coach was actually quite petite, being several inches shorter than Louise, but her excellent posture and trim frame made her seem taller than she really was.

"Let me introduce our school magazine staff." Eleanor turned and began introducing the students standing behind her. "Conor Byrne, the editor, Millicent Eddows, assistant editor, Rob Dierdorf, Hadley Gustafson and Wendy Strickland, layout and artwork, and Sherrilyn Byrne, Conor's sister and staff assistant."

Of the students, Louise only recognized the Byrne siblings. Sherrilyn Byrne, one of Alice's former ANGELs, was petite and shy, and wore her long, light brown hair pulled back from her pale face with a white bandeau.

Her brother Conor also had light brown hair, his cut close to his scalp, but there the resemblance ended. His features were much more angular, and he had a physical presence his sister lacked. Conor wasn't the largest of the boys—Rob was at least a head taller, and Hadley much wider in the shoulders—but his lean, sinewy build and controlled movements set him apart.

Sherrilyn was her usual, quiet self, but her brother seemed very alert, almost tense. *Odd sometimes how different siblings can be*, Louise thought. After the teenagers said their hellos, she responded with, "It is a pleasure to be here."

"I told the kids they could have their lunch now, if that's all right with you," Ms. Renda said to Viola as she led them over to the picnic tables.

"That's fine." Viola's expression was composed, but Louise could sense her relief.

Eleanor Renda waved her students over to two of the picnic tables, where they sat down and took out their lunches. At the same time, Viola removed a stack of books from her tote bag.

Louise carried the literary magazines she had brought to the coach. "These have a variety of layouts," she told Ms. Renda. "Would you like to look over them?"

"No, thank you," the younger woman said. "You can have the kids flip through them if you like."

Louise found the coach's reaction puzzling, but without comment went ahead and passed out the magazines to the students. She kept Jane's box aside, however, for when the youngsters had finished their lunches.

Although Viola seemed collected, she did not start her talk, but sorted through the books, checking pages she had marked and setting them in a certain order. Louise thought she might be ready to begin, but she shuffled the order of the books once, twice, and then a third time.

Louise went to her side. "Viola?"

"Don't rush me," her friend muttered as she took her bifocals from the tote bag and slipped them on. She glanced over the top rims at the waiting students. "I'll be ready in a minute."

Louise noticed a little perspiration had sprung up on Viola's forehead. Given that they were in a cool spot, with a light breeze filtering through the trees, it couldn't be because of the temperature. "Do you know what Daniel said to the lions when he was thrown into their den?"

"Get me out of here?"

"'I don't bite.'"

"Very cute." Viola glared at her.

"I could start things off with a quote by Nash," Louise offered. "Perhaps something like, 'There is only one way to achieve happiness on this terrestrial ball, / And that is to have either a clear conscience or none at all.'"

"Not bad," came one response.

"You should do standup comedy," came another.

Louise thought it was time to change tactics. *Perhaps I should not wait and just pass out Jane's goodies.*

The box contained eighteen of Jane's large sugar cookies, which were sprinkled with colorful candy confetti. As soon as Louise offered the box to the group, six eager hands emptied it in record time.

Ms. Renda refused a cookie and gave Viola a slightly impatient look. "Do you think she'll be ready to start this soon?" she asked Louise. "We've only got forty minutes left before next period."

"It should be just another minute or two." Louise followed her gaze, and saw Viola digging through her tote bag again. Trying to rush her friend would only make her more nervous, so Louise decided to try distracting the teacher. "How long have you been working at Franklin, Coach?"

"This is my first year. I taught phys ed at a high school in Pittsburgh." As the sun went behind some clouds and the shade deepened, Ms. Renda removed her dark glasses. She had brown eyes so dark they looked almost black, an unusual combination with her light hair.

"Did you work with the poetry club at your former school?" Louise asked.

"No, I've never done anything like this. I don't have time to do much more than supervise a few meetings, either." Her gaze shifted to the six students, and her lips tightened for a moment. "*They'll* have to take care of whatever is necessary to finish getting this magazine put together and published."

On their own? "Surely they will need more than supervision, Coach."

"Coach Renda is in charge of the track team." Conor, who had obviously been listening in, said. "They're headed for the regional finals in track and field, so she has to handle us and daily practice with the team. We asked a couple of other teachers to help us so that we could take the burden off Coach, but no one else had the time to spare for the club."

"I'm happy to do what I can," Ms. Renda said, sounding just the opposite, "but we have to keep our priorities straight, Conor."

He gave her an exaggeratedly innocent smile. "Agreed."

Louise felt confused. There was something very odd about the situation between Ms. Renda and Conor, and the fact that both of them were involved with this project. Yet, despite the undercurrents, they were obviously taking pains to act politely toward each other.

"My dad's a printer, so he's going to help us out with layout and binding materials," Hadley said.

Rob yawned. "Won't be much help, though. None of us except Had knows how to use them."

"Hadley will teach us," Conor said.

The other five teenagers exchanged troubled glances but didn't comment.

"Maybe you should wait and publish this thing next year," Ms. Renda suggested. "If you did, you could take your time and learn how to do it the right way."

"It won't take a year to do that," Conor disagreed.

Louise guessed that the tension between them might have been a result of the fact that they clearly did not see eye to eye about the importance of the club, or perhaps publishing the school's first poetry magazine.

The awkward silence was at last broken by Ms. Renda, who produced a decidedly artificial smile as she looked at the five other students.

"Ms. Reed is the owner of the Nine Lives Bookstore over in Acorn Hill," the coach said. "Have any of you been to her shop?"

"I have." Sherrilyn tentatively raised her hand. "Ms. Reed had copies of all the books on my World Literature Class reading list, even *Don Quixote* and *The Sound and the Fury*."

Viola overheard the remark and looked for a moment as if she would comment. Before she could get a word out, however, the other teenagers seized the topic and began chatting amongst themselves.

"Mrs. Harroway is making your class read Faulkner? That means my class will have to *next* semester." Hadley

Gustafson, a sturdy young man with the light hair and eyes that indicated a Scandinavian heritage, uttered a theatrical groan before wolfing down the last bite of his sandwich. "Can't we get class credit for working on the mag?"

"Not unless we forget about poetry and only publish essays about great writers." Wendy, an African-American girl with beautiful coffee-colored skin and large dark eyes, gathered up some orange peels and stowed them neatly in her lunch bag. "I told you to take English Comp."

"Faulkner is an *elective* on Mrs. Harroway's reading list," Conor said.

Louise could not quite reconcile the fact that Conor Byrne was a member of the poetry club, much less their magazine's editor, with his reputation as one of the area's most dedicated athletes. Over the last two years he had lettered in baseball and basketball, and was currently captain of the school's track team. Conor's father William had his son's accomplishments regularly announced in Grace Chapel's monthly bulletin, and yet there had never been a single mention of the boy's literary aspirations.

"Faulkner's a pretty tough read, Sis," he was telling Sherrilyn.

"I think I can handle it," his sister said in a low voice. At the same time she sat up, straightening her hunched shoulders and trying to project an air of confidence.

Shy, Louise decided, *but also determined to fight it*. Alice had been exactly the same way when they were girls.

"Don't worry, Sher." Rob Dierdorf, a dark-haired boy with a lanky form and a slightly crooked nose, leaned over and continued in an overloud whisper, "If it turns out to be a clunker, maybe that lady sells the Cliffs Notes too."

Viola set aside her poetry books and went to stand before the table at which Conor, Rob and Sherrilyn were sitting.

"Young man," she said to Rob, "*The Sound and the Fury* is many things, but it is not a 'clunker.'"

All of the students stopped talking and eating and stared at Viola.

"It was Faulkner's fourth novel, and his first real masterpiece," she continued, warming to her subject. "Of all his books, Faulkner loved it best, but not for the critical acclaim it received. He actually referred to it as his 'most splendid failure.'"

"You mean, he thought it was a waste himself? Wow." Millicent, a plump girl with long black hair tied back with several pastel satin ribbons, made an *O* with her mouth, exposing two rows of metallic braces on her teeth. "How awesomely humble of him."

"Nah, he was just trying to outsmart the critics," Rob quipped. He had a broad, plain face but merry brown eyes that sparkled with mischief. "What better way than to be first to stomp on your own book?"

"Despite what scholars have said over the years, I think Faulkner had few illusions about himself, or human beings, or life," Viola assured him. "Had he not chosen to write novels, he would have made an excellent poet."

"I disagree," Conor said. "Stream-of-consciousness prose like Faulkner's may accurately mirror the human thought process, but it's hard to follow and even harder to understand. So would poetry in the same style."

Louise never expected to hear such precise, analytical language from a young man best known as a stellar athlete. Clearly there was much more to Conor Byrne than met the eye.

Viola also seemed impressed, but not entirely pleased at being contradicted. "That's a very negative opinion for someone your age."

"Appreciation for clarity and simplicity is not the exclusive domain of adulthood," Conor answered in a deceptively mild tone.

Louise couldn't decide if she admired the boy's intellect and dry wit, or disapproved of how he used them. He seemed bent on challenging every statement Viola made and forcing her to defend her position.

Hadley rolled his eyes. "Here we go again. Anybody want to lend me a dictionary, so I can figure out what the heck Conor's talking about this time?"

"It's okay, Had." Wendy gave his wide shoulder a mocking pat. "I'll translate it into words of two syllables or less for you."

"I don't know, Wend," Rob said. "You might need to draw pictures for him."

Ms. Renda frowned at her students. "Why don't we save such opinions—and the chatter—for later?"

"Sure, Coach." Something unpleasant flickered in Conor's eyes before his expression turned to a blank politeness. "Sorry for interrupting, Ms. Reed."

"Never apologize for having a discerning mind, young man." Viola gave Hadley, not Conor, a look of disapproval. "Or an excellent vocabulary."

Louise decided to take a seat beside Ms. Renda and mentally crossed her fingers as the students fell silent and Viola began her talk.

"Thank you for inviting me and my friend here today," Viola said. "I know I was asked to speak to you about poetry, but I'd like to get one thing straight, right off the bat." She held up one hand, as if trying to stop traffic. "No one, especially me, can teach you anything about it."

Chapter  Four

Viola's statement nearly made Louise cough. Ms. Renda, who had been sipping some water from the bottle she had been carrying, actually choked. Sherrilyn quickly produced a paper napkin and pressed it in the teacher's hand.

"And that, boys and girls, was the shortest lecture ever given in the history of Franklin High School," Rob said, imitating a radio announcer's voice, which started Millicent giggling again.

"Oh, I'm not finished, young man," Viola said, very calmly. "Not by half." She scanned the faces of the students. "I know you six are planning to publish a poetry magazine, but do you know exactly what a poem is?"

"'Poetry is a way of taking life by the throat,'" Conor said. When everyone stared at him, he shrugged. "That was Robert Frost's definition."

"That's an excellent quotation, but I'm more interested in what *you* think it is," Viola said.

"Silly girly stuff," Hadley muttered under his breath. He caught Conor looking at him and reddened.

Millicent's hand shot up into the air, and when Viola nodded in her direction, she burst out with, "A poem is a literary work set in verse. It's usually written in lines that rhyme, with the lines in a certain sequence or pattern of repetition."

"Technically, that is correct." As the girl began to smile, Viola held up one finger. "However, a poem is more than meter, cadence, rhyme or form. It is a journey through something that must be felt, and recognized, here." She pressed a hand over her heart.

Louise felt uneasy. Viola could be very passionate about her love of books and reading—almost to the point of being theatrical—and she didn't want to watch the teenagers ridicule her because of it. Hadley was beginning to look bored, and Wendy and Rob were trading wry looks. *Please, Viola, go carefully from here.*

"So I can't teach you poetry," her friend was saying. "I can only be a guide and help you to discover it."

"Is this poetry, or a trip to the North Pole?" Wendy scoffed.

The corner of Viola's mouth curled up. "You'll have to be the judge of that, young lady."

"How are you going to, uh, guide us, Ms. Reed?" Hadley asked. "I mean, do you tap into some kind of global poetry satellite or supercomputer?"

Rob covered his mouth with his hand to smother a snicker.

"Don't need them." Viola moved over to the table and tapped the young man's temple with her finger, startling him. "Everything you need is right in here."

Wendy bent over and pretended to peer in Hadley's ear. "I think I can see something, but it's stuck behind the video game tricks and the football team statistics."

A few chuckles went around the table, and for the first time since joining them, Conor seemed to relax. As Viola continued, he gave her his undivided attention. Louise could see the influence he had on the other members of the poetry club as they picked up on his interest and also focused on what Viola had to say.

A leader on and off the field, Louise thought. *Now if she can keep his attention, the others should follow.*

"I want you to listen now," Viola said. "I want to tell you about an old abbey in the center of London. It has been an important place for more than a thousand years. The Battle of Hastings is over, and the Normans have defeated Harold and his Saxon army. Now they bring their leader, William, to the old church. It's Christmas Day, but the men are wearing armor and carrying swords, prepared for battle. There, surrounded by his Norman invaders and the conquered Saxon subjects, William is going to be crowned King of England, and nothing and no one can stop it."

"Merry Christmas, England," Rob murmured.

Louise smiled. Despite Rob's quip, Viola's dramatic retelling of the coronation of William the Conqueror had all six teenagers riveted.

"The age-old ritual of crowning a monarch begins," Viola continued. "Prayers are recited in Latin. As the crown is lifted, the Saxons—motivated, no doubt, by fear of William—and the Normans cheer and shout their approval. The Saxon voices carry to the soldiers standing guard outside, but these men are Normans, and they don't speak English. They hear the conquered Saxons calling out their good wishes, don't understand the words, and believe William is about to be assassinated."

"Uh-oh," Wendy said. "Here come the swords."

"The soldiers grab torches and set fire to the houses around the abbey." Viola made an encircling gesture. "Smoke from the burning, thatched roofs fills the church.

Thinking that the abbey is to be burned to the ground, both Normans and Saxons flee in terror. Outside, a riot begins as people fight and try to escape the flames. Yet William is determined. He has gathered his army, crossed the English Channel, led his men against the armies of Harold, fought his way inland and marched into the great city of London itself. Despite the fire and smoke and rioting outside, he does not leave Westminster Abbey. He stays until the ceremony is completed and he is crowned King of England." She paused for a moment before she added, "William will remain king for another twenty-one years."

A collective sigh escaped the students.

"Very few Saxons recorded the events of the invasion, probably because they hated the Normans and knew that William treated his enemies without mercy. Fear of the new king may be why very few Saxons wrote anything at all about William. The histories we have now weren't written until after the Normans controlled England."

"I bet they were all written in favor of the king," Conor guessed.

"There were exceptions," Viola told him. "One man, a bard named Thorkill in the service of Earl Waltheof, wrote of William after Waltheof was executed by the king for treason in 1076. He wrote it in Old Norse, perhaps to protect himself since William was still the king at the time. Still, the poem survived and was translated into English. This is what he wrote." Viola picked up a book and began to read from it.

"William crossed the cold channel
And reddened the bright swords
And now he has betrayed noble Earl Waltheof.
It is true that killing in England
Will be a long time ending."

"Wait a minute," Hadley said, in a tone of someone making a huge discovery. "I got all that!"

"Who wouldn't?" Millicent shuddered. "What a horrible prediction."

"But an accurate one," Wendy said. "There were dozens of wars after the Normans conquered England."

"Thorkill also left us a thousand-year-old clue to his master's fate in this poem. The third line, 'And now he has betrayed noble Earl Waltheof' says nothing about treason, but accuses William of betrayal. Judith, Earl Waltheof's wife, is believed by some scholars to have helped to effect this betrayal."

"Why would his wife do that?" Rob asked. "Did she hate him or something?"

Viola shrugged. "We don't know how Judith felt about Waltheof, but she probably loved her uncle. You see, she was William the Conqueror's niece."

"Yikes." Rob uttered a startled laugh. "Talk about marrying the wrong girl."

Viola set down the book and picked up another. "Now listen to another poet's view of London from a different time.

"Earth has not anything to show more fair:
Dull would he be of soul who could pass by
A sight so touching in its majesty:
This City now doth, like a garment, wear
The beauty of the morning; silent, bare,
Ships, towers, domes, theatres, and temples lie
Open unto the fields, and to the sky;
All bright and glittering in the smokeless air.
Never did sun more beautifully steep
In his first splendour, valley, rock, or hill;
Ne'er saw I, never felt, a calm so deep!
The river glideth at his own sweet will:

Dear God! the very houses seem asleep;
And all that mighty heart is lying still!

"This poem, 'Composed on Westminster Bridge,' was written by William Wordsworth," Viola told the students. "He claimed in a letter that he wrote it 'on the roof of a coach on my way to France' in September of 1802."

Hadley chortled. "Strange spot to write a poem."

"Some poets must compose whenever the mood strikes them, whatever their surroundings." Viola made a casual gesture toward Conor, who was jotting something down in his notebook.

"No poetry, only some notes, Ms. Reed," he assured her.

"I am delighted that you're taking them, young man," Viola said. "Wordsworth was actually leaving England at the time he wrote this poem. He and his sister Dorothy took advantage of the Peace of Amiens and were journeying to France so that Wordsworth could see his half-French daughter Anne whom he had never met."

Rob elbowed Hadley. "Guess it wasn't his *first* trip to France."

"Obviously not." Viola put down the second book. "Now I would like you to compare these two poems. What do they have in common?"

Millicent absently gnawed at the edge of her thumbnail. "Well, they were both written in England."

"Both of the writers were professionals," Wendy added. "Bards were paid by their masters to tell stories, and Wordsworth was a published poet."

"Two Williams: the Conqueror and Wordsworth," Rob said.

Hadley frowned. "One's about war, and the other is about peace."

"Very good," Viola said. "One other thing both poems share—as all great poems do—is that they accurately capture a moment in time. Through Thorkill's brief lament, we see a 'cold channel' and his unwanted king, William the Conqueror, 'reddening the bright swords.' This poet was a citizen of a defeated nation, forced to pay homage to a merciless invader, so naturally his poem speaks of brutality, betrayal and death.

"More than seven hundred years later, through William Wordsworth's eyes, we see a completely different picture. As he crosses Westminster Bridge, he can see the abbey that was nearly burned to the ground during William's coronation. But now we see a different London." Viola made a sweeping gesture. "Not a city of the conquered, but one that is calm and open, one that contains a 'mighty heart' and wears 'the beauty of the morning.' Each poet wrote of what he knew, and by doing so, illustrated how greatly our world changes with each passing century. When you begin putting together the poetry for your magazine, remember these similarities and contrasts."

Viola went on to give the students practical advice on how to handle the submission, editing and production stages of making the magazine. "You've been looking through the examples my friend Mrs. Smith brought, and they show how a professional editing team handles content. Always strive for the best presentation."

"Also, be sure to remember," Louise added, "that the poems you select for publication should say something about you and your time."

"We've gotten some wonderful poems already," Millicent said. Her gaze turned soft, and her voice became far away. "All about magic and miracles and making dreams come true."

"Good thing I'm doing the art work," Wendy said, flatly practical. "I'm more into mathematics and MIT and making my first million."

"*Wendy*." Ms. Renda gave the girl a pointed look.

"Whoops, sorry. I guess that didn't sound too marvelous," Wendy amended with a cheeky grin.

"The poems I like show that life is filled with meaning, and music and magnificent moments." Sherrilyn giggled shyly.

"Be nice if we could have Maseratis, mansions and mounds of money too," Rob joked, following the alliteration.

Hadley nodded. "And play linebacker for the Steelers." When Millicent scowled at him for breaking up the alliteration, he protested, "Hey, it's not my fault. I'm no poet, and besides, there aren't any positions or professional football teams that start with *M*."

Wendy jabbed a finger toward him. "This is why you're sticking to graphics and only the graphics, Mr. Sports Nut."

Louise noticed the worry that suddenly came over Sherrilyn's face, and the way she glanced at her brother. Conor wasn't writing in his notebook, and his expression indicated that his thoughts were far away from the discussion.

"What does your editor think?" Viola asked.

Hadley waved a hand in front of Conor's face. "Yo, Byrne, lower the landing gear and touch down, huh?"

"Our magazine will say that we were here," Conor said. "What we cared about wasn't stupid. It mattered. *We* mattered."

Something in the boy's voice made Louise's heart constrict. "Of course you matter, my dear."

He gave her a terribly weary look. "The question is, how much?"

A bell ringing inside the school's main building brought Ms. Renda to her feet. "I'm afraid that's the next period bell, Ms. Reed."

"I understand. Do you have any questions?" Viola asked the students.

"Do we have to go back to class?" Rob complained. "I'd rather stay out here, work on my tan."

Viola smiled at Rob. "Our friend Wordsworth also wrote about bookwork,

"Enough of Science and of Art;
Close up those barren leaves;
Come forth, and bring with you a heart
That watches and receives."

"Now there is a message I can take to heart," Rob said with a sly grin. "Go, Wordsworth!"

"Any questions about publishing the magazine?" Ms. Renda asked, eager to change the subject.

"Ms. Reed, which font reads best?" Hadley asked. "Or should we use a bunch of them?"

"That depends on your layout," Viola said.

Before she could elaborate, Wendy asked, "Is it better to have a table of contents or an index?"

"If you have room, both. If you don't, readers seem to prefer a table of contents."

Rob jumped in with, "Wouldn't a landscape format give us more print space per page?"

Before Viola could answer, Sherrilyn politely raised her hand, while Hadley and Wendy simultaneously blurted out more questions.

Only Conor didn't participate; he seemed to have

detached himself from the group again. Louise was almost convinced he was in some sort of depressed state. *But why? The boy has so many first-place trophies that his father probably had to build an entire wall of shelves to display them all.*

Ms. Renda halted the barrage of questions by blowing the whistle hanging from the cord around her neck. "We're out of time, kids. Let's thank Ms. Reed and Mrs. Smith for coming out here today."

The students' eager expressions fell, but they sincerely offered thanks and began collecting their belongings.

"Ms. Reed, we appreciate your advice," Conor said. "I was wondering if you would have time to come back to talk to us again, and help us on the actual layout of the magazine?"

Rob's expression brightened. "Yeah, you could show us how to set up the proof pages."

"I'd like to hear more on how to read poetry," Millicent put in.

"I might be able to do that," Viola said.

"Where would we meet? The classrooms are closed and locked after last bell," Wendy reminded them. "We can't bring our stuff out here, either. One cloudburst and everything would be ruined."

"How about meeting at the school library?" Millicent asked.

"The library isn't available," Ms. Renda said. "The special tutoring program is using it after school hours every day of the week."

"I guess that kills that idea," Hadley said.

"I've been planning to close my shop earlier on Saturdays," Viola said unexpectedly. "I could call Nia Komonos at the Acorn Hill library and ask permission to meet there. We could have a combination poetry reading and magazine planning meeting."

Ms. Renda shook her head. "That's a very generous offer, Ms. Reed, but I have track team practice every Saturday afternoon from one until five P.M."

"You don't have to watchdog us, Coach," Hadley said. "We'll behave ourselves."

"I hope that you would, Hadley," Ms. Renda told him. "But any extracurricular activity meetings are supposed to be teacher-supervised and take place on campus."

"That's not fair," Millicent protested. "You don't have time, and there's no place on campus for us to have the meetings."

"Couldn't the principal give us permission to have them with Ms. Reed over at the town library?" Wendy asked. "I mean, if we explained the situation and everything?"

The coach sighed. "Considering the circumstances, he might, but you would also have to obtain permission from all of your parents."

"My dad would let me go," Hadley insisted.

"The library is walking distance from my house, and Mom is always bugging me to get out of the house more on the weekends, so I'm in," Rob joked.

"I live in Riverton, so I'd have to catch a ride," Wendy said, "but I'd be willing to make the trip."

Millicent groaned. "I forgot, my folks are really busy on the weekends, and I don't drive. There aren't any buses that run out by our farm, either."

"Sherrilyn and I can swing by and pick you up," Conor told her.

Ms. Renda looked around at the hopeful faces of her students. "All right, I'll speak to the principal. If he approves the idea, and your parents send in signed permission slips on time, then you can have your first meeting this Saturday—if Ms. Reed is willing." She glanced at Viola. "I hope you know what you're getting yourself into with this bunch."

Louise wondered, too. Viola had her heart in the right place, but her tendency toward impatience, and her short temper might lead to some problems. On impulse, she said, "I could come and help with the meetings too."

Viola gave her a grateful look. "Thanks, Louise."

The next day Louise drove to Potterston to do some shopping and to pick up Alice, whose car had been giving her trouble. Her sister emerged from the staff entrance at the back of the Potterston Hospital a few minutes late.

"Sorry," Alice said as she climbed into the passenger side of the Cadillac and leaned over the seat to place her medical bag in the back. Her face was flushed, and her white nurse's uniform looked unusually wilted and wrinkled.

"Busy day?" Louise asked.

"Utter chaos. I volunteered to take an extra shift today so one of the other nurses could attend a wedding. You know what they say about good deeds." After she had clipped on her seatbelt, Alice slumped back and closed her eyes. "Three late admissions came in right in the middle of shift change, and me with two new nurses working the floor." She flashed Louise a grateful look. "Thanks for picking me up. The mechanic from the garage called and said he needs a few more days to work on my car."

Alice's car had been giving her trouble regularly over the last several weeks and had finally broken down the day before. "What did he say was the problem with it?"

"Some parts need replacing, and have to be ordered, I think." Alice brushed some stray hairs back from her forehead. "The garage called at the same time a hip-injury patient was being transferred up from the E.R. I know the poor woman was in terrible pain, but her room was just across from the nurses' station, and she was fussing so loudly that I could barely make out what the mechanic said."

"Give him the number for the inn," Louise advised her. "Jane or I can always take a message for you."

"That reminds me, could you stop at Fred's Hardware on our way home? I need to pop in for a moment and pick up a new garden hose. Jane told me the old one finally split next to the last patch."

"Of course." Louise turned onto the road leading from Potterston to Acorn Hill. "You can use my car any time you like, you know. I will only need it on Saturday afternoon."

"Oh, I don't want to put you out anymore than I already have. I can carpool with Monica Mosley from Pediatrics. She and I work the same schedule." Alice yawned and rubbed her eyes. "Where are you going on Saturday?"

"Viola Reed is meeting with the high school poetry club at the town library," Louise told her. "I volunteered to go with her and help out."

"Again?" Alice gave her a sideways look. "I thought that one talk at the school was it."

"So did I." Louise explained the unusual situation that had led to the Saturday meetings, and then asked, "Do you know anything about this Eleanor Renda?"

"Only from what Vera has mentioned about her," Alice said. "She and Eleanor were roommates in college. Evidently Eleanor was quite a track star back then."

"Was she?"

Alice nodded. "She won all sorts of championships for track and field for their school. Vera told me Eleanor even considered trying out for the Olympic team one year, but a torn muscle knocked her out of competition."

That might explain why the coach was putting the needs of the track team first. "It is a pity that the principal could not assign another teacher to supervise the poetry club."

"Oh? Why is that?"

Louise didn't want to insult Vera's friend, so she chose her words carefully. "I think with coaching the track team, Ms. Renda has enough responsibility already."

"You know how overworked and underappreciated most teachers are these days." As Louise parked in the side lot of Fred's Hardware, Alice shaded her eyes with her hand. "Look, over by those boxes. Is that the cat Viola was chasing the other day?"

Sunlight glaring on the windshield made Louise shift position. When she could see clearly, it was in time to see the scraggly form of a calico cat slip between the boxes Fred had stacked by his delivery door.

"Yes, it is." Louise switched off the ignition and reached over the seat to retrieve a plastic grocery bag from the back. "I bought some cat treats for Wendell from the pet store while I was in Potterston." She took out the canister of dried fish bits. "Perhaps we can use them to tempt her into one of the boxes."

"Good idea." Alice held out her hand for the treats. "You distract her from the front, and I'll put these in that box marked 'PVC pipe' that's tilted on its side."

"How do you distract a stray cat?" Louise asked as they left the car and cautiously made their way toward Tess.

"Speak softly to her," Viola Reed said in a low voice from

behind them, "and don't get too close or make any sudden moves."

Alice was so startled by Viola's sudden appearance that she dropped some of the treats. When she recovered, she responded, "That approach works for tired nurses, too, for your information."

"*Shhhh.* I've been following her around town for a good half hour, and I don't want to lose her again." The bookseller looked from one side of the parking lot to the other. "She's been hiding in every tight, dark corner she can find. I'm scared to death she'll climb under someone's car and try to crawl up into the engine."

"Do they actually do that?" The thought horrified Louise.

Viola waved Alice to one side, but her eyes never left Tess. "More often in winter, when it's cold out. Car engines are often nice and warm."

The three women closed in on Tess, leaving her no avenue of escape. The little calico backed up against the wall of Fred's store, her ears flattening and the fur along her spine bristling.

"Now, now, sweet little girl," Viola crooned. "We're not going to hurt you."

Alice carefully bent down and scattered some treats in the box lying on its side. The pattering sound of the food landing on the cardboard drew Tess's attention for a few seconds. Louise was close enough to see the tiny contractions of the feline's nostrils as she sniffed the air, but the animal was so tense that it would have been foolhardy to try to pick her up.

"She seems hungry," Louise whispered to Viola.

"She's starving," her friend murmured back. "Wilhelm

Wood found her trying to squeeze through a little hole into his dumpster to get at his trash this morning. The only thing that stopped her was the size of her belly."

Louise saw that Tess's abdomen appeared larger, but it might have been the result of weight loss she had suffered elsewhere on her body. The poor cat now looked as if she were made of little more than fur-covered matchsticks and wire. "She's very near her time, isn't she?"

"She is, or she may have an infection." Viola sounded grim. "Either way, we have to catch her."

Alice backed away from the box. "What should I do now, Viola?" she asked in a low voice.

"Stay where you are. If you move, she'll run that way." Viola crouched over and held out a hand.

Louise addressed the cat in soothing tones. "It's okay, Tess. I know you have good reason not to like humans, but some of us are nicer than you think." She felt a bit foolish for talking to a cat, until she thought of all the times that she had spoken to Wendell as if he were a person. *Animals may not understand the words, but they respond to a gentle tone.* "Yes, everything is all right, Tess. Please do not run away again."

The calico hissed and backed away from Viola and Louise, but when she turned to flee she confronted the waiting Alice. The alluring scent of the dried fish treats caught her attention again, and hunger drove her to take a few, hesitant steps toward the box in which Alice had scattered them.

"Go on, sweet girl," Viola urged. "Go and nibble on them. No one will chase you away."

Unfortunately at that moment, the side delivery door opened and Fred Humbert stepped out. "I thought I heard voices—"

Tess reversed direction and crouched low as if she were crawling toward the hardware store owner.

"Quick, Fred, shut that door!" Viola called out.

It was too late for that. By the time Fred reacted, Tess had made a long, low leap, bounding straight between his legs and into the hardware store.

Louise, Viola and Alice hurried past the astonished Fred and pursued Tess into the building's storage room. There was no sign of her, but the startled cries of customers from out in the store aisles gave away her location.

"Hey now!"

"Is that a *cat*?"

"Fred, you starting a pet section?"

"Watch it!"

There was a soft thud, and something fell over and bounced with innumerable hollow, bonking sounds. A different sound, the striking of a bell-like chime, triggered by a sensor whenever someone entered the hardware store, made Viola call out, "Keep the front door closed!"

Once again, the warning came too late as the chime sounded a second time. Two men walking in through the front entrance looked down, startled by Tess as she darted between them. By the time Louise and Viola dodged the customers and made it out to the street, the calico had vanished.

Chapter  Five

L ittle wretch," Viola said as she and Louise stood outside the hardware store. She sounded resigned rather than angry. "All skin and bones but for those kittens, and still she'd rather run away than trust me."

"She is certainly determined to evade capture," Louise said. "I do not wish to be pessimistic, but it may be that you cannot save this one."

"I realize that, but I have to keep trying." Viola's voice went low. "I'd do the same for any helpless animal, but for some reason Tess is special. Every time I see her scrounging around in the trash, so small and scruffy, so determined to survive, it tugs at my heart."

Viola was not a churchgoing person, and often bristled when she perceived someone to be "preaching" to her, but at the same time she was deeply spiritual in her own way.

"She is most deserving of your help, my dear," Louise said, slightly ashamed of her own doubt. "You remind me of a passage in Proverbs that says, 'Do not withhold good from those who deserve it, when it is within your power to act'" (3:27).

Viola nodded. "Does the Bible have any advice on how to catch a frightened, pregnant cat?"

"In Luke 6:38, Jesus said, 'Give, and it will be given to you,'" Louise told her. "If you keep showing Tess that you care, perhaps the good Lord will nudge her along to you."

Viola's eyes shifted to the clouds overhead. "Any time now would be wonderful, God."

When Louise and Viola went back inside, they found Alice explaining the situation to Fred as she helped him pick up the small, tin plant pots that Tess had knocked over during her flight through the store.

"I'm real sorry I scared her off, Viola," Fred told her as he restacked the pots. "Soon as I get this tidied up, I'll head on out and see if I can find her again for you."

"It wasn't your fault, and it's no use looking for her. She'll find a place to hide out until after dark. Besides, you've got a business to run." Viola sighed. "For that matter, so do I."

Fred nodded. "If I spot the little lady again, I'll give you a call."

"I'd appreciate it. Louise, Alice, thanks for trying." Viola gave them a rueful smile and left the store.

Alice righted the sales sign for the restacked plant pots. "Tess looks like she's starving, and that can't be good for her kittens. Isn't there anything else we can do besides chase her around town?"

"I'll have my customers keep a watch out for her," Fred promised. "The minute she shows her little nose around here, we'll call Ms. Reed."

Alice's expression brightened. "What if we asked some of the other merchants in town to do the same thing? You know, keep an eye out for Tess, and to call Viola when they spot her?"

"Like a neighborhood crime watch, only this would be a cat watch, if there is such a thing," Fred said, and grinned.

Alice beamed. "Why not?"

"All that, just for some grubby stray?" One of Fred's customers, a sour-faced man who had been eavesdropping on their conversation, made a sound of disbelief. "You'd be better off calling the animal control office over in Potterston. They can come out here and catch it before it hurts someone."

"The only crime this cat is guilty of is being abandoned," Alice told the man. "She's not dangerous, and she hasn't hurt anyone. The reason we can't catch her is that she's *afraid* of people."

The customer shook his head. "Strays carry all kinds of diseases. What if she has rabies and bites someone? Then you'll have a fine mess on your hands."

"There's no reason to think Tess is rabid," Alice protested.

"No reason to think that she isn't," the customer countered. "Take my advice, lady. Have that animal caught and put down before she causes you some real grief."

Before Alice jumped to Tess's defense again, Louise placed a gentle hand on her sister's shoulder. "Thank you for your suggestion," she told the man.

"Weren't you looking for some cedar mulch, sir?" Fred asked, and expertly steered the customer away from the sisters.

"Louise, how could you thank that . . . that . . . *creature*?" Alice demanded as soon as the two men were gone. "He was talking about trapping and *killing* Tess, as if it were a perfectly reasonable solution."

"Not everyone shares your love for animals," Louise reminded her, "and I suspect arguing the point would have only made him angrier."

"Well, now *I'm* angry."

"Yes, but unlike that gentleman, you are reasonable."
Louise smiled. "Now, shall we go over to the Coffee Shop
and tell June Carter about your idea? Almost everyone in
town drops in there, so she can pass along the word about
our Tess Watch to the other merchants."

"Yes, of course." Alice released a long breath. "I'm sorry,
Louise. I didn't mean to snap at you like that."

Louise borrowed one of Jane's favorite gestures and
looped her arm through Alice's. "You can make it up to me
with a cup of coffee and a slice of pie."

At the Coffee Shop, June Carter waited on the Howard
sisters and, after hearing Tess's story, readily agreed to put
out the word to the other merchants around town.

"I'll put some scraps in a dish for her out back," the
robust, cheerful June said. "Or do you think she'd prefer milk
or cream?"

"She looks so hungry I think she'd eat just about anything," Alice said.

"Would it help to try to coax her inside?" Hope Collins,
June's waitress and another animal lover, asked. "Maybe we
could put out a little trail of cheese bits from the back door
into the dry storage closet. The kitten I had when I was a girl
was like a mouse, he loved cheese so much."

"I would not recommend trying to bring her inside,"
Louise warned, and briefly described the minor chaos Tess
had caused during the time she had spent in the hardware
store. "Just leave a little something to tempt her and contact
Viola if she shows up."

June was called to the counter to pick up an order, but
Hope lingered by the Howards' table. "You know, we had a
family of raccoons raiding the garbage cans in my neighborhood a few years back, until Potterston Animal Control put
out some traps and caught them. Maybe you could borrow

one from them. Excuse me." Hope moved down to the next table to refill a waiting customer's coffee.

"Why does everyone want to call Animal Control?" Alice grimaced. "They might have to put Tess and the kittens to sleep."

"Try to think positively, dear. You know that that is not necessarily true. Animal Control deals with community problems resulting from negligent animal ownership," Louise said. "If Tess is healthy, the Animal Control officer will likely take her to the Humane Society shelter in Potterston. Calicos are rare, and new kittens are very appealing, so there is little reason to expect they won't be adopted."

Alice grimaced. "*If* she's healthy."

"Loving animals does not excuse one from behaving responsibly. If Tess is carrying a communicable disease, then she presents a danger to other animals and possibly humans." Louise sighed. "I want to see Tess and her kittens live just as much as you and Viola do, Alice, but we must be sensible. If Tess was carrying a disease, and infected a child trying to pet her, how would you feel?"

Alice's brown hair bobbed as she shook her head. "A child would never get close enough to pet her."

"Very well, how would you feel if Tess wandered over to Grace Chapel Inn? Wendell is very friendly, and persistent. We let him roam freely on the property, so Tess would likely encounter him. If she is infectious, he would never have a chance."

Alice swallowed hard. "I never thought of that."

"Caring for animals does not give us the entitlement to violate the rights of others," Louise said gently. "We must keep things in perspective, and temper our compassion with wisdom."

Alice nodded reluctantly. "I understand, and if it comes to that, I'll call Animal Control myself."

Louise covered her sister's hand with hers. "We will do our very best not to let it come to that."

∽

Viola called Louise on Friday to confirm that Ms. Renda had obtained permission from Franklin's principal and the students' parents to have the poetry club meet at the Acorn Hill Library the next day.

"Nia Komonos is putting a table, an overhead projector and a tape recorder in the reading room for us," Viola said.

Louise wasn't surprised to hear this, as Nia, their new librarian, was very considerate of the library's patrons. The need for the equipment, however, perplexed her. "Why will we need all those things?"

"To inspire the poetry club, and to show them how to accomplish certain production and publishing tasks," Viola said, sounding excited. "Oh, and come prepared to read your favorite short poem out loud. The kids will be bringing theirs."

"How short? What are you planning, Viola?"

"No more than twenty lines." The bookseller laughed. "As for the rest, you'll see."

∽

Before Louise left for her meeting the next day, she stopped by the front desk to check the inn's schedule.

"Mr. and Mrs. Landry are spending the day in Riverton, and will check out tomorrow. Mr. Merrick checked out this morning," Alice, who was sorting some paperwork and receipts, told her. "Our next reservation doesn't arrive until tomorrow, so we have everything under control. Go to your meeting in peace."

Louise eyed the door leading to the kitchen. "I think I will check on Jane before I go."

The phone rang. "I don't think she's back from the market yet," Alice said before she answered it.

Jane walked into the kitchen at the same time Louise did, her arms filled with grocery bags. More bags crowded the counter by the refrigerator. "Hi, Louise."

Considering that they only had two guests presently staying at the inn, there were an unusually large number of bags. "What is all this?"

Jane's expression turned to one of chagrin. "I should never go shopping when I'm hungry. Especially on the day the new produce shipment arrives at the General Store."

"You should have eaten more at breakfast this morning," Louise gently scolded as she came over to help her sister unpack the bags. The exotic-looking vegetables Jane had purchased made her frown. "Goodness, what are these?"

"Impulse buys," Jane said in a morose voice. "Bok choy, purple cabbage, kai lan, luffa, pingtung eggplant and snow peas. Plus jasmine rice and other goodies." From another bag she removed a bottle of red-tinted oil, a large bag of rice and several packets of spices. "Everything I need to try out some new recipes." She gave her a hopeful glance. "You and Alice do like Chinese food, don't you?"

Accustomed to her sister's inclination toward adventure, especially in cooking, Louise smiled. "We will now."

"Good, because you're going to be eating it for at least the next three days." Jane produced a wry laugh and began separating the colorful vegetables. "The only thing I couldn't find was Chinese chives, but I can ask Craig Tracy to order some seedlings for me. They're eaten like a vegetable in Asia, and you can make a spray from them that prevents mildew in the garden."

"I see." Louise tried to imagine eating something that could ward off mildew and shuddered. "What prompted you to buy all this?"

"It's my own fault. The farmer's market didn't have the little cucumbers I wanted for this half-sour recipe I found in mother's cookbook, so I thought I'd stop in town to see if the General Store had them. You know how I've been nagging the manager to bring in some different types of veggies and other foods. Well, he ordered a trial selection to see how they'd sell." Jane chuckled. "Next thing you know, I was standing in line with an entire cart full of Asian delights."

Once all the bags were unpacked, Louise surveyed the curious-looking produce. Normally such foreign vegetables would have intimidated her, but Jane was such an accomplished chef that she had no doubt that whatever she made with them would be delicious. The amount she had bought, however, was rather daunting. "We may have to invite Aunt Ethel over for dinner several times."

"Or the local detachment of the National Guard. I wonder if they like Chinese food." Jane turned to look at the wall clock, making her long dark ponytail sway. "Aren't you supposed to be at the library soon?"

"I can spare a few moments." She examined some golden brown, gnarled-looking roots that had a sharp but pleasing scent to them. "These smell rather familiar. What are they?"

"Fresh ginger root. It's much tastier than the powdered variety." Jane wrapped them in parchment paper. "I might make some cookies or crystallize pieces of them in sugar. Ginger root is supposed to be good for nervous stomachs."

She placed them in the refrigerator's vegetable bin. "Speaking of nervous, is that how you're feeling about your poetry club meeting?"

"No, although I am concerned about Viola." Louise washed a head of purple cabbage and shook it off before placing it in a perforated vegetable storage bag. "I am not sure if she offered to host these meetings because she wants to help the students, or because . . ."

"She wanted to show up Ms. Renda?" Jane asked. "Now, now, Louise. Most days Viola may be as friendly as a hedgehog with a migraine, but she's not the vindictive type."

Louise dried her hands on a kitchen towel. "That is a remarkable observation, considering all the negative things you had to say about Viola the other night."

"Alice and I talked about it, and you were right. I wasn't being fair to her. You know, I'm beginning to think that Viola is a lot like the Big Bad Wolf, all huff and puff." She caught Louise's expression and grinned. "You're not to repeat that to her. I'll be barred from her bookshop for life."

"I would not dare." Louise opened the spice cabinet and began putting away the various bottles and jars left on the counter.

"Meeting with these kids will be good for her. She needs to get in touch with the younger generation." Jane took a bottle of garlic-honey dressing from her sister's hand. "Let me do that. Go on, now, before you're late." She made a shooing gesture.

Louise had never consciously selected a favorite poem from the many she enjoyed reading, but one that always made her feel better about life was the obvious choice. So armed with a volume of Shakespeare's sonnets, she drove into town.

For years, the Acorn Hill library had provided a modest collection of books and a quiet haven that many of the town's residents sought out for reading or study. Ever since their elderly librarian had died, her replacement, a young woman from Pittsburgh named Nia Komonos, had done much to revitalize the town's little library. Louise thought it was like watching a replanted garden grow and burst into bloom.

In the sunniest corner by the front windows, Nia had created a new children's section by replacing the old wall stack shelving with low, long wooden shelves open on both sides and painted with bright primary colors. The shelves, which were the perfect size for the library's smallest patrons, were stocked with picture and board books, and arranged so that they formed a three-sided reading area. Nia had also moved the school-style furnishings to another section and put out some low plastic play tables and small bean bag chairs. A row of larger chairs lined the opposite side of one of the partition-forming shelves, so that parents could sit in relative comfort to watch their preschoolers. Nia also had recruited several volunteer grandmothers and grandfathers to come in and read to her youngest patrons during the library's new weekly "Story Hour."

Louise had never paid much attention to the children's section, but the imaginative way that Nia had remodeled it drew her gaze now.

Posters featuring famous authors and books now decorated the walls, and a centered, square glass case held interesting objects related to the library's monthly theme, also one of Nia's ideas. In keeping with the current month's theme of patriotism, Nia had arranged a number of books about the men and women who had sacrificed so much in order to serve their country, and the wars they had fought. There were also some medals and ribbons, lent by members of the local branch of the American Legion, and some small American flags.

Louise thought it was an excellent way to remind the town of their history. Acorn Hill had seen many of its young men go off to war, never to return, and she liked to see that their memory was honored.

Vera Humbert had lent Nia one of her antique quilts for display as well, Louise saw. She had seen the red-and-white church quilt, originally made to aid the Red Cross during World War I, on display at the Humberts' home many times. Vera had told Louise that the names, embroidered in red and gold thread on the quilt's oblong patches, had been purchased by donating a nickel or dime to the Red Cross fund. Although the quilt was eighty-five years old and was worn and faded, hundreds of names were still perfectly readable. Across the top the makers had embroidered "United We Stand" in large, beautifully scrolled letters.

Louise stopped to admire the quilt. Like so many other treasured heirlooms, it became more fascinating as the years passed.

"It's lovely, isn't it?" Nia Komonos came over from the checkout counter to greet her. The small garnet earrings she wore sparkled against her dark brown hair and matched the dark red jumper she wore over her long-sleeved white blouse. The outfit went beautifully with her coloring, which was dark and vibrant, thanks to her Greek ancestry. "The moment I saw it, I had to beg Mrs. Humbert to let me borrow it for our display."

"Vera does have the loveliest collection of quilts in town." She glanced around but saw no sign of Viola or the poetry club. "Have Ms. Reed and the students from Franklin arrived?"

"Yes, I put them in our new study room." She gestured toward the south end of the building, where the administrative office was located. "Let me go with you."

Over the last month Nia had rearranged other areas in the library, Louise saw, to make optimum use of the available shelf and floor space. Armchairs flanked small side tables, providing spots for patrons to sit and read, and a row of student cubicles offered study and work space along the back wall, where it was quietest. There were also three desks with computers with Internet access.

Louise wasn't inordinately fond of computers, but Jane had taught her that they were standard equipment in most schools now, and that some children learned to type before they could write. It made sense to have them available here, where the kids could use them for study and homework projects.

"One of our regular patrons telecommutes from home for a large computer supply company in Potterston," Nia told her. "He just upgraded his home system, so he donated the old computers he had sitting around the house to the library."

"They do not look very old to me," Louise said, admiring the efficient-looking equipment, one of which was similar to the modern computer that Jane had installed at the inn after she had moved back home.

"They aren't. The gentleman who donated them told me that his job requires him to work with the very latest technology, so his company gives him a brand-new computer every six to eight months." Nia paused to answer a question from a young boy looking for reference books for a school project, and directed him to the appropriate shelf. "I'm hoping to wheedle another donation out of him just before Christmas."

Louise smiled. "Next you'll be telling me that the library has a Web site."

"Not yet, but I am working on Mayor Tynan about using some of the town budget to purchase the domain on the Internet *for* our Web site." As they walked, Nia absently rearranged a chair here and there and scooped up a magazine left on a table. "When he does, I'm planning to ask your sister Jane to help me with the site."

The young librarian sounded optimistic, but that was in keeping with her bright, gregarious personality. Louise also had no doubt that Nia would achieve her goals with little difficulty. Where the library was concerned, she was becoming a force to be reckoned with.

"This was the old records and card file room," Nia said as she led Louise down a narrow aisle to a door marked with a new sign that read STUDY ROOM—QUIET. "Since the county has computerized our index, we don't need to keep all those boxes of paper and records. The walls are well insulated, so I thought we would use it for meetings, study groups and so forth."

One of the library's teenage volunteers came up to them. "Ms. Komonos, there's a lady with an overdue book at the desk who doesn't want to pay her fine. She says the return slip was stamped wrong."

"Of course she does." Nia rolled her eyes. "I'd better get back up front. If you need anything, let me know, Louise."

Chapter   Six

The six members of the Franklin Poetry Club were sitting around a rectangular desk while Viola spoke to them from the front of the room. Unwilling to disrupt her friend, Louise silently slipped inside and sat in one of the empty seats.

"Poetry is unlike any other art form, both in the writing and in the understanding of it," Viola was saying. "If you consider novelists as the architects of literature, then it's easy to imagine their books as mansions. Poets, on the other hand, are more like painters, as they use words not to build, but to portray. Each poem is an intimate portrait of something—an event, a person, a place, even a feeling."

"Well, we've got some more portraits to look at," Wendy said, and lifted a folder containing loose papers. "These are a few late submissions we've gotten in from the kids at our school."

"And we have to read all that?" Hadley groaned. Today he was wearing a Steelers football jersey and matching cap, as if to emphasize his love for the sport.

"Why join a poetry club if you hate reading it?" Rob asked.

Hadley's expression changed. "Oh, I like some poetry. The stuff I don't like is what we have to read in class. It sounds like it's written in a secret code. I've got to write a paper on part of this one guy's poem, and I don't understand half of what he's talking about. Why didn't he use, you know, like plain language?"

"Poetry enables us to see our world and each other through someone else's perspective," Viola replied. "Because a poem takes you directly into that other person's thoughts and emotions, quite often it's difficult to understand. Based on when they lived, where, and what sort of experiences they have had, not to mention their native language, their point of view might be dramatically different from your own." She looked at Hadley. "What was the name of the poet and the poem you found so difficult?"

"It was a book-long poem by some guy named Chaucer."

Louise disguised a wince by fluffing the short silver hair at her temple. Naturally a boy so modern-thinking and involved in sports would find Geoffrey Chaucer's *Canterbury Tales* nearly incomprehensible.

Viola was also sympathetic. "That is a tough one. *Canterbury Tales* is a very long poem, and it was written in a type of English that hasn't been spoken for hundreds of years."

"That's what I mean," Hadley said. "How can you relate to something you can't even translate? Couldn't the guy just write it in plain English?"

"For Chaucer, that was plain English," Viola assured him. "Keep in mind that this particular poet lived in a world that no longer exists, and which had many odd things in it that are completely foreign to us. Priests often spoke in Latin, merchants spoke French, some country folk even used the language of the Vikings. Their world was nothing like ours. For instance, how many of you have had a conversation with an armored knight about chivalric behavior? When was the last time you and your families went on a pilgrimage to a famous shrine?"

"My folks took me and my sister to Disney World in Florida last summer," Rob said, making the other teenagers laugh. "Does that count?"

"Only if you write a poem about it, and then try to imagine what someone five hundred years from now will think of it," a straight-faced Viola told him. "It's safe to assume that they won't have Mickey Mouse as an icon of their culture. So what do you think people in the distant future will make of our devotion to a three-foot-tall, costumed rodent?"

Rob scratched the back of his head. "That we all badly needed glasses?"

The discussion continued for several minutes as the students eagerly traded remarks on how they and their era would be perceived by their distant descendants. Viola didn't appear to mind at all, and Louise took pleasure in listening to the bright minds wrestle with the new idea.

"Okay, you guys," Conor said at last. He turned to Viola. "We'd sit here all day and pick apart something, if you let us."

"Yeah, shut up already, Had," Wendy said.

"No problem," the fair-haired boy said. "I've got plenty to write for my paper now."

Sherrilyn raised her hand as if she were still in school. When Viola nodded to her, she asked, "You were going to read one of your favorite poems, weren't you, Ms. Reed?"

"I will, and you're going to analyze it. It's one that was written by our old friend William Wordsworth." Viola picked up a slim volume. "We're going to a secluded grove in the

English countryside now. There's a man sitting there, a man who just returned to his homeland, and this is what he is thinking about." Viola opened the book to a page marked with a ribbon and began to read.

> "I heard a thousand blended notes,
> While in a grove I sat reclined,
> In that sweet mood when pleasant thoughts
> Bring sad thoughts to the mind.
> To her fair works did Nature link
> The human soul that through me ran;
> And much it grieved my heart to think
> What man has made of man.
> Through primrose tufts, in that green bower,
> The periwinkle trailed its wreaths;
> And 'tis my faith that every flower
> Enjoys the air it breathes.
> The birds around me hopped and played,
> Their thoughts I cannot measure:—
> But the least motion which they made,
> It seemed a thrill of pleasure.
> The budding twigs spread out their fan,
> To catch the breezy air;
> And I must think, do all I can,
> That there was pleasure there.
> If this belief from heaven be sent,
> If such be Nature's holy plan,
> Have I not reason to lament
> What man has made of man?"

Viola closed the book and regarded the students. "That poem was William Wordsworth's 'Lines Written in Early Spring.' It is a classic representation of his work, and typical of English romantic verse, which explores the similarities and contrasts between aspects of nature and mankind. Wordsworth loved nature." She paused and scanned the faces of the students. "What is your first reaction to it?"

"He sure loved to complain," Wendy said.

"That he did, and he was very good at it. You could call him the eighteenth century's most prolific whiner." Viola's gaze shifted. "Rob? What did you think of it?"

"He liked nature more than hanging out with the guys, maybe," the boy said. "Not exactly the jock type, huh, Conor?"

Conor didn't reply, but his expression darkened.

"Maybe he had some bad experiences," Sherrilyn said, diverting everyone's attention from her brother.

"Wordsworth regularly found that human beings came up short when compared to the rest of nature. He perceived the natural world as filled with great happiness and joy, while the world of mankind existed in the exact opposite state." Viola passed the book, opened to the poem, around the table. "Imagine Wordsworth as a student at Franklin, and submitting this poem for your consideration. What would be your reaction?"

"I'd accept it," Millicent said at once. "It's simple, beautifully written, and still makes you think."

"Same here, only I'd tell him to use a pen name," Rob drawled.

Sherrilyn frowned. "Why?"

The boy made a face. "Come on, Sher, a guy who writes about primroses and periwinkles? He's just asking for some *severe* ragging."

Conor didn't laugh with the other students, and when the mirth died down, he said, "It's a pretty poem, but Wordsworth's views are wrong."

Louise, who like Viola had always enjoyed Wordsworth's poetry, asked him, "What do you find wrong with them?"

"The natural world isn't happy or joyous." His gaze shifted to the window. "It may appear to be, but it's very unemotional and businesslike."

"Give us a practical example," Viola said, encouraging him.

"They're all around. You only have to look." He pointed to a black and orange striped butterfly, which was flitting over the flowers growing in Nia's window box. "It's beautiful, but see what's watching it?" He pointed to a cobweb stretched over one corner of the window. A large spider sat in the center of a barely visible web. "If that butterfly blunders into the web, it's a goner. You can't idealize the surface beauty of nature and ignore the constant life-and-death struggles taking place behind it every second of every day."

"If everything in nature is too busy surviving to feel happy," Hadley chimed in, "then everything in nature must be pretty depressed. You'd feel right at home, Conor."

"That's not true," Millicent said, looking indignant. "I mean, the notion that things in nature have no emotions. Our dog just had puppies, and you can tell by the way she treats them just how much she loves them."

"Animals care for their young out of instinct, not emotion," Conor argued. "What separates man from all the other creatures is his capacity for sentiment. It is what makes us the most unnatural creature in nature."

Louise wondered whether a public library was the place to debate Creation, but felt she had to respond to the boy's cynical view. "Sentiment is not the sole line of separation. There are many aspects of human existence that elevate us above the animals, like faith and hope."

Conor shrugged. "If you're lucky enough to have them."

Louise felt completely taken aback. The young man's careless remark sounded bland, but there was a bleakness to it that hinted at personal pain. Was this the reason Conor had not been to church? Had he somehow lost hope, and with it his faith in God?

"I've noticed a lot of poetry is about man and nature," Sherrilyn said, again drawing the group's focus away from her brother. "Is that a common theme, Ms. Reed?"

"It is. Many types of environments—however unsentimental they may be—inspire us." Viola looked at Millicent, who had raised her hand. "Yes?"

"Maybe Wordsworth wanted man's nature to be more in tune with what he thought the rest of nature offered," the girl guessed, "so he wrote the poem to communicate that to people."

"He's not addressing anyone in particular in the poem, though," Rob said. "He's just sitting in a grove by himself, brooding."

"A poem is a form of address," Conor said with a trace of condescension. "You don't have to start them like a letter you're writing."

"Sounds to me like Wordsworth can't relax and enjoy himself," Hadley put in. "He's too tense."

"Or he's feeling guilty about something," Sherrilyn said. She flushed as the other students looked at her, but lifted her chin. "I mean, he condemns man, but he's a man, too. Whatever man does reflects on him too."

"You said Wordsworth had just returned to his homeland, Ms. Reed," Wendy said. "Where was he before he wrote this poem?"

"I thought someone might pick up on that little clue I dangled," Viola said. "Wordsworth composed this poem immediately after returning to England from a visit to

France. He was actually in France during the time of the French Revolution."

"But why would he feel guilty about escaping such a horrible war?" Millicent asked. "You'd think he'd be celebrating or something."

"I'd be popping open a couple bottles of champagne," Rob said.

"William Wordsworth had supported the idea of revolution in France," Viola told the students. "He had believed the cause was just, and had publicly spoken in favor of those in revolt."

"Then he went and saw what the revolution was truly like in person," Sherrilyn said softly.

Wendy took in a sharp breath before releasing it slowly. "Poor guy. Imagine how guilty he must have felt."

Viola nodded. "So beneath the obvious meaning of love for the beauty of nature, and regret for the ugliness of man at his worst, there seems to be a deep and heartfelt sense of shame. In this poem, Wordsworth might not have been complaining as much as he was grieving, for man and for himself." She closed the book. "Now it's your turn to read your favorite poems. Who would like to go first?"

"I will," Wendy said, and took out a sheet of notebook paper. "This poem is 'Love and Friendship,' written by Emily Brontë.

"Love is like the wild rose-briar;
Friendship like the holly-tree.
The holly is dark when the rose-briar blooms,
But which will bloom most constantly?

The wild-rose briar is sweet in the spring,
Its summer blossoms scent the air;

Yet wait till winter comes again
And who will call the wild-briar fair?

Then scorn the silly rose-wreath now
And deck thee with the holly's sheen,
That when December blights thy brow
He may still leave thy garland green."

Wendy grinned and folded the paper. "That's my favorite poem because it reminds me that friendship is just as important and as lasting, if not more so, than love." She elbowed Rob, who was making a face. "It does, lame-brain."

"I bet that attitude will change, soon as you and your boyfriend make up," he predicted, earning another jab.

Viola cleared her throat. "An excellent reading, Wendy, and a rare poem by Ms. Brontë, who was better known for her great novel, *Wuthering Heights*. Millicent, why don't you go next?"

Louise was surprised when the seemingly frivolous Millicent read "Nightpiece," a serious and subtle poem by James Joyce.

"There, now," Hadley said when she had finished reading. "I didn't understand hardly any of that."

"Neither did I," Millicent admitted, "but I loved the sound of the words, so I looked them up. A thurible is a container made of metal, also called a censer, made for burning incense. You hold it in your hand or on the end of a chain, and the incense is burned at an important service like a Catholic Mass."

Louise admired the teenager's persistence. "James Joyce was Irish Catholic, so the word was a familiar one to him."

"What's a verge, and a nave, and a starknell, then?" Hadley demanded.

"A verge is a boundary. A nave is the hub of a wheel. There is no such word as starknell, but I think he meant it as *star knell*, two separate words that he ran together. A knell is a tolling of a bell slowly and solemnly, like at a funeral. It's also a mournful or ominous sound. So a starknell would be the same thing, except coming from the stars instead of a bell."

"James Joyce liked confusing his readers," Viola put in. "He told an associate that history was like a game, where you make people line up. You whisper a phrase in the ear of the person on one end of the line and have them pass it along in the same way. By the time the last person in line hears the phrase, it comes out completely different from how it began."

"Joyce also called his novel *Finnegans Wake* a 'night-piece,'" Louise said. She had personally grappled with his many, difficult works in college, and admired anyone who had the nerve to study the often exasperating poet and novelist. "It was his code word for something no one could understand easily."

"What do you think it means, Millicent?" Viola asked.

"Well, I think the key line is 'the adoring waste of souls.' The poet is looking at life, which he thinks is pretty pathetic." The girl made a face. "Joyce can be pretty mean, but maybe he meant our faith helps us to rise out of the void of life, like the smoke from the incense burner."

"*Sheesh.*" Hadley rubbed his face with one big hand. "Good thing you had a dictionary close by."

Wendy patted his shoulder. "Sometimes you have to make an effort, Had."

The readings continued. Rob contributed a short, comical limerick by an anonymous modern poet, and Hadley recited an enthusiastic tribute to his favorite football team, which had been made into a song by some area fans.

"If song lyrics rhyme, they're poetry too," he said after the other students booed his selection. "And there's nothing wrong with them being about sports."

Wendy laughed. "'We'll kick their butts all over the field come Sunday' is hardly lofty, inspirational material."

"Ms. Reed said poetry is a portrait in time. In this time a lot of us guys like sports," Hadley stubbornly insisted.

"We'll reserve that debate for another time, Hadley. Sherrilyn, would you like to go next?" Viola asked.

Conor's sister flushed and looked down at her hands. "Mine is 'The World's Need' by Ella Wheeler Wilcox. It's pretty short, but I like what it has to say.

"So many gods, so many creeds,
So many paths that wind and wind,
While just the art of being kind
Is all the sad world needs."

Viola smiled. "That is a belief that I can support wholeheartedly."

After discussing the simple but devastatingly direct philosophy of Sherrilyn's poem, Viola turned to the girl's brother. "That leaves you, Conor."

"My favorite poem was written by Emily Dickinson," Conor said.

"Ho-ho, a chick poem!" Hadley crowed.

"Not particularly," Conor replied. "There's no title for the poem, but then, she never titled any of them.

"Because I could not stop for Death,
He kindly stopped for me;
The carriage held but just ourselves
And immortality.

We slowly drove, he knew no haste,
And I had put away
My labor, and my leisure too,
For his civility.

We passed the school where children played
At wrestling in a ring;
We passed the fields of gazing grain,
We passed the setting sun.

Or rather, he passed us.
The dews drew quivering and chill,
For only gossamer my gown,
My tippet only tulle.

We paused before a house that seemed
A swelling of the ground;
The roof was scarcely visible,
The cornice but a mound.

Since then 'tis centuries; but each
Feels shorter than the day
I first surmised the horses' heads
Were toward eternity."

In the sepulchral aftermath of the reading, no one spoke
for a few moments.

"Wow, Con," Rob finally said. "Could you have picked
something a little *less* uplifting, maybe?"

The other students' expressions ranged from puzzled to
uneasy, except for Sherrilyn's. Louise was startled to see tears
in the girl's eyes, and the edge of her teeth set in a trembling
lower lip.

"Doesn't anyone want to analyze it?" Conor said. Although his question was provocative, there was more misery than defiance in his eyes.

Wendy grimaced. "No, that's fairly self-explanatory, as poems go."

"Emily Dickinson was one of the greatest American poets of the nineteenth century," Viola said in a suitably somber voice. "She was also a reclusive spinster who lived with her father. After she died of Bright's disease, a debilitating disease of the kidneys that likely caused her years of chronic pain, her poems were found written on scraps of paper she had packed away in boxes and trunks. She never showed them to anyone, and during her lifetime published only two poems."

"No wonder she's so depressing." Rob made a face. "Are all her poems like that?"

"Many are. She was unusually sensitive to matters of life and death." Louise knew that some teenagers often had an exaggerated interest in the subject of death, but Conor's choice disturbed her on a different level. *It is time for another point of view.* "Viola, I would like to read my favorite poem, if I may?"

Chapter Seven

Years had faded the cloth cover of Louise's collection of Shakespearean sonnets from a dark forest green to the color of sun-drenched ferns. Most of the gilt had been scoured away from the embossed lettering on the spine, and the page edges had turned a faint yellow.

There was no need for Louise to mark her favorite sonnet, for the book fell open naturally to the page that she had read so often.

"When, in disgrace with fortune and men's eyes,
I all alone beweep my outcast state,
And trouble deaf heaven with my bootless cries,
And look upon myself and curse my fate,
Wishing me like to one more rich in hope,
Featured like him, like him with friends possess'd,
Desiring this man's art and that man's scope,
With what I most enjoy contented least;
Yet in these thoughts myself almost despising,
Haply I think on thee, and then my state,
Like to the lark at break of day arising
From sullen earth, sings hymns at heaven's gate;

For thy sweet love remember'd such wealth brings
That then I scorn to change my fate with kings."

Louise set down her book. "William Shakespeare wrote this sonnet in the sixteenth century, around the time plague caused the theaters in London to be closed. His plays had been featured in those theaters, so he was out of work. At the same time, a famous dramatist named Robert Greene attacked Shakespeare, defaming his work and calling him an 'upstart crow.'"

"Ouch," Rob said.

"No one likes to be criticized, naturally, but it is particularly wounding to poets, who invest such emotion in their work that enduring any vicious name-calling is particularly painful." Louise nodded toward the folders containing the poems submitted to the club for consideration. "Please remember that when you compose your rejection slips."

"Hey, everyone's heard of Shakespeare, even me," Hadley said. When everyone gave him puzzled looks, he added, "Anyone ever heard of Robert Greene?"

"Success is the best revenge." Viola smiled. "Tell us why this is your favorite poem, Louise."

She thought for a moment. "I think it has to be its stirring optimism. The sonnet speaks about the despair everyone feels at some point in his life, and how important it is to rise above the trials and tribulations we endure."

"Heaven can certainly be deaf," Conor muttered.

There was a hallmark of pain too fierce to be concealed. Did Conor believe his prayers to be ignored? "No, Conor, it only seems that way. God always listens. The pain we feel comes from within, from our own sense of disappointment, which is a common enough reaction when we face adversity."

"Like when we compare ourselves to people who are better off," Millicent said. "We all want to be beautiful, and wealthy, and have lots of friends."

Rob gave her a dubious look. "Who wouldn't? Bring on the pals, the millions, and"—he felt his long nose with his fingers—"the plastic surgeon."

"That is why envy is one of the seven deadly sins," Viola said. "It can do such damage to us. Consider the paradox in the line, 'With what I most enjoy contented least.' Emptiness instead of fulfillment. Shakespeare reminds us what little value something has when we take no pleasure in it. That is, without question, the scourge of envy."

"But Shakespeare doesn't feel better until he thinks about someone he loves. Doesn't that make him a bit codependent?" Wendy asked.

"We don't have to go through life alone, unless that's the way we want it," Viola answered.

Louise nodded. "If the thought of someone we love raises our spirits, and keeps us from hating ourselves, is that not the best sort of dependence, if it is such?"

"Who was this guy talking about, anyway?" Hadley wanted to know.

"No one knows," Louise admitted. "Shakespeare never identifies his love by name, or even what sort of love he feels toward this person. It could be the bond shared with a parent, an abiding passion for a spouse, or the joy found in a loving friendship. The universality in this poem is that it applies to every sort of love we experience."

"Maybe in the sixteenth century it did." Rob turned to Hadley. "I like you, man, but I ain't flying around like a lark when I think about you."

"Same here, buddy." Hadley clapped him on the shoulder.

"Oh, come on, you guys." Wendy exhorted. "I think Shakespeare *is* talking about a friend in this poem, Mrs. Smith. Real friends don't care what kind of job you have, or how rich you are. They like you for you, and they stick by you when things get tough."

Louise looked at Conor, and noted that some of the strange sadness, which had no place in the eyes of one so young, had disappeared. "Remembering that is what saves us from despair, and gives us the hope we need to persevere during hard times."

The door to the study room opened, and Ms. Renda came in. She was dressed in her coach's uniform. "Sorry to interrupt, but the librarian said I'd find you here, and I need to speak to the club right away."

"Please, come in and join us." Viola gestured to an empty chair, but the coach merely closed the door and stood by it.

"Thank you, but I have to get back to the track as soon as I make this announcement." Ms. Renda took a folded slip of paper out of her trouser pocket. "As you know, the finances for our extracurricular activities come out of the same general school fund each year, and we've been waiting for word from the accounting office on how much is available for the remaining school year." She held up the paper. "This is the bad news. The budget for the fund has been drastically cut."

"How much money is left?" Conor asked.

"Not enough to cover the combined cost of printing the magazine *and* ordering the new uniforms for the track team next year, which have to be paid for in advance." She handed the paper to Wendy. "One of these expenses will have to be eliminated."

"May I see that, Wendy?" Conor took the paper and studied it. "The club and the team have an equal share of the fund. There is enough money left for us to publish the magazine."

Ms. Renda's jaw tightened. "I'm sorry, I didn't explain this properly. If the poetry club uses their portion of the fund, there won't be enough left to pay for the team's uniforms."

"Doesn't the team have uniforms?" Millicent asked.

The coach nodded. "The ones we have need replacing before the next school year starts."

A peculiar sort of triumph lit up Conor's face. "That would be the team's problem, Coach. Not ours."

"You know we're going to take the regional championships this year," she told him with exaggerated patience. "We'll need those uniforms for the state-level competitions in the fall." When the boy didn't react, Ms. Renda sighed. "Conor, you were a member of this team. You know how important this is for the school."

"Can't the school budget a little extra for uniforms?" Wendy asked.

"The principal has already extended our budget to cover traveling expenses and accommodations for the team when we're out of town." The coach looked around the room. "I know publishing your magazine is important to you, but it can wait until next year. These uniforms can't."

"Oh really!" Viola glared at Ms. Renda.

Louise, wanting to head off a heated exchange, was grateful when Rob deflected animosity with a question.

"What about doing some fund-raising?" he suggested. "The school band has car washes and candy bar drives to buy their new uniforms."

"The team can't afford to take off from practice now," the coach said. "The uniforms have to be ordered within the next two weeks. There's no time to raise the money we need."

"Why should we wait?" Conor stood up abruptly. "What makes the track team better than us? Why are they more worthy of the fund money? Why should we give up our objectives just so they can reach theirs?"

"That's not what I said—"

"But it's what you *think*, isn't it?" The boy stormed out of the room.

"I'm sorry, Coach," Sherrilyn said as she got up to follow her brother. "He's . . . he is . . . he didn't mean it." She fled the room.

"Excuse me." Coach Renda went after the Byrne siblings.

A silence hung in the air for a few moments, until Viola took charge of the situation. "You'll need time to think this over—and perhaps have Ms. Renda change her mind—so let's call this meeting to a close, and reconvene next Saturday."

"If there still *is* a poetry club next Saturday," Millicent said. She didn't sound optimistic.

"Conor isn't going to bail on us," Rob assured her. "He's told us that from the beginning, and I believe him."

"So do I." Wendy threw down her notebook. "The heck with the track team."

"Wend!" Hadley looked scandalized.

"I'm serious. Conor's right. It's not fair that we should have to give up our magazine just so that they can look good running around at the state championships." She planted her hands on her hips. "We deserve our share of the fund, and I'm not letting the coach take it away from us."

"Then we'd better be prepared to fight for it," Rob predicted, "because it appears that Coach Renda wants that money just as much as we do."

∽

The day after Viola's first library meeting with the poetry club, Louise accompanied her sisters and aunt to services at Grace Chapel. Their late father, Daniel Howard, had been head pastor at the little church for so many years that it was practically an extension of their home. It was such a presence in the lives of the Howard family that the three sisters had borrowed the church's name to christen their inn.

"I'm afraid it may get hot today," Jane said as they entered the church and walked up to the pew that they were accustomed to occupying. "Did you see how blazing blue the sky is? Not a cloud in sight."

"I don't see Roland or Edna," Ethel fretted. "Edna was supposed to find someone to take over her turn hosting the Craft Klatch."

Since Ethel had taken on the responsibility of coordinating all of Grace Chapel's committees and groups, she often helped with changes in monthly arrangements.

"I see Roland's sister over there, Aunt," Louise said. "Perhaps she can tell you where her brother and Edna are today."

"Yes, Sarah would know. I'll be right back." Ethel left her Bible on the pew beside Jane and made her way to where Sarah Jones was sitting.

Rev. Kenneth Thompson came to the front of the church, which the decorating committee had adorned with bunches of new spring flowers and leafy potted ferns. The tall, dark-haired pastor had come to Acorn Hill from a busy parish in downtown Boston.

Louise was very fond of their pastor. Although he had not been the church board's first choice to replace Daniel Howard as head pastor at Grace Chapel, he had proved to be just as caring and concerned about the community as her father had been. With quiet friendship Rev. Thompson had already helped her and her sisters to deal with many adverse situations. The Howards now considered him one of their dearest friends.

Being at church was a spiritual minivacation for Louise. She enjoyed sharing worship with the other members of the congregation, many of whom were old friends, and Rev. Thompson's sermons never failed to revive her sense of spiritual balance. This Sunday she had expected to find the same, but not even the pastor's clever interpretation of Psalm 62 brought her the usual sense of serenity.

Her gaze strayed time and again to where the Byrne family sat. Sherrilyn and her parents listened attentively to the sermon, but once again Conor was conspicuously absent.

Something was keeping Conor Byrne out of church, perhaps even away from God. But what could it be?

Louise had seen hints of Conor's hidden anguish too often to ignore it further. In her heart, she knew that she could not. He might be suffering a spiritual crisis, one that so many teenagers endured as they outgrew the unquestioning trust of childhood and began to see the world through adult eyes. On the other hand, it might be something far more ominous. All Louise knew was that the more she thought about him, the more she became convinced that the young man was in dire need of help.

She gazed at Conor's parents and sister. They appeared calm, almost stoic. No hint there. *What can I do but pray for him?*

Prayer was another haven that Louise was happy to seek. *Heavenly Father, You protect us always with Your gifts of peace and understanding. If Conor has lost his way, please help him find the path back to You. Make his life whole and happy, and embrace him with Your eternal compassion. Show him the peace that comes from knowing Your light and Your truth.*

Turning the matter over to God restored some of Louise's inner tranquility, but she decided to seek additional, earthly counsel. After the service, she stayed behind and asked the pastor if he could spare her a few moments to discuss a problem.

"Of course, Louise." Rev. Thompson's smile warmed his austere features and revealed the kindness in his eyes. "I was going to straighten up the book room. Would you mind if we talked in there?"

Grace Chapel's book room, which contained a small but interesting library of Bibles, biblical studies and other Christian reading material, had been one of Daniel Howard's favorite places. Louise could not count the number of times that she had discovered her father sitting in one of the comfortably shabby armchairs, reading a Bible story to one of the congregation's children or spending time in his own studies.

Rev. Thompson had made some changes to the room. There were two more floor lamps and a shallow work table set in one corner. The mild disorder of the shelves was gone, the books now neatly put away. Small labels on the shelf edges indicated they were now grouped by subject matter and then alphabetically by author.

"Nia Komonos would enjoy what you have done with our book room," Louise said idly. "She is as dedicated to organization as you are."

"You were at the library yesterday, weren't you?" Rev. Thompson asked.

"I was helping Viola Reed. She's meeting there with the Franklin High School Poetry Club once a week." She sat down with a sigh. "At least, I think she is. There are some problems, and they're part of the reason I needed to speak with you."

The pastor closed the door so that they would not be disturbed, and sat down in the chair opposite Louise's. "One of the problems would be Conor Byrne, I imagine? His father mentioned to me that Conor had gone to your meeting at the library."

She nodded. "Conor was not in church today."

"No. The boy hasn't been attending services for quite some time now." Rev. Thompson clasped his hands and rested his elbows on his knees. "He is a troubled young man."

"I knew something was wrong with him, the first day that I met him." She met the pastor's steady gaze. "Have you spoken with him or his parents? Is there anything we can do?"

"I have provided some counseling for a member of his family, but I can't be more specific than that." He gave her a regretful look. "As with all the people I counsel, I must respect their privacy."

"I understand, and I have no desire to intrude on a confidence. There is likely nothing that I can do but pray for him." A shift in the pastor's expression caught her attention. "Or is there something more?"

Rev. Thompson rose to his feet and went to the window. He stood looking out at the field beyond the church for several moments before he spoke again. "When I was in school, I had a very good friend named Chuck who wanted to be a writer. He had talent, but his stories were so dark and frightening that he couldn't get them published. No one knew that his father was an alcoholic who abused his mother. None of us realized that what he was writing was a silent cry for help, until it was too late." He glanced back at her. "Just before we graduated, Chuck killed himself."

"How terrible!" Louise pressed a hand to her mouth. "I am so sorry."

"I was devastated, but I did learn something from that tragic friendship," Rev. Thompson continued. "Chuck taught me to be more aware of others, of the pain that some people carry around inside and suffer in silence. When I notice that someone is struggling with such a concealed burden, I do whatever is possible to convince him to talk about it. We can't always help our friends with whatever burdens them, but sharing in the knowledge of it is far better than watching them bear it alone."

"Is the same thing happening to Conor?" Louise couldn't help asking. "Is he thinking of . . ." She couldn't bring herself to use the word *suicide*. That such an intelligent and gifted young man might consider such a horrific act chilled her to the bone.

"No, my friend, and I apologize for making you think that," Rev. Thompson said quickly. "All I can tell you is that I have repeatedly tried to share Conor's burden, but I can't reach him. He needs help, but he will not accept it from me. Whoever can get through to him must be someone who pays attention, who cares without reservation, who is there for him without judgment. Louise, you might succeed where I have failed and restore hope in his heart."

It was a daunting proposition, especially as Louise had no idea what was causing Conor's pain. Yet at the same time she felt resolved to do her best. "Let me try, Pastor."

Chapter Eight

The day followed Jane's prediction and turned very warm, so much so that Louise felt somewhat weary by the time she had returned from Grace Chapel. Fortunately, as much as possible, the Howard sisters reserved Sunday as a day of rest, and so planned the bulk of their household tasks for Monday through Saturday. Mr. and Mrs. Landry had signed out by noon, and their expected guest, Arthur Sheldon, helped by arriving on time with plans to do nothing more than sleep off a case of severe jet lag.

"I'll probably stay in bed until morning," Arthur told Louise as he signed the guest register. The tractor salesman's face appeared drawn and tired, and his voice rasped with weariness. "I've spent the last two weeks jaunting between airports from L.A. to Philly, and frankly, I'm bushed."

"Your room is ready, Mr. Sheldon, and we will see to it that you are not disturbed," she assured him.

"A little noise won't bother me, but don't drive a tractor past my window. I'll be tempted to come down and sell you a better one." He refused help with his one bag and trudged upstairs.

Louise began sorting out the week's receipts, but her heart wasn't in the task, and she was grateful when the phone rang. "Good afternoon, Grace Chapel Inn, Louise Smith speaking."

"It's Viola," her friend said. "The poetry club is meeting at the library tomorrow after school is out. Can you make it?"

She eyed the calendar. No new guests were scheduled, she had no piano students, and Alice was off duty. "Why tomorrow?"

"The kids need our help with this fund business, and Ms. Renda doesn't have a scheduled practice." Viola made a disparaging sound. "I'll have to close the shop an hour early, but we *certainly* wouldn't want anything to interfere with the track team's schedule."

"Now, Viola." The second phone line rang, but Jane picked it up in the kitchen, so that Louise did not have to put Viola on hold. "I am sure Ms. Renda is doing the best that she can."

"You keep thinking that, Louise. Can you make it to the meeting?"

Louise thought of Conor, and her promise to Rev. Thompson. "Yes, I will be there."

Alice emerged from the parlor, where she had been reading, and came to the desk. "Was that Aunt Ethel?"

"No." Louise felt disgruntled, although she didn't know precisely why. She did not have to get in the middle of the developing animosity between Viola and Eleanor Renda. She had enough to cope with; there was no reason to allow herself to be used as a buffer.

"I thought she might call," Alice said. "Aunt Ethel wanted to speak to you after church, but evidently she couldn't wait and left for town a few minutes before you came home."

"That was Aunt Ethel just now on the other line," Jane said as she walked out of the kitchen. "She's over at Edna Grassnickle's. You're not going to believe this."

Worry over what the pastor had told her—and over what would come of the meeting with the poetry club the next day—left Louise with little desire to deal with more mundane matters. "What is it now?"

"Edna broke off the engagement with Roland," Jane said. "She's not going to marry him."

"Oh no!" Alice gasped. "How terrible! No wonder they weren't in church today."

Jane nodded. "Auntie said Edna was pretty devastated."

Louise felt a surge of impatience. "I am sure that our aunt will take a few minutes to console Edna before she calls everyone in town to inform them of the news."

"Is that right?" Jane inspected Louise's face. "I know it's hot out, Louie, but warm weather generally doesn't make you catty."

"I am busy. I am *not* being catty."

Alice came around the desk. "Why don't you let me fill out that paperwork, Louise?" Her voice took on the soothing note of calm competence with which she spoke to her patients. "I have the time, and you can have a rest."

"You had the front desk yesterday." Louise strove to keep from snapping. "Today it is my turn. I do not *need* a rest."

"Don't you? Won't do our business much good if you scare off all the guests with that attitude," Jane drawled.

"My attitude has nothing . . ." Louise stopped and stared at her youngest sister for a moment. Jane looked very self-righteous, ready to do battle. Alice appeared deeply concerned. She could only guess what her own face reflected.

"It's all right, Louise," Alice said, giving Jane a warning look.

Jane merely folded her arms. She was not going to budge until she had some satisfaction.

Why am I taking out my temper on my sisters? "Very well." It was better to retreat than fight, Louise told herself, and she would do better to find a quiet space to sit and think. And calm down. "You can take over, Alice. Excuse me."

Seeking solace in her room upstairs proved fruitless. She was just too agitated to rest. She tried to read but soon found herself pacing the floor as she mulled over what to do about Conor.

What could she do? She was fifty years older than Conor Byrne, and while she enjoyed the company of young people who appreciated her devotion to music, she had nothing in common with an athlete-turned-poetry-editor, certainly not one as edgy as Conor could be.

Besides, how could she relate to whatever was causing him such anguish, if there was such a source? If Rev. Thompson, with his natural compassion and empathy, had not been able to reach Conor, what chance did she really have?

Then there was this business of Viola and Eleanor Renda. Were there ever any two people more opposite? No wonder they were starting to dislike each other. Yet they were the only help the poetry club could expect. How was she to manage keeping them from arguing in front of the students, if it came to that?

A gentle knock called Louise from her thoughts. "Yes?"

"It's Alice. May I come in for a minute?"

Naturally it was Alice. After the sharp words she had exchanged with Jane, their youngest sister was likely in the garden, yanking weeds and pretending that they were Louise's hair. Feeling as worn out as their recently arrived guest, Louise went to open the door.

Alice stood waiting outside. She was smiling, and in her hands she held a cup of tea and a plate crowded with fresh peach slices and one of Jane's oversize fruit-and-nut muffins. "I come bearing snacks. I thought they might work better than aspirin."

"Oh, Alice." She took the cup and plate from her sister, remorse evident in her expression. "I am so sorry that I lost my temper that way."

"Jane is too. She sent the muffin." Alice came in and closed the door gently behind her. "I don't want to be nosy, but are you upset about something? Something besides Aunt Ethel and her grapevine newsflash, I mean?"

"Yes and no." She set down the peace offering and dropped onto the edge of her bed.

Alice sat beside her. "Want to talk about it?"

"No, thank you, my dear." Confiding in her sister was tempting, but under the circumstances Louise felt as constrained to silence about Conor as the pastor had been. "This is something I must deal with on my own."

A gentle arm came around her. "If you change your mind, remember that two heads are better than one. Well, maybe not in the movies. Things with two heads in the movies are always awful."

Louise uttered a reluctant chuckle. "You always make me laugh, even when I am feeling utterly dismal."

"That's what sisters are for." Alice gave her a half-hug with her arm before rising. "I'm going to beat a tactful retreat downstairs to work on Jane now. She's whipping something into a fine froth in the kitchen. I'm hoping it's not egg whites. I'm not a fan of meringue on pie, but I'll have to eat a piece to be polite. Call if you need me."

After Alice had left, Louise drank a little of the tea that her sister had brought and broke off a piece of the muffin. She had always been easily moved toward anger, and Jane's occasional pushing often brought out her temper. *How fortunate we are to have Alice. No matter how angry we are with each other, she always steers us in the right direction.*

What she herself had said to Conor the day before came back to her: "There are many aspects of human existence that elevate us above the animals, like faith and hope."

And his bleak response echoed in her thoughts too: "If you're lucky enough to have them."

Other things the boy had said came back to her. "What we cared about wasn't stupid. It mattered. *We* mattered. The question is, how much?"

All that Conor seemed to care about now was poetry, and publishing the club's magazine.

Poetry.

Louise quickly set down her teacup and hurried downstairs. Jane and Alice had left the kitchen and were finishing up the paperwork she had left out, and as she reached the desk Jane began to apologize.

"Louise, I'm so sorry I—"

"I am sorry too, dear, and it was all my fault. Thank you for the muffin. I love you dearly, you know." After rushing all that out, and leaning over to kiss the astonished Jane on the cheek, Louise turned to Alice. "Do you recall that lesson you had planned for your ANGELs meeting, oh, about two months ago? It was something about poetry and the Bible."

"Yes. It was about the poetry *of* the Bible, actually," Alice said.

Jane looked surprised. "Is there a lot of poetry in the Bible?"

"About a third of the Old Testament is written in poetic form," Alice told her. "The Book of Job is considered by some scholars to be one of the greatest poems in all literature."

Jane frowned. "But it doesn't rhyme."

"It is not that sort of poetry," Louise told her, and then asked Alice, "Do you still have your notes on that lesson?"

"Sure. I keep all my lesson notes filed in my planner." Alice gave her a puzzled look. "Would you like to read them?"

"I would like to borrow them, if I may."

Alice smiled. "Of course."

Jane gave her a dubious look. "Are you feeling all right, Louise? You look a little rattled."

Love for her sisters welled up in Louise's heart. "I have never been better."

∞

Viola met Louise at the door to the library the next day. She looked down at the notes Louise was carrying. "What's that?"

Louise smiled. "Something I would like to talk about, if there is time."

"I don't know. This could be the last meeting we have." Viola fiddled with her collar.

Her friend was wearing a comfortable peach short-sleeved blouse paired with matching cotton knit slacks, but her neck was conspicuously bare. "Where is your scarf?" It was the first time in memory that Louise had seen her without her trademark accessory.

"I simply forgot to put one on," Viola admitted.

Louise spotted a long, thin white scar on Viola's neck, in an area usually covered by her scarves. "You must have had your mind on other matters."

"Probably. This school fund business had me so upset that I barely closed my eyes last night. It's not right to do this to these kids."

Louise had not realized that Viola had such strong feelings on the subject. "I think it may be out of our hands."

"Not if I can help it." Viola marched into the library, leaving Louise to trail in behind her.

"Good afternoon, ladies." Ms. Renda stood waiting with Millicent, Conor and Sherrilyn. "The others should be here shortly."

Nia came over and greeted them, obviously curious. "I have your group scheduled for next Saturday." Her gaze bounced between Viola's stern face and the coach's somewhat bored expression. "Did I make a mistake on the date?"

"No, this is an impromptu get-together," Viola told her. "I should have called you, but I didn't know about it until yesterday."

"It's not a big deal. If you need the study room on Monday afternoons as well as Saturdays, I can reserve it for you," the librarian said. "Just give me a week's notice so that I don't lend the space out to another group."

Conor gave the coach a challenging look, then turned to the librarian. "We will, thanks, Ms. Komonos."

The other members of the poetry club arrived while they were talking with Nia, and by silent mutual consent the entire group went back to the study room.

"I have to get back to school for a meeting, so I can't stay," the coach said as soon as the students were settled in their seats.

"This won't take long," Conor said. "In an effort to be fair, the principal has decided to split the funds evenly between the poetry club and the track team. There is still enough in our portion for us to publish our magazine."

"Barely, Conor, and it leaves the team without enough money for the new uniforms." Ms. Renda turned to address the other students. Conor assumed a bored expression and sat back, making a show of it, drawing the other teenagers' attention to him.

"As I said on Saturday, I know how important this magazine is to you kids," the coach assured them, "but our track team needs to practice, not fund-raise. This is the first shot Franklin has ever had at a state championship, and you all know how excited the entire student body is about it."

"Sports are usually more popular than poetry with the students, I take it," Viola said coolly. She tugged absently at her collar.

Hadley made a comical face. "Well, yeah, naturally. I mean, it's *sports*."

Ms. Renda nodded. "The point is, our athletes do not have the same luxury of time after school that the poetry club has. They have to practice several days a week. What time they have left is devoted to studying and homework. All I am asking is that the poetry club wait until next year to publish your magazine, and give your portion of the fund for this year to the team."

"No," Conor said at once, before anyone else could comment. "It's our money, and we're using it *this* year."

Ms. Renda gave him a long-suffering look. "We've been over this a hundred times, Conor. It'll be hard enough for the team to compete at the regionals without you. Don't be spiteful."

Viola frowned. "You're on the track team, Conor?"

"Until a few weeks ago I was, yes." The boy regarded Ms. Renda with something of a smirk. "I was your star runner, wasn't I, Coach?"

The flippancy with which he said that disturbed Louise. Why was he seeming to take sides against his former teammates? What had transpired to cause him to quit? Was it responsible for his attitude?

"You can have your place back on the team any time you like," the coach assured him.

His smile turned enigmatic. "I'm tired of running."

Ms. Renda looked at Viola with something like anger in her eyes. "Ms. Reed, can you give me a little help here?"

"I sympathize with your needs, Coach Renda, but I also think Conor is right," Viola replied bluntly. "The poetry club deserves their share of the school fund as much as your track team does."

"This magazine will do nothing for the school," the coach barked. "No one is going to give out awards for poetry."

"I guess you never heard of the Pulitzer Prize," Wendy murmured.

"Poetry is just as important as your team's uniforms," Viola snapped. "These students' goals are of equal value. You can't discriminate against them because of your own prejudices. Try to see it from these kids' point of view."

"I'm not prejudiced." Now Ms. Renda sounded furious. "I'm only asking them to be realistic." To Conor, she said, "Don't you know what will happen if you insist on using your portion of the fund? The other kids at school will find out about it and make your lives miserable."

"Like they don't already?" Hadley asked, looking pained.

"Maybe they will," Conor said. "Or maybe they'll realize

that there are other things in life that are just as important as trophies."

Viola nodded her agreement. "If the student body is so dependent on the team's performance, let them come up with the money for the new uniforms."

"We don't have time to raise the money," Ms. Renda responded through clenched teeth.

"I hate to interrupt," Louise said, not feeling in the least bit sorry for derailing the escalating argument, "but there are other ways to solve this problem."

Conor, Viola and the coach stared in her direction.

"You have indicated that the track team has no time to fund-raise," Louise stated. "The poetry club is under pressure but still could handle the job. I would recommend giving the track team the money they need for their uniforms out of the poetry club's share of the fund. The club can then raise the rest of the money to publish the magazine on their own."

The suggestion made everyone gape at her.

"We could do that," Wendy said in a cautious tone, as if the idea were highly explosive. "Makes sense, doesn't it?"

"Everyone would feel pretty nice toward us if we did," Rob pointed out. "We'd be able to raise some of the money from donations from the kids at school."

"We could have car washes after last period in the back parking lot," Hadley put in.

"Or a pizza party in the cafeteria," Millicent said. "We raised almost a hundred dollars for the glee club that way last year."

"We could sell advertising space in the mag, like the professional ones do," Rob said. "My dad is always buying them for his car dealership. He'd be good for a few bucks."

Sherrilyn gave her brother a pleading look. "It wouldn't

be that hard, Conor, and we still have some time before we have to go to the printer."

Conor was silent as he considered the matter. At last he said, "It appears that I'm outvoted. We'll give the team the money for the uniforms."

Louise studied the boy's face. It was a blank mask again, as devoid of emotion as his voice. She almost would have preferred to see and hear anger. *Conor, what is wrong? Why are you shutting yourself away from everyone like this?*

"I'll speak to the principal." Rather than sounding pleased, Ms. Renda seemed somewhat miffed by Conor's remark and the group's generosity. She made a point of checking her watch. "I have to get back to school now. I'll see you all tomorrow."

Conor's dislike of Ms. Renda had never been hidden, but as the teacher left the room, Louise could feel a definite wave of animosity from the boy. *Maybe she is the reason that he quit the track team and was so adamant about not sharing the fund money.*

"Do we have to go now?" Millicent asked. "If I go home, my mom's just going to make me do chores, and I think it's my turn to muck out the stalls."

Wendy grinned. "My ride doesn't get here for another hour."

"Our progress has been so steady that I hadn't planned anything for today, but"—Viola eyed Louise—"I think my friend Mrs. Smith has something she'd like to discuss."

"I do." Louise opened the folder Alice had given her and took out the ANGELs handout that she had altered slightly before making copies for the group. "I thought you might be interested in hearing about one of the oldest collections of poetry in the world. Hadley, would you be kind enough to pass these around?"

"Sure." He took the stack and started dealing the copies like cards to the other students.

"Maybe you have your notes mixed up, Mrs. Smith," Rob said a moment later. "This handout has a bunch of Bible verses listed on it."

"The Bible is what I plan to talk about." Louise smiled at the confused looks that earned her. "I know that in a public school you are not permitted to take part in religious practice. However, examining the Bible here as a historical example of poetry does not violate that rule."

Conor gave her a suspicious look. "Are you sure about that?"

"I feel reasonably certain of it," Louise said, keeping her tone casual. "But if any of you finds what I have to say offensive, please feel free to tell me, and I will end the discussion immediately."

Conor's belligerent expression suggested to her that he might do just that.

The handouts Alice had made up for her ANGELs lesson listed a number of passages from the Bible that Louise had annotated with a few alternate choices, carefully selected for content as well as structure.

"The 'Song of Moses' and the 'Song of Miriam' in Exodus are two of the world's oldest existing poetic works. You can find them in your handouts. Both poems, which were written as hymns by Hebrews, may date as far back as the twelfth century B.C."

When she paused, Rob whistled. "That's pretty old."

"Who did you think wrote it?" Conor demanded. "Bob Dylan?"

Uneasy laughter swept around the room, but died off as quickly as it had erupted.

"Scripture has many ancient poems incorporated in it,"

Louise told Rob, ignoring Conor's scowl. "About one-third of the Old Testament is written in poetic form, which includes entire books like Psalms, Proverbs and Lamentations."

"But the Bible doesn't rhyme," Millicent said, unknowingly echoing Jane's observation from the day before.

"Structured elements that are commonly found in modern poetry, like rhyme schemes, only appear infrequently in Hebrew poetry," Louise said. "Instead the authors of these books often used what are called parallelisms. This is where the poet repeats the content of a line, contrasts it, and otherwise uses it to convey a sense of thought rhythm. The words alone are not as important as the arrangement in which they are used."

"No, the words aren't important at all," Conor muttered under his breath.

"Can you give us some examples, Mrs. Smith?" Millicent asked. "I'm still not sure what you mean by parallel-lel- whatever it was."

"Parallelisms." Louise said the word slowly so that the students could hear all of the syllables. "Some are synonymous, which means that they repeat an idea over and over through rewording. Take the first two lines of Psalm 24. 'The earth is the Lord's, and everything in it, the world, and all who live in it; for he founded it upon the seas and established it upon the waters.'

"Other parallelisms are antithetic, which means the exact opposite. One idea is contradicted by another. We see this in the first two lines of Proverbs 13. 'A wise son heeds his father's instruction, but a mocker does not listen to rebuke.'"

Millicent's smile framed her braces. "That makes it a lot clearer."

"If it doesn't relate to today's poetic forms, and the Bible doesn't," Conor said, his tone scathing, "what's the point in talking about it?"

"You were looking for greater understanding of poetic expression and for ways to evaluate the poetry you have for your magazine," Louise pointed out. "I cannot think of better or more inspiring examples of the variety of poetic expression than that found in the Bible."

"I agree," Viola said. "How many of you have actually read the Bible? All of it?"

Conor didn't move an inch. Sherrilyn, Wendy and Millicent raised their hands. With a sheepish look, so did Rob.

"My folks are big on Bible study," he told the other students. "We always read excerpts to each other on Sunday nights. My mom starts with Genesis in January and keeps going until we finish up with Revelations in December."

"I think that is a marvelous way to study the Scriptures," Louise told him.

"Man, is there anything that *doesn't* have poetry in it?" Hadley wanted to know.

"You mean, besides your soul?" Wendy retorted.

"All right, children," Viola said, sounding like a stern but fond parent, "let Mrs. Smith finish."

"If you reference the Bible verses that I have listed on the handout, you will find excellent examples of parallelism in the books of the Bible," Louise said. "Read them and observe how the words and ideas are arranged. The poetry of the Bible is not always obvious—nor is the inspiration that it provides—so you have to look hard to recognize it, but once you do it will change the way you think about verse." *As well as other things,* she hoped in Conor's case.

Chapter Nine

With that the poetry club meeting ended, and the teenagers departed with a promise to return on Saturday for their next meeting. Viola decided it was too late to reopen her shop and planned to go home instead.

"Do you have to get back to the inn right away?" she asked Louise as they walked out of the library.

Jane and Alice had things well in hand, since they had only one guest left at present and no one else expected until the following week. "No, not immediately. Why?"

"I put a chicken to stew in the crock pot this morning. Come and have dinner with me, or I'll be eating the leftovers until I grow feathers."

Her friend always issued invitations as if they were made solely for her own benefit. Viola was a self-sufficient woman, content to live by herself with her cats, happiest when engrossed in one of her books. Yet despite her off-hand invitations, Louise suspected she enjoyed entertaining select company, and she felt privileged to be one of the few people often invited to Viola's beautiful home.

"I would be happy to," Louise said. "I'll call the inn so that no one will be concerned about me."

Louise always enjoyed family dinners with her sisters, especially since Jane was such an accomplished and inventive chef, but dining at Viola's home was something of a special event. It might have been because of the formal dining room, which as a result of the Victorian architectural design of Viola's house had walls that formed a pentagon. The shape of the room contributed to its air of grandeur. Certainly Viola's mahogany table was a thing of beauty. It was so lovingly polished that it reflected every curve of the English hunting horns that made up the unusual brass chandelier hanging overhead. The carved backs of the table's matching chairs and the fine tapestries covering the seats could have easily graced the room of a great estate.

Yet it was the mood and the company more than the surroundings that made dining at Viola's a pleasure. She set an elegant table, with fresh flowers from her garden gracing the center in a lovely crystal vase. For her place settings, she put out fine bone china made in Staffordshire and brought over from England by her ancestors. Most people were surprised, as Louise had been, to discover that Viola used it as regularly as someone else might use everyday stoneware.

"Why have such beautiful china," Viola once asked Louise, "and only use it a couple of times a year?"

The china's pattern of hydrangea blooms, in misty, dream-like colors of pink, magenta and lavender, was one of the loveliest Louise had ever seen. Tapered ivory candles cast a soft golden glow over the table, the light condensing to glitter in the facets of fine, lead crystal glasses. Even the quality of the napkins was not overlooked; Viola insisted on using linen instead of paper and folded the napkins, like her scarves, into inventive shapes.

Viola's stewed chicken turned out to be coq au vin, the

delicious French dish in which the humble bird is simmered in a light wine sauce with fresh vegetables and fragrant herbs. Slow cooking had rendered the meat so tender that it literally fell from the bones.

The food was so good that neither woman made much effort at conversation during the meal. Viola did urge Louise to eat as much coq au vin as she could, but also warned her to leave room for dessert. After she cleared away their dinner plates—refusing Louise's offer to help—she brought in a large, clear glass bowl with a fitted lid. Through the sides Louise saw six layers of custard, sponge cake, cream and a variety of fresh berries.

Now she was sorry that she had eaten so much of the delicious chicken. "Is that what I think it is?"

"English trifle," Viola identified it as she set it on the table. "There's so much that I'll have to send some home with you for your sisters. I made it last night."

"I marvel at how Jane finds contentment in the kitchen. Do you also enjoy preparing such delightful dishes?"

"I might if I had someone else to clean up and wash the dishes. Otherwise, it can be fun for a few minutes, then sheer drudgery for an hour." Viola picked up a triangular, scoop-bottomed cake server and used it to cut wedges in the trifle's luscious layers. "I know I don't need the calories, but it made me feel better to make it. At least I'm not like that Ms. Renda, ignoring kids she's supposed to be helping."

"They do not seem to pay a great deal of attention to her, either," Louise pointed out. "'Children aren't happy without something to ignore / And that's what parents were created for.'"

Viola eyed her. "Don't you dare quote Nash at my table."

"Forgive me, the temptation overcame my good sense."

Louise held out her dessert plate, upon which Viola deposited a generous portion of trifle. "I do think that Ms. Renda's responsibility to the track team has her under a great deal of pressure."

Viola made a disparaging sound. "She's probably just like every phys ed teacher I had in school, only interested in the athletic students and what trophies and awards she can get through them."

"I did not know that you were not athletic in school."

"I was overweight and uncoordinated," Viola said, her tone matter-of-fact. "Oh, I tried at first to play the games and do the exercises, but I either came in last or ended up in the nurse's office with a horrendous gash or bruise on some portion of my anatomy. Eventually the other kids began refusing to have me on their teams. Finally, after I was seriously injured, my grandmother had a word with the administration, and I was permanently excused from physical education classes."

"Did you really suffer a serious injury?"

Viola lifted a hand and touched the long, white mark on her neck. "Yes, I fell into a fence trying to catch a softball. The fence collapsed, and a jagged edge caught me here. Another inch and I'd have bled to death." She dropped her hand. "Do you know, my phys ed coach stood over me and yelled at me for a good minute before one of the other kids screamed and made him realize that I was hurt?"

Now Louise understood why her friend had allowed herself to bristle with antagonism toward Ms. Renda. "I am sorry, Viola."

Her friend made a dismissive gesture. "It was a long time ago."

"I do think there is more we can do to help the poetry

club," Louise continued carefully. "The fact that Ms. Renda seems uninterested in doing more is the first thing we should try to change."

Viola's eyebrows rose. "How?"

"Rather than working against her, why not try to gain her cooperation?" Louise spread her hands out, palm up. "We could begin with asking her to help with raising the money the club needs."

"Since they donated their money for the track team's uniforms, she should feel guilty enough to do something," Viola said with a certain amount of satisfaction.

"Undoubtedly." Louise decided to change the subject before her friend went off on a rant regarding the Franklin coach. "What did you do after you were excused from phys ed in high school?"

"I helped the school librarian when she needed me, or I sat in the library and read." Viola picked up her spoon and dug into the trifle on her plate. "You could say my inherent clumsiness and hatred of sports contributed a great deal to my love of reading."

The picture of a much younger Viola sitting by herself and reading a book popped into her mind. It was a lonely image. "Still, you must have felt left out."

"I was *overjoyed* to be left out." She hesitated, and then added gruffly, "I was never the type of girl to make friends easily anyway."

On impulse Louise said, "I wish we had gone to school together. I think you and I would have been good friends."

Viola looked across the table at her. "Why, thank you. That has to be the nicest thing anyone has ever said to me."

"You are most welcome."

"You may seem stern at times, Louise, but you are really

sweet, aren't you? Even when you go to the trouble of spiking a poetic study with recommendations for Bible study that might console a bruised dreamer," Viola tacked on smoothly. "That was very well done. Conor's suspicions were nearly dispelled by the end of your talk. Another five minutes on parallelisms and I think he'd have been completely fooled."

Louise was speechless.

Viola took her plate and gave her friend a second helping of the trifle. "I don't know if it will be enough to help him, though. That boy is in serious trouble, and like you, I think he needs to find his way back to spirituality. But I don't think you can do that for him now, unless you drag him kicking and screaming."

Louise picked up her spoon, poked at the trifle, and then set it back down. "You cannot force someone to turn back to God, and how did you know about Conor's problems and what I had intended?"

"I may not be a church person, but I've studied the Bible for years," Viola reminded her. "I don't know what his problems are, exactly, but I'm beginning to sense some desperation in whatever is driving that boy to act the way he does. As for you, well, you aren't always as subtle as you think. The coffee should be done brewing by now." She rose and went into the kitchen, returning with cups of decaf coffee for them both.

Louise accepted hers with thanks, and then asked, "What do you think is driving Conor to be so contrary?"

"Cross-purposes. What he wants is at odds with what he's expected to do." Viola passed a bowl of sugar cubes and a small pair of silver tongs to her. "I never went through a rebellious stage when I was a girl—my grandparents would never have permitted it—but I know exactly how that boy feels."

"I am sorry, but I cannot see any similarity between the two of you," Louise confessed, "other than your love of poetry."

"My grandparents held a very traditional, very conservative attitude about the roles women were allowed to assume in life. The English blood showing through, I suppose." Viola added some cream from a small pitcher to her coffee. "They were very supportive of my love of books—they encouraged me to read at every turn—but when I talked about opening my own bookshop, they told me I was being foolish. Permitting me to study to be a librarian was as far as they were willing to let me go."

"So you studied library science to please them."

"To placate them," Viola said. "I'm sure they were hoping that I would work as a librarian for a few years, meet a nice boy, get married, have children, take care of my kids and my housework, and forget about my dreams. What every nice girl was expected to do."

"You refused?"

"Not precisely. I became a librarian, waited, and saved every penny I could. They were old, my grandparents, and before long they passed on. As soon as they did, I left the library and went to work at a bookshop in Philadelphia in order to learn the business. That, and inheriting my aunt's estate, gave me the means to open Nine Lives."

Louise nodded. "I admire your determination, but how does this relate to Conor's situation?"

"Conor isn't waiting or placating or putting up with anyone's expectations. Something has happened to make him abandon all that and to pursue what he wants now." Viola used the edge of her spoon to nudge one last raspberry into a smidgeon of custard on her plate. "I asked his sister if he

was playing any sports, and she told me he had quit everything. All he cares about is this poetry club and publishing
this magazine."

"But what could make him do that?" *Surely not his loss of
faith.*

"I don't know, but whatever it is, it's made him turn his
back on everyone and everything." She ate the raspberry with
a bit of cream and custard and sighed. "Trifle is always better if you let it sit overnight."

An enormous black and white domestic shorthaired cat
wandered into the dining room. With a single graceful movement, he leapt up onto the table beside Louise and inspected
her plate.

Viola snorted. "I swear, they can smell cream through
concrete walls." To the cat she said in a sharper voice,
"Gatsby, get down."

The big tomcat gave her an indignant look with his large
golden eyes before bounding back down to the floor and
sauntering off. He used his head to nudge open the swinging
door that led to the kitchen, and disappeared through the gap.

Louise smiled. "Very obedient."

"Only when it suits him," Viola said. "Nine times out of
ten, I'd have had to pick him up and carry him out of here to
keep him away from your plate."

Louise thought of an earlier remark from her friend.
"You said that the Bible verses I referenced might not be
enough to help Conor. Is there anything you can do?"

"Me?" The thought seemed to startle her.

"You feel an affinity with him," Louise stated. "You have
recognized important aspects of his character."

Viola shrugged. "It doesn't take a genius to notice that
someone is in pain, Louise."

"I have the feeling that Conor is far more intelligent than anyone has ever guessed, that he has been disguising this behind his sports accomplishments, to appease his parents, perhaps. I also think that you are correct about his desperation. Conor Byrne desperately needs someone to talk to."

"That someone being me." Viola sounded faintly ironic. "I am no counselor like your Rev. Thompson, Louise."

"You do not see yourself and Conor as I do. What was that line Joanne Woodward said in *The Long, Hot Summer*?" Louise pretended to think for a moment. "Ah, now I remember, 'One wolf recognizes another.'"

"Such flattery! I can't remember ever being compared to a character as volatile as Ben Quick, someone accused of being a thief and a barn burner." Viola laughed. "Keep that up and I'm not giving you any of my trifle to take home."

Louise looked at her plate, from which she had cleaned nearly every crumb of dessert, and then held it out. "In that case, I would like to have another helping, please."

∽

"The Tess Watch is up and running," Alice announced cheerfully as she came down for breakfast early the next morning. "June Carter, Craig Tracy, Sylvia Songer and a bunch of other people in town have agreed to call Viola whenever there's a sighting."

Jane grinned and put a plate of whole-wheat toast on the table before returning to the stove, where she was scrambling eggs. "Is this a cat, or a UFO?"

"Simply calling Viola may not help to catch Tess," Louise warned as she retrieved a pitcher of orange juice from the refrigerator. "Remember what happened outside Fred's Hardware."

"Alice told me about that," Jane said as she seasoned the

eggs with fresh parsley and rosemary. "Sounds like Tess is determined to hang on to her freedom, whatever it takes. How are you going to keep her from running away?"

"The cat shelter in town has some large cardboard carriers that are given to people when they adopt a cat. They're boxes that have air holes, reinforced sides and a handle-type lid that keeps the cat from jumping out." Alice began buttering the toast. "If we could just get her to climb into one of those, and someone was on hand to close it up, then we'd have her."

"You cannot know where Tess will be until someone calls," Louise pointed out as she arranged Jane's honeydew and cantaloupe slices on a small platter. "When she sees anyone approaching her with a carrier, she is sure to run."

"What you need is a mousetrap," Jane said, bringing her skillet to the table and portioning its contents among their three plates.

"You want to use *dead mice* to catch her?" Alice made a face.

"No, silly. You bait something, as you would a mousetrap. You know"—Jane placed the skillet back on the stove before she came to sit down—"make a cat-type mousetrap."

"Hold that thought for a moment, if you would, dear." Louise held out her hands, which her sisters took in theirs. "Dear Lord, with Your bounty before us, we take joy in this day. We give You thanks for all the blessings that will come our way. We ask that You watch over us with every passing hour, for without Your love we would be lost, now and forever. Amen."

"Amen." Alice gave her a curious look. "Isn't that the Grace you wrote for Thanksgiving one year, when we were little girls?"

She nodded. "One of my few attempts at poetry."

"It's really nice. I like it." Jane squeezed Louise's hand before releasing it. "Say it again sometime, will you? Now let's talk about making a mousetrap that catches cats."

As the three sisters ate breakfast, they discussed Jane's idea and how best to make and bait a safe trap that would secure the timid calico.

Alice knew of a certain fish-based cat food that Wendell adored, and theorized it might have the same attraction for Tess. "It's made of salmon, and every time I open a can, Wendell becomes so impatient he jumps up on the counter before I can set his dish down."

Louise thought of what Gatsby had done at Viola's house the night before. "Is there something else cats find irresistible?"

"Oh yes." Jane retrieved the catnip they sprinkled on Wendell's scratching post to encourage him to use his claws on it rather than on their furniture, and read the label. "It says here that if your cat is not eating the way he should, you can sprinkle a little catnip on his food." She handed the container to Alice. "So to cover all the bases, we should make a dish of the soft food Wendell likes, spiced up with a little catnip, and put it inside one of the shelter's carriers."

"But where do we put out the carrier?" Alice asked.

"We should borrow several," Louise suggested, "and leave them around town at the places where Tess has been spotted previously."

Alice, whose car was back from the garage, volunteered to obtain the carriers from the town shelter. Jane and Louise prepared the catnip-spiked bait, which smelled so appealing to Wendell that he wove in and out around their ankles meowing piteously until they allowed him a taste.

"I hope Tess feels the same way about this stuff," Jane

said as they placed the concoction in small disposable containers. She bent over and took a whiff. "Whew! I love herbed fish, but this sure doesn't smell the same."

Ethel Buckley entered the kitchen carrying a large white garment bag over her arm. She stopped in her tracks and drew back, nearly dropping the bag as she clapped a hand over her mouth and nose. "Good Lord, what is that awful stench?"

"Cat bait, Auntie." Jane took out plastic wrap and began to cover the offending dishes. "We're trying to catch that little calico Viola's been after."

"Well, wrap that up quick or you'll have to fumigate the entire house."

At the same time, their guest, Arthur Sheldon, appeared in the door. "Something smells good in here." When the women stared at him, he grinned. "Must be you ladies, because it surely isn't that cat food."

Alice explained the situation as she escorted Mr. Sheldon to the dining room, and Jane started making his breakfast, leaving Louise to deal with their aunt.

"Now what do you have there?" she asked her aunt. "Something that needs to go to the dry cleaner's?"

"No, I need to store this in one of your closets temporarily. Would you help me find a spot?" Ethel hurried out of the kitchen.

Louise followed her out into the hall. "Are those winter clothes?" She knew her aunt had plenty of closet space at the carriage house, so she was confused as to why she would need to keep something stored at the inn.

"No, it's Edna's wedding dress. Where can I hide it?"

"Why do you have Edna's wedding dress, and why must you hide it?"

Ethel placed the garment bag on the reception desk, looked around as if checking for eavesdroppers, and then said in a low voice, "I have to, or she'll tear it to ribbons."

Louise tried to imagine the eighty-three-year-old Edna tearing anything to ribbons. And failed. "Why would she do such a thing?"

"Roland." Ethel's voice dropped another notch. "Edna had Sylvia make her this dress months ago, because she was counting on Roland to propose. Why he did when he was . . . you didn't hear what he did to her, did you?"

"No."

"Edna went over to his house and found him in a compromising position with another woman." Ethel paused dramatically. "A much, much *younger* woman."

"Oh dear."

"Edna looked through the front window to see if Roland was napping—you know how he falls into a snooze at the drop of a hat—and there he was, standing in the living room *giving her a kiss*," her aunt whispered. "Poor Edna went straight home and locked herself in the house and hasn't come out since."

Louise felt sorry for the elderly woman, so rudely upset. "Have you suggested that she speak to Rev. Thompson?"

"I'm working on that. She's so shaken, poor thing, she can't think straight. I'm afraid that if she tears up this dress, she might hurt herself with the scissors or something." Ethel sighed. "She's threatening to come over to the carriage house to get it back, so I thought I'd hide it here for a spell."

"Aunt, why not suggest that she donate the dress to the clothing thrift shop over in Potterston?"

"She says it's a symbol of her love for Roland, which is why she wants it in shreds." Ethel rolled her eyes. "Can I put it in your bedroom, maybe? I don't think she can climb all those stairs."

"Let me take it." Louise draped the garment bag over her arm. "I will keep it safe until Edna and Roland work out their problems."

"He's been calling her every half hour since she broke off the engagement, but she just hangs up on him. I'm hoping he doesn't show up on her doorstep." Ethel grimaced. "Maybe I should go back over there and take all the scissors out of the house too."

Chapter  Ten

The shelter in town gave the Howard sisters five card-board cat carriers, which they baited and set out in places where Tess had been seen. Alice told the members of the Tess Watch about the traps, and gave them instructions on how best to approach the calico if she took the bait. Now all they had to do was wait and hope that the stray would come out of hiding.

"I've also told the merchants on the Tess Watch how to scoop her up as soon as she's inside one of them," Alice told her sisters.

Disappointment came on Friday, when June called the inn. She had reported a Tess sighting to Viola, but not without some bad news to go with it.

"Little thing looked like a wraith, although from the size of her belly I'll guess that she hasn't had her kittens yet," June told Louise. "I watched her creep into the carrier, but she only took one whiff of the bait before she backed right out again."

"She did not eat any of it?"

"No, although she has to be starving." A note of curios-ity entered June's voice as she asked, "What type of food did you put out for her?"

"It is made of salmon, and we added some catnip to it," Louise explained.

"Oh, then it's the catnip that's driving her off," June said with a faint chuckle. "Some cats can't stand it, you know. My mother's tabby won't touch the stuff."

Louise's heart sank as she thought of the four other containers, carefully baited with the same mixture of food. "We will have to try something else."

After Louise related the problem to her sisters, Alice suggested that they replace the food right away, before Tess found any of the other bait. "If we don't, she might associate the carriers with something she doesn't like, and refuse to go near any of them."

Jane agreed. "I've got a cake in the oven, so I'll stay here and hold down the fort."

Alice stopped at the General Store to pick up more cans of cat food, and as she and Louise exited the store, Sylvia Songer met them outside.

"I thought I saw your car, Louise. I called Viola's shop but apparently she's out to lunch." Sylvia pointed in the direction of her own shop, Sylvia's Buttons. "That cat you're trying to catch is in the back of my place. I think she crawled under the hedge to take a nap."

Or to have her kittens, Louise thought. "Thank you for letting us know, Sylvia."

"I put a carrier just on the other side of those bushes," Alice said.

"We should replace the food in it before she wakes up," Louise advised, somewhat afraid of what they might find when they checked the hedge. "If she has had her kittens, Alice, will we be able to move them into a box?"

"I think so." Alice frowned. "Knowing Tess, though, we should try to lure her into the carrier. If she's had the kittens, we can put them in a separate box, and reunite them once we get them to Viola's."

"I took the food out this morning and discarded it," Sylvia told them. "June spread the word about the catnip problem, so all of the carriers are empty now."

The three women walked together down the street to the shop, discussing Tess and the various ways to catch her and to deal with the kittens if they had been born.

"You might be able to scoop her up while she's sleeping," Sylvia suggested. "She'll wake up, of course, but she might be groggy enough to let you put her into a box. The kittens will be so small and helpless they won't be a problem."

Louise frowned. "Should we try the new food, or attempt to pick her up while she's asleep, Alice?"

"I don't have anything to put her in but the container we left at Sylvia's," her sister said, "so let's try the new bait first."

Sylvia led them around the side of her shop to where a short hedge grew against the building's back wall. "With her colors, it's a little hard to see her," she whispered, "but she was right in there." She pointed to a small hole at the bottom of the hedge.

Alice bent down. "I can't tell if there are any kittens." She moved closer.

Louise was ready to suggest that they leave the stray alone when she saw a familiar red pickup truck with a white topper on the back parked out at the curb. "Alice, the Animal Control Officer is here."

"We can't let him take her," Alice cried.

"I will handle this. You and Sylvia stay here." With what she hoped was a convincing smile, she stepped around the corner and met a tall, solid-looking man as he walked down the side of the building. "Good afternoon, Officer O'Hara."

A former Marine, Jack O'Hara still wore his bright red

hair in a military-style crew cut, but he had grown a luxuri-
ant mustache that over the years had acquired a distinct, han-
dlebar shape to it. He looked like an old-time police officer,
and despite his flamboyant mustache still projected an
impressive aura of authority.

"Mrs. Smith." Jack seemed surprised to see her. After
all, Louise was standing in an alley.

"I was just out for a walk." That much was true. She had
walked from the store. "I have not seen you since the grand
opening at our new cat shelter. How are you?"

"As well as can be expected." He consulted a clipboard
he was carrying. "I had a report called in to my office this
morning about a stray cat around here. Have you happened
to see a calico anywhere in the immediate vicinity?"

"Why, no," Louise said honestly. "I have not." The sound
of rustling leaves behind her made her produce a small, faked
cough. "Will you be looking around town for Te . . . for her?"

"That's my job." He glanced over her shoulder and then
studied her face. "Are you all right, Mrs. Smith? You seem a
little . . . off balance."

"Oh no, I am fine. I was just talking to my sister about
your son, Jack." Louise took his arm in what she hoped was
a friendly fashion and subtly steered him back toward the
street. "He's twelve now, isn't he?"

Jack chuckled. "No, he's a very surly eleven. What has
Jack been up to that you would talk about, ma'am?"

Louise went blank. The only thing she knew about Jack
O'Hara Jr. was that he was friendly with one of her piano students. "Oh, you know. That thing that happened with
Charles Matthews." Charles was in enough scrapes that it
was reasonable to assume that young Jack might be involved
in one of them.

"I told those boys if they went swimming in that pond

that they'd likely come out covered with leeches. At least they came to me after, instead of my wife. She would have skinned my son alive." Jack released a fatherly sigh. "How did you hear about that?"

Being unable to tell the truth made Louise uncomfortable, but she had to carry on. "You know, I . . . I cannot recall." She took a step toward the street. "You know how unreliable the memory becomes as the years pass."

"I see." Jack didn't budge. "If you don't mind me asking, Mrs. Smith, what were you doing wandering around back there behind the building?"

She was going to spend a long time praying for forgiveness tonight. "I was . . . looking at Sylvia's hedges, actually. I think they're nicely shaped. Very . . . hedge-like."

"Are they now?" He took another look. "That stray might be hiding back there in them. I should take a look."

"Oh no." Louise clutched his arm. "I saw no cats at all. When I was back there, looking at the hedge."

Jack frowned. "Maybe I should take you somewhere you can sit down. You're looking a little pale."

"I am perfectly fine, thank you." She began to move again toward the street, and as she hoped, Jack went along with her. In fact, he kept a firm grip on her arm as they walked, as if he expected her to stumble. *This is what I get for pretending to be a doddering old woman.* "This cat you are looking for is a calico, you said?"

"Yes, ma'am." As they came to the front of the building, he peered down at her. "Maybe you should let me take you home."

Sylvia chose that moment to emerge from the front door of her shop. A delicious waft of cool, air-conditioned air came with her. "Louise, I thought that was you. Come in and see the new trims I've just gotten in." She gave Jack a sunny smile. "Jack, how nice to see you. Can I interest you in some silk tassels or hand-crocheted lace for Alison?"

Alison O'Hara was also an avid seamstress, Louise knew, and made most of the clothes that she, Jack and their three boys wore. Jack's smartly fitted uniform attested to her skills with fabric and thread.

Her husband didn't appreciate all her efforts, however. "Thank you, Ms. Songer, but she has a whole room filled with her sewing things. One more bolt of anything and it'll start spilling over into my den." He nodded to Louise. "You have a good day now, Mrs. Smith. Try to get on home and get some rest."

"Thank you, Officer O'Hara," Louise said, reining in a sigh of relief.

Louise and Sylvia watched as Jack climbed into his truck and drove off. Sylvia waved before she pulled Louise into the shop and leaned back against the door. "The coast is clear, Alice. He's gone."

Louise's sister emerged from the back workroom. "So is Tess. No kittens, by the way. Her belly is as big as ever."

"Who called Jack O'Hara about Tess?" Sylvia asked. "If he catches her, she'll go right to the pound."

"There was a horrible man over at Fred's hardware the last time we tried to catch her," Alice said. "I bet he's the one who called Jack."

"We do not know that for sure, Alice," Louise reproved her. "What happened to scare Tess away?"

Alice grimaced. "When I heard you talking to Jack, I made a grab for her. She slipped right through my hands and took off again."

"Try leaving out some of the new food in the carrier

anyway," Louise said, feeling exasperated with herself and Alice. "She may return."

"I'll call Viola the minute I see her," Sylvia promised. "But what are we going to do about Jack O'Hara? He's a professional."

"We'll simply have to catch Tess before he does," Alice announced. As they left Sylvia's shop, Louise put a hand on her sister's arm. "Alice, I want to save Tess as much as you do, but Sylvia is right. Jack O'Hara is very experienced at handling stray and dangerous animals. It may be that he will catch her."

"I know, but I can't give up hope. Hope is all we ever really have." Alice smiled. "Come on, we have four more traps to rebait."

Louise had finished folding the final load of laundry and was about to retire to her room for the evening when Jane intercepted her on the way upstairs.

"Viola's here, and she needs to talk to you," Jane said in a low voice. "She wouldn't say about what, but she seemed a little upset. I asked her to wait in the parlor."

"Thank you, dear." *What on earth is Viola doing here so late?* Louise knew that as a general rule her friend went to bed very early.

Jane nodded. "Can I bring you two anything? Some tea, maybe?"

"No, it is a little late for that." A glance at the clock confirmed that it was well after eight. "I do not think she will be here long."

Louise found Viola sitting in the parlor. She was skimming restlessly through one of the *Country Living* magazines that

Jane had left out on the coffee table for the guests, but she put it down as soon as Louise came in. "I'm sorry for not calling first, but I was out driving around and I needed to talk to you. So I came here."

"It is no trouble." Louise closed the door and came to sit across from her. "You look shaken, Viola. What has happened?" She thought of Jack O'Hara and the little calico. "Is it Tess?"

"No, I haven't seen her for a while. I received a call from Ms. Renda this afternoon." Viola's voice became strained. "Conor Byrne was in a fight at school today."

Louise was concerned, but not surprised. Conor had been like a powder keg with its fuse burning. "Tell me what happened."

Viola repeated what the coach had told her. While in the locker room, Conor had been drawn into an argument with another student, a member of the track team. "This other boy, Jason, was a friend of Conor's before he quit running, and he began harassing Conor about the poetry club. Conor said some disagreeable things about the track team's recent performance. One thing led to another, and the boys got into a shoving match."

Louise closed her eyes briefly. "Was anyone hurt?"

"No, thank heavens. Ms. Renda told me that a teacher and another coach were able to break up the fight before it became too serious, but both boys were sent to the principal's office." Viola grimaced. "Jason apparently admitted to starting the fight—I gather he was proud of the fact—and the principal decided that Jason, not Conor, was the one to be punished."

"In what manner?"

"Jason has to spend two days a week helping Conor and

the other kids from the poetry club raise funds for their magazine." Viola fussed with the side of her hair, smoothing the short strands. "Ms. Renda was livid, as was Conor."

Louise thought it over. "Tailoring the punishment to fit the crime, I presume. I am sure Jason does not appreciate it, but the poetry club could use another person to help them fund-raise. It does not sound so bad."

Viola shook her head. "The principal also decided that Jason must attend the poetry club meetings every Saturday, along with Ms. Renda. He has cancelled Saturday track team practice until further notice. I think you can safely call that a punishment for Ms. Renda as well. The principal was not happy that she has been sacrificing time she should be spending with the poetry club in order to concentrate on the track team."

That would turn an unhappy situation into an intolerable one. "I can see why you are upset."

"Louise, I understand the principal's motives—he obviously thought this would help the poetry club—but you know what will happen. This Jason will be on hand to spoil things for the poetry club meetings, while Ms. Renda . . ." Viola's expression turned gloomy. "It's as if Conor is the one being punished. He doesn't need any of this on his shoulders right now."

Louise saw that Conor's plight wasn't the only reason Viola had come to see her. "Neither do you, my friend."

"I hate it when you read me like an open book." Viola lifted a hand and touched the silk scarf around her neck.

"It is terrible, what is happening to Conor and what happened to you," Louise said quietly. "Only be careful not to let bad memories influence your feelings."

"How can I help it?" Viola threw up her hands. "This boy

is being victimized in almost the exact same way I was. It's as
if everyone keeps piling weight upon weight on top of him.
Something has to give, and it won't be that Ms. Renda. She
has a core of cold steel."

"Taking the road less traveled is never easy, as we both
know. As for Ms. Renda, well, I cannot say. She is a teacher,
and she knows better than to take sides against her own students, whatever their interests may be." Louise thought
about calling the coach, or perhaps Conor's parents, but she
worried that one or both parties might not welcome what
they could regard as an intrusion. That might only create
more pressure on the boy. "What can I do?"

"I don't know, Louise." Viola rested her forehead against
her palm. "I truly don't."

"Should we cancel the meeting tomorrow? I can call Nia
and Ms. Renda first thing in the morning."

Viola's head snapped up, as if she might jump at the suggestion, but she caught herself and lapsed into silence. "No,"
she said at last. "Conor needs someone on his side. It's why
I was driving around aimlessly tonight. I know how he feels.
He's all alone in this."

Louise suddenly thought of how her sister Alice had
come to her after the quarrel she had had with Jane. "He
needs someone to confide in, too. Someone who understands
his feelings. You could reach him, Viola. I know you could."

"No," she said at once. "I've never counseled young people. I wouldn't know what to say."

"You care, and you speak from the heart." Louise tried
to think of a comparison. "When you think about it, Conor
is a little like Tess. Alone, afraid, unwilling to let anyone
help. He is by himself, hiding from whatever is hurting him.
The difference is that you can talk to Conor, and he will

understand what you say. And you share so much, Viola. You both have the same type of intellect, the same love of literature, the same sensible outlook on life. He respects you. You can see it on his face whenever he listens to you."

Doubt appeared in Viola's shrewd eyes. "But if I were to say the wrong thing this time—"

"You will not. You could not." She thought of the many children to whom she had given piano lessons over the years. Despite the differences of age, temperament and talent, Louise rarely had any trouble communicating with her students. Music had paved the path for many friendships with young people in her life.

Viola stared at her. "You have such faith in me."

"It is not misplaced, I assure you." Louise reached across and took her friend's hand. "Conor needs someone to have the same faith in him."

The bookseller nodded slowly. "I'll talk to the boy after the meeting tomorrow."

"In the meantime, we will try to keep everyone on civilized terms, whatever that may require." Louise's gaze strayed to the bookcase, and her eyes twinkled. "I could bring my Ogden Nash book if you need a topic for the discussion."

Viola burlesqued a wide-eyed look. "You mean that Hades has frozen over and no one told me?"

They were still laughing as Louise walked her out to her car.

Chapter Eleven

J ason Gerber was a dedicated athlete and loyal member of the track team, and he hated being forced to attend the poetry club meeting. That was evident from the moment he walked into the study room at the library.

Not that it would be easy to mistake Jason for anything else, Louise thought as she was introduced to the sullen student the next day. Rather than typical casual clothes, Jason had decided to wear his Franklin letter jacket over his track sweat suit. His expression was decidedly hostile.

"How long does this thing last?" he demanded.

"It should be no more than an hour." Louise indicated an empty seat next to Millicent, who had the least hostile look on her face.

The rest of the poetry club regarded Jason the same way they would a rattlesnake that had slithered into their midst.

"Ms. Renda is going to be a few minutes late," Conor said carelessly, "so if you want to get started, Ms. Reed, feel free to go ahead."

Viola glanced at Louise, who nodded.

"Mrs. Smith talked to you briefly about the Bible as a poetic work. I'd like to talk today about how styles of poetry have evolved over time."

Jason slouched back in his seat and muttered something Louise couldn't make out.

Millicent heard it, and turned to glare at Jason. "I'm trying to listen, so if you don't mind, please be quiet."

Jason gave her a startled look. Clearly he wasn't expecting to be corrected so politely, or by such a sweet-faced girl. Quickly he resumed his expression of angry boredom. "Yeah, whatever."

"May I continue?" Viola asked pointedly. "Poetry springs from a variety of influences. Early Romantic poets like our friend Wordsworth deviated from a type of writing that was intended to describe an external source, and instead they focused on the feelings invoked by the source. Poetry became contemplative and open to individual interpretation."

"Wouldn't it be more like music instead of painting, then?" Wendy asked.

"Good question. What are your thoughts on that?" Viola asked the other students, touching off a round robin of analysis.

The animated discussion kept Louise interested, but Jason Gerber refused to participate, and Ms. Renda remained missing. Jason did not interrupt Viola again, but he shifted position, thrummed his fingers on the table top, and stared off into the distance.

"Now I'd like to read a poem written by John Keats," Viola said, drawing Louise's attention back to the talk. "This is 'Ode on a Grecian Urn.'"

Viola read the haunting poem, and the grace and mystery of the words seemed to captivate the teenagers. Even the antagonistic Jason, Louise noted, was listening closely as Viola reached the end of the poem.

"When old age shall this generation waste,
Thou shalt remain, in midst of other woe
Than ours, a friend to man, to whom thou say'st,
'Beauty is truth, truth beauty'—that is all
Ye know on earth, and all ye need to know.

"As you see, the last two lines of the poem are written in plain language and"—Viola nodded in Hadley's direction—"are simple to understand."

"For once," Hadley said. "Bring on more of this Keats guy, please, Ms. Reed."

Viola smiled at him. "For Keats, the concept that 'truth equals beauty equals truth' suffices as the pinnacle of human knowledge and experience." She closed the book from which she had read and held it between her hands. "Yet as basic as this idea is, its meaning and importance have been disputed almost from the moment Keats wrote it. Alfred Lord Tennyson considered them among the finest lines of poetry of all time. T. S. Eliot called them an ugly blight on an otherwise lovely poem. Why do you think these lines aroused such strong reactions in people?"

"Maybe the idea seems too simple," Millicent said. "Some people think simplicity means stupidity."

Jason opened his mouth as if he wanted to second that, and then closed it without saying a word.

"Beauty is supposed to be shallow, as in skin-deep," Rob said. "Truth isn't."

"I don't think Keats meant beauty as in physical appearance," Sherrilyn said hesitantly. "He could have meant it in the purest sense. The beauty of life."

"The beauty of life is a mask," Conor said rather harshly, "and perfection, well, that can offend as much as it thrills."

His sister stared at her sneakers. "No one's perfect, Con," she said faintly. "We can only try to be."

"*You* can try." His eyes glittered with thinly veiled hostility.

Louise saw how Sherrilyn seemed to crumple in the face of her brother's anger. A pang of guilt struck her as she remembered speaking just as sharply to Alice and Jane. *Why do we take out our tempers so often on those we love?*

"I'd like to read something, if I may, Ms. Reed," Wendy said. "We've gotten in some really decent submissions lately, and I'd like to get everyone's take on a couple."

"Please," Jason said. "It'll put me to sleep. I could use the nap."

"We wouldn't mind that," Sherrilyn said sweetly, "as long as you don't snore or drool on the table."

The other students laughed, and Jason turned faintly red before subsiding back into his brooding silence.

Wendy took out a selection of six poems, and passed them around the table. Everyone took one except Jason, who silently passed the stack of poems on to Millicent.

"Oh, I'm sorry," Wendy said to Jason. "I didn't know you couldn't read."

"Wendy." Viola's voice held a warning tone. "No one has to read if he would rather not."

Jason almost gave Viola a grateful look, then remembered he was supposed to be angry and scowled.

"I'd like to read this one first," Wendy said, "because I think it was written in honor of our track team. It's titled 'Competition.'"

"How brilliant." Jason twirled a finger in the air.

Wendy ignored Jason. She lifted the paper and began to read.

"We live our lives like runners;
We give no one a chance.
So hard to find a reason,
Go on reaching, then pursuing.
I hear your footfalls next to mine.
Will we ever go beyond this road?
We say the past is behind us,
Never looking back to see.
I never thought I'd be this way
And all I know is paid but we
Run forever toward that line,
Where they promised us an end
And we know they lied so many times.
Is it the sound of our own hearts
That moves our feet, or is it
That our hearts would break
If we stopped for only one feeling?
I know you're there, I listen
For the sound of you against the stones.
I've heard you quicken, falter
And to know you're there is more
Than I could hope, for gone
Are the safe paths and loyal friends.
Except for you, companion,
As we run,
As we run."

Rob grinned. "He should have called it 'Fast Times at Franklin High.'"

"Who wrote it, Wendy?" Millicent asked.

"Some kid who's been submitting poems anonymously." Wendy put down the paper. "The other five I passed out were typed on the same typewriter. They're as good, if not better, than this one. Go ahead, read them."

The students took turns reading the other five poems aloud. Each was a detached but detailed observation of life, mostly cynical, sometimes painful, and as bitter as the runner poem.

Louise noticed that Jason seemed very interested in what was being read after Wendy had finished the first lines of "Competition." By the time Rob read the last of the poems, Jason was intently studying the other students' faces. When he noticed her watching him, however, he scowled and slouched back into his pretense of indifference.

Too late, Louise thought, but kept the smile from her lips and said nothing.

"They're not very lyrical, are they?" Millicent said. "But I like them. They're real, from the heart."

"I think they're a little cynical for a high school kid," was Wendy's comment. "Do you think one of the teachers submitted these?"

"A teacher would sign them," Rob said. "Heck, a teacher would probably assign them as homework."

"The voice sounds too young to be a teacher's," Millicent said. "This is someone our age. Maybe someone who wanted to make the track team"—she glanced at Hadley—"and couldn't."

The fair-haired boy shook his head. "It's not me, Mill. Seriously. I have trouble thinking up two more lines to go with 'Roses are red / Violets are blue.' I don't think it's a kid. I mean, have any of you guys ever used the word *footfalls*?"

"Maybe you meant to write *footballs*," Rob joked.

Hadley discreetly elbowed him.

"It's decent," Jason mumbled.

Viola zeroed in on him. "Did you have a comment, Jason?"

"I said, it's decent. It's all right, for poetry." He ducked his head and fiercely studied the pattern of the Formica tabletop.

Conor smiled a little at his former teammate. "Liking it won't kill you, Jase."

The door to the study room opened, and Ms. Renda came in.

As if in a panic, Jason shot to his feet. "Coach, do I really have to listen to this—"

"Sit down, Jason." Ms. Renda's tone brooked no opposition. To Viola she said, "I'm sorry I'm late. There was some confusion at the school, and I had to drive out there to talk to some unhappy parents who showed up thinking that the track team would be having practice." She gave Conor a hard look.

"I'm glad you were able to make it in time to hear Conor's reading," Viola said.

Conor stopped glaring back at the coach and turned to Viola. "Sorry, Ms. Reed, but there's some kind of mix-up. I haven't prepared anything."

"I'd like you to read, just the same." She handed him the book of John Keats's poems. "It's the poem at the top of the page that I marked."

Conor opened the book to the indicated passage and, after examining the page and giving Viola a quick look, began to read.

"When I have fears that I may cease to be
Before my pen has gleaned my teeming brain,
Before high-piléd books, in charact'ry,

Hold like rich garners the full-ripened grain;
When I behold upon the night's starred face
Huge cloudy symbols of a high romance,
And think that I may never live to trace
Their shadows, with the magic hand of chance;
And when I feel, fair creature of an hour,
That I shall never look upon thee more,
Never have relish in the faery power
Of unreflecting love!—then on the shore
Of the wide world I stand alone, and think
Till Love and Fame to nothingness do sink."

As soon as Conor had uttered the last line, Jason snorted. "'Faery power.' That's what you think is more important than the team, Con? Real cute."

Conor put down the book and ignored Jason entirely. "Had, would you give Millie and my sister a ride home?" As soon as Hadley indicated that he would, Conor picked up his backpack. "I've got to go, Ms. Reed. Thanks." He walked out.

"I'll be right back." Viola went after him.

Viola and Conor's departure left a wake of angry silence. It swelled as the teenagers glared at the source of their displeasure.

"Way to go, Jase," Rob finally said.

"Shut up, Dierdorf."

"Gentlemen." Louise had no desire to referee a fight. "If you have nothing kind to say to each other, please say nothing at all."

"Yeah, is that all you can do, Jason?" Wendy demanded. "Harass Conor?"

"I'm not the one reading poems about Tinkerbell," the sullen boy countered.

"Oh, you're so clueless," Millicent said complacently. "Faeries were extremely powerful creatures in Celtic mythology. They could level cities, turn the seas inside out and keep the sun from rising. You think they were all like Tinkerbell?" She snorted. "Some faeries were as big as mountains."

"Who cares?" Jason shrugged. "It's girl stuff."

"Perhaps we should direct our attention back to John Keats," Louise suggested. "Any comments, thoughts or opinions relating to the poem?"

"He's afraid to die," Hadley said. "I got that much out of it."

"Me too," Millicent chimed in.

"I don't think he's afraid of dying per se," Wendy argued. "He's afraid of dying before he has a chance to do some things, like write and fall in love and be famous."

"Aren't we all?" Rob said with a dramatic sigh.

"Excuse me, Mrs. Smith, but may I be excused?" That came from Sherrilyn, who rose and left the room as soon as Louise consented. She passed Viola, who returned without Conor.

"What's your take on this Keats poem, Mrs. Smith?" Hadley asked.

"Keats was not afraid of dying," Louise said. "He was facing it. The last lines show exactly how. 'Then on the shore / Of the wide world I stand alone, and think / Till Love and Fame to nothingness do sink.' That is what he did to separate himself from his fear, and face it, and, in essence, divorce it."

"To add a bit of biographical data, John Keats was trained to be a doctor, but gave it up to write poetry," Viola tacked on. "He was poor, born to a family of commoners, and highly unpopular with the critics largely because of his background. He wrote this particular poem in January 1818. He was nursing his brother Tom through the last stages of terminal tuberculosis. They called it 'consumption' in those days. It was highly contagious, and while there were some limited treatments, there was no cure. People died of the disease in the hundreds of thousands."

Millicent gasped. "Oh, the poor man."

"Keats died of the same disease three years later, in Rome, at the age of twenty-five," Viola told her. "He probably knew when Tom died that he had contracted the same disease by nursing his brother."

"So he wrote the poem to cope, right?" Hadley made a sympathetic sound. "Rotten luck."

"When you're putting together your magazine, go with what you feel is right, and remember what a wise man once said, 'Science is for those who learn; poetry, for those who know.'" Viola took the book that Conor had discarded and held it up. "As a doctor, John Keats would have tried to stave off death. As a poet, he made himself face it. In any case, the man knew death before death knew him."

Viola ended the meeting there and congratulated the students for the progress they had made on the magazine. "I think we can see some light at the end of the tunnel."

"I've got to do this every Saturday?" Jason complained over-loudly.

"Oh, you don't just get to listen to great poetry," Hadley said, clapping the other boy on the shoulder. "You get to help us raise the money to print our own."

Jason groaned and closed his eyes.

Ms. Renda lingered, waiting impatiently until all the students had left before addressing Viola. "Ms. Reed, I'd appreciate a word with you."

"I have to get back to my shop, Ms. Renda," Viola said, matching her testy tone.

"I'll stop in there after I catch up with Jason and speak to him about the rescheduled practice times." The coach stood. "Is that acceptable?"

Louise caught Viola's eye and nodded.

The bookseller straightened her shoulders. "Naturally, you can stop in my shop. My hours of operation are posted on the sign in the window."

"Fine, then I'll see you in thirty minutes." Ms. Renda left without waiting for an acknowledgment and let the door bang behind her.

"Well." Viola snatched up her books. "I may close early today."

∽

Louise was glad she had insisted on accompanying Viola to her shop. Sherrilyn Byrne was waiting on the bench outside the front door, and as soon as she saw them she jumped to her feet.

"Ms. Reed, Mrs. Smith, I thought I'd take a chance and come over and see if you were here. I need to talk to you both." There were wet tracks on her pale cheeks, and the fact that she hugged herself tightly with her arms didn't hide her trembling. "It's about Conor."

"Come inside, my dear." Louise put an arm around the girl as Viola unlocked the door and then ushered her in.

Viola nodded toward the back room where she kept her files and took her breaks. "Let's go in the back. I have an electric kettle, and I think we could all use a cup of tea. You do drink tea, dear?"

Sherrilyn nodded and smiled weakly.

Louise prepared the tea while Viola calmed the teenager by introducing her to Ahab and Diver.

"Ahab I found on a trip to a booksellers' conference in Baltimore," Viola told the girl. "He lived in the garage where the hotel guests parked their cars, and one of the attendants told me the old reprobate had actually survived being run down by one of the guests." Viola leaned down to give the arrogant Ahab a fond scratch on the top of his head. "He came right up to my car, and when I opened the door, he jumped in. My vet said it was because I smell like cats, but I think he just decided to adopt me."

"Where did you find Diver?" Sherrilyn asked, sniffing a little as she bent down to pet the plump, attention-loving feline.

"Diver is a hand-me-down kitty. He used to live with a lady down the block from me. Her mother moved in with her, but the old lady was allergic to cats, so Diver had to move out." Viola looked at the big tabby and crooned, "But he's much happier with me, aren't you, baby?"

Diver made a rumbling sound in response, coaxing a smile from Sherrilyn. "Does he always talk back to you like that?"

"Always, don't you baby?"

Diver rumbled again, and added a small, complacent meow afterward, as if to underscore his response.

"I wish I could have a cat. We had a dog when I was little, but he passed away two years ago." Sherrilyn took in a quick, shuddering breath.

"We have plenty of cats looking for good homes at the shelter," Viola told her.

"Thanks, Ms. Reed, but it's not a good time right now to ask my folks. It's not as if . . . I could . . ." Her face crumpled and she began to sob.

Louise set aside the tea mugs she had ready and searched for some tissues while Viola put an arm around the distraught girl. At last she found a box and pressed several into Sherrilyn's hand.

"I'm so sorry," the girl gasped when she could catch her breath. "I didn't mean to bawl my eyes out like this. It's just that poem, and Conor, and everything." She made a helpless gesture.

"If you would rather not talk about it," Louise began, but Sherrilyn shook her head violently.

"Everyone will know about it soon anyway. About why Conor quit the track team. Why . . ." Sherrilyn used a tissue to blow her nose and mop up her tears before she went on. "See, my brother has always been good at sports. That's the trouble. Our father was a star athlete, and he wanted Conor to be just like him. I don't think Conor liked sports all that much, but he wanted to make our father happy, so he went out for everything."

"What did Conor like?" Viola asked gently.

"Reading, and writing. He really likes poetry." Sherrilyn grimaced. "My father doesn't think too much of that. He says that kind of thing is for girls, not boys."

Louise restrained a sigh. That explained a little of Conor's conflicted attitude. "All this time Conor has been playing sports to please your father?"

The girl nodded. "He played everything. Soccer and baseball and football—you've seen how many times he's been in the papers—and he was good. I never knew that someone might not like something they were really good at, but Conor never complained much. Not until my father wanted him to try out for track. It was the only thing my father hadn't done, you know, run competitively. When my brother made the team, my father was so pleased."

"But Conor wasn't," Viola guessed.

"Con was happy that my father was happy, I think. Like always. But Conor had trouble after the practices and the meets. Running made his right knee hurt, so bad that he had to ice it down every night." Sherrilyn's mouth tightened. "My father kept telling him that it was normal. That all athletes had to endure that sort of thing."

"He was in pain every night?" Louise looked distressed.

The girl nodded. "Last month he got up one morning and he couldn't walk right. It was like he couldn't straighten out his leg. It was right before an important meet, and my father, well, he said Conor could wrap his knee with a flexible support brace and go to the doctor afterward." Sherrilyn swallowed hard. "It was terrible, Mrs. Smith. After the meet, Conor took the brace off and his knee looked wretched. It was all swollen up, and he was in so much pain that night that he couldn't sleep. That was the last time Conor ran for the team. He quit the next day."

"Did your parents take Conor to the doctor?"

"Conor didn't tell my parents about how bad his knee had gotten. He hid it from them. I think he was afraid of what the doctor would tell our father. My father was too mad about Conor quitting to realize how badly he was hurting. My mother finally saw how bad Conor's knee looked one day when he was changing, and she took him to the doctor." Fresh tears welled up in Sherrilyn's eyes. "The doctor thought it was an injury, you know, from too much track practice, until he had x-rays taken of Conor's knee last week."

Louise went still, as did Viola. "What did they find, Sherrilyn?"

"A tumor, growing in his knee." She took another tissue

and pressed it against her eyes for a few moments until she was able to speak. "So Conor has to go into the hospital this week for tests. To see if the tumor . . . if he has . . . if it's c-c-cancer."

Cancer. An icy tremor of fear ran through Louise. Cancer was what had killed her husband, Eliot. *But Conor can't have cancer. He's only a boy.*

A choked sound made Louise turn to see Eleanor Renda standing in the doorway. From the look on her face it was obvious that she had been listening for some time.

"Why didn't he tell me?" the coach asked in a strangled voice.

"He did." Sherrilyn's expression changed from one of sorrow to one of anger. "Conor told you his knee was bothering him a bunch of times. You saw him limping too." She glanced at Viola. "I know, I was at the practices. I was watching him."

"He never said he was in that much pain. The one time he was limping, he made it sound as if he had a muscle strain. I would never have . . ." Ms. Renda shook her head, at a loss for words.

"I am sure the doctors will do everything they can for him, Eleanor," Louise said. "Do not blame yourself."

"I can't believe this. Conor is too young, too talented. He can't—" Abruptly Ms. Renda turned and strode out of the store.

"She's just like my father," Sherrilyn said sadly. "All she cares about is what Conor can do on the field. Never mind that it made him sick."

"No, my dear girl." Louise put a hand on Sherrilyn's shoulder before Viola could say anything. "I am sure that is not the case. Your father and Ms. Renda simply did not realize the seriousness of what was happening to Conor. If they had known, they would have seen to it that he received the proper treatment at once."

"Doesn't matter now anyway," the girl said dully. She looked up at Viola. "I think that poem Conor read today helped him, though. He's been so strange since the doctor found the tumor in his leg. I thought he would be angry or sad, but mostly he just keeps his feelings locked away. You can talk to him and he doesn't even hear you."

"I am sorry we didn't know, Sherrilyn," Viola said. "I asked him to read that poem—oh, how I wish I had chosen another—because I thought it might help him face his fears. I had no idea he was coping with anything so dreadful as a tumor."

"Conor didn't want anyone to know. He made me promise not to tell anyone until after he went into the hospital. He'll be really angry if he finds out I told you. And now that Ms. Renda . . ." the girl lapsed into a miserable silence.

"Conor has carried this burden long enough," Viola said firmly. "So have you."

Louise could think to do only one thing. "I would like to have a prayer now, if we could?" When Sherrilyn nodded, Louise took her hand. She was slightly startled when Viola also joined hands with them. "Heavenly Father, You are our light, our strength, and our hope. We need You in our lives, to guide us and to heal us. We ask that You bestow Your blessings on Conor Byrne, and help him through this terrible ordeal. Please also inspire us with the ways and means with which we can help Conor. We are all Your children, safe in the love You show us, and we trust in You above all things. For the Truth that is Your Son, Christ our Lord. Amen."

Chapter Twelve

While Louise spoke with Sherrilyn about what could be done to help her and her brother and family, Viola called Isabel Byrne. Conor's mother had thought that her son would be driving her daughter home from the meeting, but after Viola explained the situation, Mrs. Byrne immediately agreed to pick up Sherrilyn.

When she arrived at the bookshop, Viola and Louise met her at the door.

"I am so sorry to hear about Conor, Isabel," Louise said. Viola echoed her condolences.

"Thank you for that, and for looking after Sherrilyn. I haven't been able to give her much time lately. Coping with Conor and his father has taken all my energy." Isabel gave Louise a weary look. "Some days it seems like there just isn't enough of me to go around. I only wish she had come to me and let me know how upset she was. I'd have made the time."

"She was probably trying to spare you." Louise glanced at Conor's sister, who was still sitting in the back room. She had Diver on her lap and was idly petting him. "Sherrilyn loves her brother very much."

"She adores him. That's why she's taking this so hard." Isabel pressed a hand to her temple. "Good Lord, we all are. I never dreamed that one of my children would ever get cancer."

"You don't know that for sure yet, do you?" Viola asked.

Isabel shook her head. "The tumor must be biopsied before the doctor can say for sure."

"We will pray that all goes well, Mrs. Byrne," Louise said. "I think that if you can give Sherrilyn something to do— even ask her to cook dinner or do some housework—that may keep her mind occupied."

"I never thought of that." Conor's mother gave her a wan smile. "Thank you, Mrs. Smith."

"You are very welcome," Louise assured her. "If you would like, Sherrilyn can stay with me and my sisters at the inn, any time."

"Or she can come and stay with me," Viola added. "She's a sweet girl, and it would be no trouble at all."

"I may take you up on one of those offers, if it turns out that Conor must have surgery." Isabel took a deep breath, blinked a few times, and then called to Sherrilyn. When the girl came out of the back room, she put a comforting arm around her. "Come on, honey, let's go home."

When the Byrnes had departed, Viola locked the front door of the shop. "I can't believe this is happening. That boy is only seventeen years old."

"Unhappily, cancer does not discriminate by age." Louise's own husband had died of the disease, but not as a young man. At least Eliot Smith had had time to know something of life, explore his beloved music and help her raise their daughter Cynthia. If Conor had cancer, he might not have the chance to do any such things.

"What I'd like to know is why Ms. Renda didn't detect this problem earlier." Viola whipped up a hand. "Before you defend her again, remember what Sherrilyn said. Conor told her he was in pain. The woman is trained in physical education. She should have recognized the warning signs."

"Ms. Renda is a coach, not a doctor," Louise said gently. "She made a mistake in not paying closer attention, but she is not perfect, Viola. No one is."

"I would have noticed. I would have done something about it."

"We do not even know what Conor told her," Louise said. "Likely he described the same sort of thing that her other athletes complain of."

Viola looked unconvinced. "If he had gone to the doctor sooner, none of this would be happening."

"Alice has told me that tumors are routinely difficult to detect until they are large enough to seriously impair the patient. Had Conor gone for treatment, his doctor might have made the same mistake." She smiled at her friend. "It is not fair that Conor should be made to suffer so much at such a young age. But really, Viola, blaming Eleanor Renda will not change anything. All we can do is provide what support we can for the Byrnes and pray for them. God will look out for him, I know He will."

"You pray, Louise." Viola collected her purse. "I'm going to find Conor and talk to him."

"Viola." When the determined woman looked at her, Louise thought of a thousand things to say. She settled for, "Leave your anger here. He doesn't need that."

"No, of course he doesn't." Her friend's shoulders slumped. "I wish I could give him my health, such as it is. I would, you know. I've lived long enough."

"No, you have not." Louise touched her cheek. "Not nearly enough, my friend."

∽

Louise returned to Grace Chapel Inn to find Alice and Fred Humbert working together on the front porch. Next to them they had Wendell's purple plastic cat carrier, in which the family's pet was regularly transported to the veterinarian's office for his check-ups and shots. Arthur Sheldon was sitting in one of the rocking chairs. The tractor salesman was sipping a glass of iced tea and observing Alice's and Fred's efforts.

"Afternoon, Mrs. Smith," he greeted her, and grinned. "Fine day to sit around and watch someone else work, isn't it?"

Louise smiled. "That it is, Mr. Sheldon."

"Hi, Louise," Alice said as she straightened. Small beads of perspiration gleamed on her forehead, but she grinned like a child. "Guess what we're making?"

Louise regarded the carrier and the oddly hinged mesh panel Fred was fitting to the front. "It looks like Wendell's carrier, but what have you done to the door?"

"We've turned the carrier into a cat-trap to catch Tess." Alice motioned to the front. "It's perfectly safe, according to Fred."

"When she goes in, her weight will trip this latch," Fred said, pointing to the pressure-sensitive mechanism hooked to the mesh panel. He triggered it, and the panel swung down and sealed off the open end. "Voilà, you got yourself a stray cat."

"If only you could make a man-sized one of those for my next convention trip," Arthur said, and chuckled. "I could bait it with country fried steak and rebate slips."

Fred laughed aloud.

Louise contemplated the trap. "I take it the cardboard carriers we set out around town failed to do the job."

Alice grimaced. "Yes, June and Rachel Holzmann both tried to capture Tess in the carriers by their shops, but she ran as soon as they approached her. This way we can catch her without getting near her."

For a moment Louise thought of Conor, trapped by his pain, unwilling to trust anyone enough to allow them near. *Dear Lord, please let Viola help him. Let Conor trust her enough to confide in her, and lean on her. It will break her heart if he pushes her away.*

"Louise? Is something wrong?"

"I am sorry, my thoughts were wandering." She forced a smile. "So where will you place your trap?"

"Sylvia Songer told me she thinks that little critter's taken to sleeping in her hedge," Fred said. "I think your best bet would be to set it up behind her shop."

While Fred and Arthur Sheldon remained on the porch, discussing the latest trends in tractors, Louise accompanied Alice back to town, where they found Sylvia Songer had already closed her shop for the day.

"I know Sylvia would have no objections, and I can call her and explain as soon as we return home, but should we leave the trap out overnight?" Louise asked.

"I don't think anything will hurt Tess. The carrier will protect her from any animals, and she'll have food. Hold the panel for a moment, if you would, Louise." Alice placed a soft terry-cloth rag next to the dish of cat food within the carrier.

A rustling made Louise look sideways. The unmistakable shine of cat eyes glittered back at her from under the hedge.

"Alice," she whispered. "I think she is over there, watching us."

"Back away very quietly," Alice advised, doing the same.

Louise went to the corner of the building with her sister, and held her breath as the hedge's leaves twitched. "She can smell the cat food," she murmured.

"Yes, I think so. *Shhh*."

Two minutes passed before the small, scraggly calico crept out from under the hedge. It was Tess, sniffing a patch of ground directly in front of the trap that they had set. With relief Louise saw that the stray still had not delivered her litter.

"Come on, sweetie," Alice said under her breath. "Walk into the nice safe carrier and let us catch you."

For a moment it looked as if Tess would do just that. She stayed crouched low to the ground, almost crawling as she inched closer to the opening of the carrier.

Louise held her breath. *Yes, yes, go inside. Let us save one lost soul today.*

A low, grating growl came from the other side of the hedge. Tess arched her back and hissed as she turned toward it.

"No, not another one," Alice groaned.

A larger spotted cat stalked forward, making Tess back toward the carrier. The intruder was almost as dirty and scraggly as the calico but had more weight and definitely displayed more aggression.

"It is the food," Louise said with a sinking heart. "The other cat smells it too."

"They'll fight over it." Alice took an involuntary step forward and her shoe slid on some gravel.

Tess's head snapped in their direction, and her eyes

narrowed as she saw them. The larger cat chose that moment to charge her, and the little calico scampered off.

"No!" Alice hurried after her, scaring off the larger cat in the process. By the time Louise had caught up with her sister, both strays had vanished.

∞

That Sunday after church, Rev. Thompson sought out Louise.

"Louise, may I have a word with you?"

She thought immediately of Conor and turned to her sisters and aunt. "If you can manage without me, I need to speak to the pastor."

"This is becoming a regular weekly meeting," Jane teased. "Of course, go ahead. We'll hold brunch until you get home."

Alice gave Rev. Thompson and Louise a searching look. "Would you like to join us, Pastor?"

"Thank you, Alice, but I have a prior engagement in an hour," Rev. Thompson said.

After the pastor had finished trading farewells with the last members of the congregation to leave the church, Louise accompanied him to the book room.

"Isabel Byrne called me yesterday," he told her without preamble. "She told me everything that happened after the poetry meeting, and gave me permission to discuss the family's troubles with you."

"It is such a sad situation." Louise sat down and rubbed her forehead. "I did not sleep very well last night from thinking about it. I was worried, too, when I did not see any of the Byrnes at services today."

"Conor was admitted to Potterston Hospital this morning

to get ready for his pre-op tests," the pastor told her. "His family is there with him now."

Louise stiffened. "He is not in any more danger, is he?"

"No, but his parents have been concerned about his state of mind. Evidently Ms. Reed went to the house to speak to him, and he became very emotional." Rev. Thompson frowned. "She was quite distraught as well."

"I knew she was going to speak to him." Louise ducked her head. "We should not have interfered."

"No, I think that her visit had a positive effect. Whatever Ms. Reed said to that young man, it broke through the wall of indifference he had built around himself. I think it was the best possible thing to happen." He produced a cheerless smile. "I only wish I had good news about his tumor."

"Is it . . . do they know if it is cancer?"

"The biopsy will be performed tomorrow, and it will be several days before the pathologist's test results are back. A surgeon and an oncologist examined Conor's X-rays, and they made their recommendations to his doctor and parents. The tumor is such that there is only one treatment that will save his life." Rev. Thompson placed his hand on hers. "If this tumor does test positive for cancer, then the surgeon must amputate Conor's leg immediately."

Oh, dear God. From what Sherrilyn had revealed, Louise had known Conor's condition was serious, but this sounded so final. "Sometimes, Pastor, it is very hard to be a person of faith. That God could allow such a thing to happen to such a young boy . . ."

"We can't question God's plan, Louise. At times like these, we can't even hope to comprehend it." He gave her a sad smile. "We can only pray and trust in Him."

"Does Conor know? About the amputation?"

"Yes. The doctor insisted he be told. If necessary, the surgery will have to be performed this week." The pastor's eyes shadowed with sorrow. "I am providing what consolation I can for Conor and his parents. Since you know him a little better, I was hoping that I could impose on you to accompany me to the hospital tomorrow to see the boy."

"You do not even have to ask that, Pastor." Louise went with Rev. Thompson weekly to visit patients at the hospital. "I will do whatever I can."

"We will bring what comfort we can, and trust in God to see us through." He patted her hand. "When I spoke to Sherrilyn last night, she seemed to think that Conor's coach, Ms. Renda, might also need a friendly ear. Can you tell me how she is involved?"

Louise related the tension that had existed between Conor and Ms. Renda, and how the teacher had reacted upon hearing the dreadful news. "I do not know which church she attends, if any, but she was deeply shocked and could be blaming herself. I wanted to speak with her, to reassure her, but she left so quickly that I fear I was of little help to her."

Rev. Thompson glanced at his watch. "I would call her this afternoon, but I have an appointment with Ms. Grassnickle, and after her, Mr. Jones."

"I will see if I can reach her." Vera Humbert would know Ms. Renda's phone number. "Are Edna and Roland still at odds?" That seemed so trivial compared to Conor Byrne's situation that Louise could scarcely summon an ounce of compassion for either party.

"When last we spoke, Edna told me that she would rather run Mr. Jones down with her car than speak to him again. Roland in turn advised me that he would not marry Ms. Grassnickle if she were the last woman on earth." His expression turned wry. "I think there is still time to work things out so that they can celebrate a June wedding."

∞

Ethel, in the company of Lloyd Tynan, her special friend, had a much different opinion to share on the Jones-Grassnickle nuptials when Louise returned to the inn. "She can't say his name without making spitting sounds. I've never seen Edna this riled up over a man."

"Has Edna had that many boyfriends?" Jane teased as she set a plate of crisp seafood crepes on the table.

"Of course not," Ethel said. "Edna's a widow, like me, but her husband died very early in their marriage, and she's been on her own since then. Roland's the *bachelor*." She said the last word with significant emphasis.

Louise used her fork to move the food that Jane had served her, and pushed it around her plate. She could not bring herself to eat. Three terrible words seemed to echo in her mind, destroying what little appetite she had: *cancer, surgery, amputation.*

"Now, Ethel, not all bachelors are reprobates," Lloyd Tynan, mayor of Acorn Hill, reminded her. "Remember that I've never been married."

Ethel's eyebrows arched as she regarded her good-natured beau. "Are you taking his side?"

"I've known Roland Jones for better than thirty years, and he's always conducted himself like a gentleman." The mayor held up his hands. "That's all I'm saying."

"Maybe there's been some sort of mistake," Alice said, which prompted Ethel to repeat every detail of the incident that had caused Edna and Roland to call off their wedding.

Louise barely heard them. Her head had been throbbing

since she left the church, and she suspected that another of her infamous tension headaches was setting in. She contemplated the food that she had barely touched on her plate, and then looked up to meet Jane's concerned gaze.

"Not hungry?" Jane asked gently.

Cancer, surgery, amputation. Louise shook her head slightly. "I believe I will save this for later. Excuse me." She picked up her plate and carried it into the kitchen.

She was covering her plate with plastic wrap when Arthur Sheldon entered to put a box of fudge that he had bought in town in the refrigerator. "For my wife," he explained to Louise. "If I keep it in my room, the ants will surely get at it."

She gazed at him blankly. "We have ants?"

"No, ma'am, but they've been known to follow me around the country and nibble at the treats I buy my wife." He winked at her.

Jane came in after Arthur had left, and Louise gave her a strained smile. "I am fine, dear. It is only a headache."

"You can't fool me, Louise. You're dead white."

Cancer, surgery, amputation. Death?

"This is *not* only a headache." Jane came to stand beside her.

Louise was not the type of woman to burst into tears easily. So when she found herself in Jane's arms, sobbing quietly as she poured out what Sherrilyn and the pastor had revealed, Jane knew how terribly upset Conor's misfortune had made her sister. When the words ran out, Louise only wept and wished the world away.

"We need a few minutes," she heard Jane say over her head, as if to someone coming into the kitchen, but not even that could stop the misery from spilling out of her.

No one questioned Jane, nothing further interrupted Louise's outburst. Jane's steady arms guided her over to one of the kitchen chairs. There she sat, one of Jane's arms cradling her shoulders, until at last she felt the terrible sorrow lifting from her heart and she could stem the tide of tears.

"When I was in San Francisco," Jane said quietly, "I worked with a wonderful dessert chef. His name was Ryan, and he was just a kid, maybe twenty-two years old at the most. I think the kitchen manager hired him straight out of culinary school. He was talented, a genius. His cakes were perfectly fluffy, and his pies melted in your mouth. He made puff pastry so light it practically floated off the baking sheets. He also worked like a galley slave, making sure his desserts were perfection."

Jane rose and went to the stove, where she put on the kettle, and then returned to sit beside Louise.

"Ryan started coming to work with a cough. He thought it was because of the flour and other dusty ingredients he worked with. But the cough got worse, and he went to see an allergist." Jane's gaze became distant. "It wasn't an allergy. It was lung cancer. He didn't smoke, he didn't get it from working in a kitchen. He just got it. I know the doctors tried their best, but he died of it anyway six months later."

Louise put her hand over Jane's.

"I had a hard time understanding it. Why it happened. I still don't, not really. Ryan was such a sweet kid. He had a gift, he was willing to work hard, and he had his whole life ahead of him." Jane's voice went soft. "And then he was gone. Just like that."

"It was like that with Eliot." Louise cleared her throat and pressed the handkerchief against her cheeks. "There one moment, and then gone. But Eliot had a life. He had me and Cynthia, and many happy years."

"I bet Kenneth told you that it's part of God's plan, didn't he?" At her nod, Jane's mouth tightened. "That's the part I don't get. Why does the fact of good people dying young like that have to be a part of the plan?"

"We cannot judge God. We can only ask Him to be merciful." Louise felt the pain in her temples easing; perhaps crying had relieved the source of her headache. Usually it was the exact opposite, so it puzzled her for a moment. "Jane, did you visit your friend Ryan in the hospital? Did you console him?"

"Every day that I could."

"What did you say to him?"

"I talked about work. I made jokes about the sous chef because he was such a pompous little tyrant. I told him stories about you and Alice and Father. Sometimes I held his hand and just sat with him." She ducked her head. "Sometimes—a lot of times, actually—I prayed with him."

"And that was enough? That helped him?"

Jane went to the stove and prepared two cups of tea, and then brought them to the table. "I think my showing up, you know, being there, helped him the most. He always thanked me for coming to see him, and he was always so glad to see me when I came back." She wiped a tear from her own cheek. "Even at the end, when he was on continuous pain medication, he always smiled at me when I came through the door."

Louise choked back a sob. "I have to go with Rev. Thompson to see Conor Byrne."

Jane added sugar to Louise's cup before she offered it to her. "Are you up to that?"

"Yes." She summoned up her composure. "I will go and

see him as often as I can. I will try to make him smile. I will be there with him." And that would have to be enough, since the rest was in God's hands.

Jane took the teacup from her hands so she could hug her again. "I know you will, sweetheart."

Chapter  Thirteen

I'm going to see Conor during visitors' hours tonight," Viola Reed told Louise over the phone the next morning. "I'm glad you and your minister are visiting him today. He needs friends around him now."

Louise had to agree with that. If not for Jane's perceptive heart, she would still be holding her own emotions in, and probably making herself sick with them. Too much of what was happening to Conor Byrne reminded her of those terrible weeks after she had learned that Eliot had cancer. "Has Sherrilyn told the other members of the poetry club?"

"She said that she would when she saw them at school today." Viola sighed. "I should feel better after my latest confrontation, but I don't."

Louise's hand tightened on the receiver. "You mean, when you spoke with Conor?"

Viola had already related what had happened when she had gone to the Byrne residence. Conor had been his usual, sullen self, until Viola removed her scarf and told him how she had acquired the scar it hid. Conor had tried to act nonchalant at first, but the sight of the old injury seemed to break something loose inside him. He had wept for the first time since learning about the tumor in his knee.

"No, I think that was a good thing," Viola said. "He needed an outlet, and I provided him with one. When I referred to my latest confrontation, I meant when I went to see Ms. Renda. I got her address from Vera and went to her house yesterday."

Louise caught her breath. "You did not."

"Wild horses couldn't have kept me away."

"Oh, Viola." She closed her eyes briefly. "I hope you did not say anything that you will regret."

"I was tempted, but I managed to control myself," her friend said dryly. "Ms. Renda told me that she has resigned as moderator of the poetry club."

Louise caught her breath. In this misfortune there was more than one victim. "She resigned because she feels guilty over what is happening to Conor."

"We all do," Viola said bluntly. "But she is taking it very personally and blames herself for not noticing his condition earlier. She even talked about resigning from her job, until I talked her out of it."

"*You* convinced her not to quit?"

Viola made a slightly miffed sound. "Don't sound so shocked. From what the kids have told me, she's an excellent phys ed teacher. I have been known to be understanding, too, every blue moon."

Louise smiled. "I am proud of you, my friend."

"Yes, well, don't congratulate me just yet. Things are only going to get harder on that woman if Conor's condition takes a turn for the worse."

"I think you and I should invite Ms. Renda to have tea

with us at the inn so that we can boost her spirits." Louise recalled what the teacher had told her about her schedule. "The track team has no practice on Thursday, and Conor's test results will probably be back by then."

Viola was resistant to the idea at first, but Louise talked her around. When she ended the call, Louise called Franklin High and asked to speak to Ms. Renda, who, as luck would have it, was working in her office that period.

"Hello, Mrs. Smith." Eleanor Renda's voice sounded flat and lifeless. "What can I do for you?"

"Ms. Reed and I were wondering if you would come and have tea with us on Thursday at Grace Chapel Inn. We can meet at four o'clock, if that is convenient for you?"

"Why?"

"We would like to talk about the poetry club," Louise said, carefully casual.

"I can't see what good that will do." A harsh note entered the teacher's tone. "I'm sure Ms. Reed has told you that I wanted to resign as their moderator."

"Yes, she did, but there are still some arrangements with the meetings to be discussed." She would have to remember to bring up the subject when they did meet or the woman would think that she was careless with the truth. "Until a new moderator is appointed, we will need to consult with you."

There was a long silence, so long that Louise thought she might have to make up another excuse.

At last Ms. Renda said, "Oh, very well. I'll see you on Thursday." And ended the call abruptly.

Louise replaced the receiver on the telephone cradle and smiled to herself.

"Rev. Thompson just pulled up the driveway." Jane walked up to the reception desk with a vase of fresh flowers. "Do you want me to go with you? Alice said it would be fine with her."

"That is all right, dear." Louise looked into her sister's discerning eyes. "You are not to worry about me."

"Sisterly right. Goes along with nagging you about eating your veggies and getting enough sleep and all that." Jane removed a bright orange carnation from the vase, snapped the stem off and tucked it into the lapel of Louise's jacket. "There. That looks better."

Louise tucked her chin in to look down. "How does an orange flower go with a powder blue suit?"

"Orange is a happy color, and I say it goes just fine." Jane gave her a winsome grin. "Trust me."

"Always."

∽

Visiting the hospital on a Monday seemed odd to Louise. She and Rev. Thompson went together to visit patients on Fridays, and knew the nurses and clerks who worked that day. Today Louise recognized very few.

"Conor's room is in the surgical area," the pastor told her as they stepped into the elevator.

"I thought he might be in pediatrics." Although Conor was a teenager, that was the ward to which most minors were admitted, unless they needed specialized treatment or surgery. "They must be expecting the worse."

"I believe they are preparing for it."

Conor's room was in a quiet corner, and the smiling nurse who greeted them from the surgery station told them to go right in.

"He hasn't eaten much, but he's in fairly good spirits,"

the nurse said. "Unusual kid, though. He'd rather read books than watch the television."

Before they reached the door to Conor's room, Louise put a hand on Rev. Thompson's arm. The memory of how she had cried the day before nagged at her conscience. "I may have to step out for a few minutes."

"I understand."

Conor was not lying on the hospital bed, but sitting in one of the visitor's chairs by the room's only window. He was dressed in a patient gown and a light, white-and-blue striped robe. A book lay open on his lap, but instead of reading, he was staring out at the sky.

"Hello, Conor," Louise greeted him. "Would you mind some visitors?"

He turned and looked at her. His eyes were faintly red-rimmed, and his face seemed much thinner. The smile he gave her, however, seemed genuine. "Not at all, Mrs. Smith. Hi, Pastor Thompson." He closed the book and set it aside.

Louise saw that Conor had been reading Viola's collection of John Keats's poetry. She took a discreet, steadying breath. *I will not think of Eliot. I will not weep. I am here to be of help to this child.*

"Conor." Rev. Thompson went over and shook his hand. "How are you feeling?"

"Okay, I guess, but after the latest round of procedures, I can't hide my limp anymore." He got up from the chair slowly and reached for a cane nearby. "I'm supposed to keep my weight off my leg, too, so I have to use this." With the awkwardness of someone not used to relying on a cane for balance, he made his way over to the hospital bed, where he sat on the edge after offering his chair to Louise, who thanked him but remained standing.

"Have they scheduled your test?" Rev. Thompson asked.

"The doc was by earlier. They're going to take the biopsy in a couple of hours." He glanced at the door. "My folks went downstairs to get something to eat."

"Ms. Reed said she would come by to see you tonight, after she closes the bookshop," Louise told him.

Conor nodded. "She called me this morning too."

As they chatted about inconsequential things, a shaft of sunlight crept across the room. It illuminated Conor's face, making him look even younger than he was.

For a moment Louise thought she might have to leave, and then the warmth of the same sunbeam touched her face. *God's love*, she thought, *is in the room. He is here, with this child. Whatever happens, He will not abandon him.*

Somehow she had to find the words to communicate that knowledge to Conor.

Rev. Thompson asked Louise if she wanted some coffee, and she gratefully accepted. He left them in order to find one of the hospital's vending machines.

"I didn't expect Pastor Thompson to come to see me," Conor admitted when the minister had left the room. "The last time I talked to him, I said some pretty nasty things."

"Rev. Thompson is a very understanding man," Louise assured him. "He will not hold that against you."

Conor nodded slowly before staring at the window again. "He wants to talk to me about God again, doesn't he?"

"That is part of his job, but you do not have to talk about anything. I know Rev. Thompson came here today as your friend." She smiled. "As I did."

The boy began to say something before he closed his mouth and turned away.

She felt the warmth of the sunlight like a gentle but insistent caress. It reminded her of what she had thought. *No, it reminds me of what I know. I must tell him.* "God is here, Conor. He is here with you. Whether you choose to believe that or not. He will never abandon you."

Conor's mouth twisted. "Don't worry, Mrs. Smith. I do believe in Him. Now more than ever."

The way he spoke of God made Louise curious. "I had thought your absence from church meant that you were having some difficulties with your faith."

"I couldn't go back to church. Not after . . ." He gazed at his knee.

Louise was struck with a sense of urgency. Whatever Conor had been thinking, he had not told anyone. "Not after what, Conor?"

"This. This is the kind of thing God does best, isn't it? Punishing people for thinking bad thoughts?" He put a hand on his knee. "If I'd gotten hit with a lightning bolt during practice, it couldn't be clearer."

Why would the boy think that God was punishing him? "Cancer is a disease, my dear. It is a terrible and very frightening thing to face, but God did not do this to you. No matter what you were thinking."

Conor hung his head. "How would you know?"

"My husband Eliot died of cancer." When the boy stared in shock at her, she nodded. "He did not deserve it, I assure you. He was a good man who always tried to follow the teachings of Christ and help others. He loved his family and music and life. If cancer was, as you said, a punishment from God, my husband would never have gotten the disease."

Rev. Thompson slipped into the room and stood aside, listening.

Unaware of the pastor, Conor began rocking a little back and forth. "But I prayed for it. I prayed."

Louise could hear guilt trembling in the boy's voice. The same guilt she had felt after Eliot had died. One terrible night, she had even prayed for God to take her so that she could be with her husband again. "What did you pray for, Conor?"

"I prayed for it to stop. All of it. I didn't want to do it anymore."

Suddenly Louise recalled what Sherrilyn had said about her brother. *"I never knew that someone might not like something they were really good at ... Conor never complained much ... Con was happy that my father was happy ..."*

"You asked God to help you stop running," she guessed, "and you believe this tumor was His answer to your prayer?"

Conor gave her a stricken look. "Yes," he whispered. "I didn't mean to, but when I made the track team I was already so tired of it. Being a jock like my dad—I never wanted that. Then my knee started hurting and I prayed for it to stop. The pain and the sports. I prayed that God would let me be injured so bad that I wouldn't be able to run anymore." His voice broke, and he covered his face with his hands. "I didn't want cancer. I didn't want to lose my leg. I only wanted to stop."

"Conor, look at me. Look." Gently she put her hand under his chin and raised his face so that she could look into his eyes. "Your prayer did not do this, Conor. God is not punishing you. This tumor is something that just happens. Sometimes there are reasons—environmental reasons, for example—but most of the time disease simply strikes at random. Oh, Conor, our God is a God of love and forgiveness. Hurting the innocent is not His way."

Doubt shadowed his eyes. "Even if I prayed to be hurt?"

Louise brushed his hair back from his forehead. "You know the saying about prayer, that sometimes the answer is

'No'? I can guarantee that in some cases, like asking God to hurt you deliberately, that the answer is *always* 'No.'" She looked up at Rev. Thompson, who nodded his approval and came forward to rest his hand on Conor's shoulder.

"There is something you can do to make things right with God, if you would like to," the pastor said.

Conor glanced at him and nodded mutely.

"Ask God for forgiveness for doubting Him, Conor," Rev. Thompson said. "Reaffirm your faith in Him. Open your heart and accept His love back into your life."

"How do I do that?"

"There are many ways. I have always done so with the Lord's Prayer." He sat on the other side of the boy. "Let's pray together. Our Father, Who art in Heaven, hallowed be thy name . . ."

As Louise repeated the words of the comforting prayer, she heard Conor doing the same. His voice was thready at first, but gradually it grew stronger, as if the prayer were healing some part of him from the inside out.

Seeing the new hope in Conor's eyes made Louise believe that God was doing just that.

∾

Despite the garage's best efforts, Alice's little car began to have engine problems again, so Louise volunteered to help her sister take her craft supplies over to Grace Chapel on Wednesday evening for Alice's weekly ANGELs meeting.

"I have nothing planned, and it has been ages since I have spent an evening with you and your girls," Louise told Alice.

Alice frowned. "But I thought you were visiting Conor Byrne tonight."

Louise had been over to the hospital as often as she could since the day Conor had been admitted. The biopsy of his tumor had been performed, and now there was nothing to do but to wait for the results. Unfortunately, the hospital's chief pathologist was on vacation, leaving only the assistant pathologist on duty. Conor's mother had told her that the report might take another week.

"Viola Reed is visiting Conor tonight, as well as Rev. Thompson," Louise informed her. "Since Conor's parents and sister also spend their evenings at the hospital, I thought it might be a bit crowded in his room."

Indeed, Conor's room was seldom anything but packed with visitors. After his sister had made his condition known, the poetry club insisted going en masse to see their friend, and stopped by every day after school to check on his progress. What surprised and pleased Louise was that the track team also took the time to visit their former teammate.

The day before, Jason Gerber had come into the room with several other team members while Louise was visiting, and he had blanched at the sight of the dressing and brace on Conor's knee.

"It's not as bad as all that, Jase," Conor drawled. "Get a good look at it while you can, though, 'cause in two weeks it might not be here."

"Man, I am so sorry about this." Jason came over and shook Conor's hand in the sideways fashion teenage boys seemed to prefer. "Why didn't you say something?"

That was nearly everyone's reaction to learning of Conor's condition.

"I was saving it as a surprise. Surprise!" Conor leaned over to look at the other members of the team who were hovering near the door. "Well, if you're going to suck up to me, get in here."

"The ANGELs will be talking about Conor tonight." Alice said to Louise, pulling her out of her thoughts. "Would you be willing to say a few words to them?"

"I would be happy to, but why are you talking to the ANGELs about Conor?"

"Several of the girls have older siblings who go to Franklin High School," Alice said. "They've heard a lot of rumors, and I would like them to get the facts straight. Also I think it would be good for the girls to do something for Conor. Usually we make get-well cards, but I thought since he likes poetry so much that I would ask them write some funny poems for him."

Louise smiled. "I think he would enjoy that."

Alice's youth ministry was something she took very seriously. She prepared carefully for every meeting, and she liked making the ANGELs meetings fun for the girls. That night she had a topic sheet listing the Bible verses that they would be discussing, along with boxes of craft supplies for the girls to use for a new project. Jane sent along a small cooler of fruit juice boxes and a pan of her pecan-studded white chocolate brownies as refreshments.

The Howard sisters had just finished setting up the Assembly Room when Louise heard the sound of several girls' voices coming from the church.

"Did someone arrive early?" she asked Alice. They still had fifteen minutes before the meeting was to begin.

"Mrs. Matthews must be carpooling for the soccer team this week." Alice put down her planner. "She always drops off Sissy and a couple of the other girls early so she can take Charles and his friends to a night practice."

Yet when Alice and Louise walked up to the church, there was no sign of the girls.

"Sissy?"

"Over here, Miss Howard," an excited voice called.

Louise and Alice followed the voice, and found Sissy Matthews and two other girls hovering about the pipe organ, hunched over as if looking for something.

"What is it, girls?" Alice asked.

"It's a kitten, Miss Howard," Sissy said. "We saw her walking down one of the pews and followed her over here. I guess she got scared when we tried to pet her because she went right under the console. She has funny colors, like a patchwork quilt."

"Could it be?" Alice hurried forward, bent down and peered under the pedals of the enormous pipe organ. "Was she orange and white and black?"

"It was hard to see," one of the other little girls said. "She ran so fast."

"She has a fat tummy, though," another girl put in. "And she's awful dirty and she smells, Miss Howard. Like she's been sleeping in a garbage can."

Louise knelt to see if she could spot the wayward calico. "Could she have come all this way from town, Alice?"

"I don't know. Maybe." Alice scooted to one side and reached under the organ's console, searching blindly by touch. "That big spotted cat might have chased her out of town."

"Good evening, ladies," Rev. Thompson's deep voice said, making all of them turn suddenly. "Did someone lose something?"

"It's Tess, Pastor, Viola's elusive calico." Alice said as she got to her feet. "We think she's crawled under the pipe organ."

"There is one way to flush her out right away, if you'll stand back." When Louise, Alice and the girls moved away, the pastor turned on the console's power switch and pressed a single key. A sonorous high "C" note rang out, vibrating through the organ's polished pipes.

A small bundle of orange, white and black fur flew out from under the organ and darted through the girls' legs.

"There she goes!" Sissy followed, giggling as the cat bounded up and raced along the narrow edge of a pew.

"Be careful, girls, don't frighten her," Alice urged as she pursued her ANGELs and the calico.

"Don't try to grab her, children," Rev. Thompson warned as he also went after the little cat.

Louise decided to let the others give chase, but shook her head as the girls dodged around Alice, trying to corner the frightened calico. "I do not think this was such a good idea." To the girls, she called, "Do be careful!"

Once again the cat proved too elusive for her determined pursuers. As another of the ANGELs arrived at the door, Tess darted out of the church's entry and disappeared into the night.

"Oh, she's gone!" a disappointed Sissy wailed. "Why did she run away?"

Louise exchanged a weary look with Alice. "She is a stray cat, Sissy. Quite often they are frightened of people."

"But isn't she the cat all the people in town are trying to catch?" another girl asked.

"Yes. Her name is Tess, and we have been helping Ms. Reed from the bookshop try to catch her," Alice said. "She is going to have kittens soon, so we would like to help her."

Immediately the ANGELs gathered around and began asking about Tess.

"Did she run away from home?"

"When will she have her kittens?"

"Can I ask my parents if I can have one, please, Miss Howard?"

Alice answered their questions as best she could and described the efforts to save the little calico.

Sissy Matthews asked, "Why don't we join the Tess Watch? We could help, Miss Howard."

"Well, I suppose you could," Alice said. "If any of you see Tess, you can call me at the inn, or Ms. Reed at the bookshop."

"You must be cautious, though, girls," Rev. Thompson advised them. "Tess is afraid of people, and she has lived out of doors for so long that she may have become feral. Feral cats are just like any wild animal. If she thinks you are a threat to her, she will do what she can to defend herself."

As they led the ANGELs back to their meeting room, Alice glanced at Louise. "I think Tess will be having her kittens soon. She may have come into the church to hunt out a nesting spot."

Louise nodded. "Perhaps instead of traps, we should have the Tess Watch put out some birthing boxes."

Chapter  Fourteen

L ouise went to town on Thursday to pick up groceries for Jane, and decided to stop by the Nine Lives Bookstore to remind Viola about their tea with Eleanor Renda that afternoon. She found the bookseller chatting with an older woman customer.

Viola had dressed in one of her more sober suits, a conservatively tailored charcoal gray jacket and matching skirt. The stiff lines of her icy white blouse were relieved by a dove gray silk scarf, yet she had draped that simply and tied the ends with a plain box knot.

Armor, Louise decided, *against Ms. Renda, or against what Viola believes Ms. Renda represents. I will have to remind Viola that this is to be a friendly meeting, not a joust.*

The customer speaking to Viola had her back to Louise, but her diminutive stature, frail limbs and halo of thin, bluish-silver hair made her identity unmistakable.

"Hello, Viola, Ms. Grassnickle," Louise greeted them.

Edna Grassnickle gave Louise a cool look and did not immediately discontinue her conversation with Viola. "I told Florence I had a mind to drive over to Potterston and buy myself one of those BB rifles. And here I see Daniel

Howard's oldest girl, looking as if butter wouldn't melt in her mouth." She turned slightly. "Well, Missy. Did your busy-body aunt hide my wedding dress in that inn of yours?"

"No, Ms. Grassnickle," Louise answered calmly. She couldn't remember the last time she had been called "Missy" but was fairly sure Edna had been the one to do it. "I did."

"I never. I should call the sheriff and have him search the place," the old lady said, shaking a thin finger under Louise's nose. "I could have you and Ethel Buckley hauled off to the hoosegow for possession of stolen goods. Then we'd see how cheeky you'd be, eh?"

Louise could imagine her doing just that. "If you feel that strongly about it, I will have the dress returned to you tomorrow. It only seems a shame that you would destroy Sylvia's beautiful work when another woman might be able to make use of it." *If there are any tiny, four-and-a-half-foot-tall women in the immediate vicinity who are planning to be married.* Louise rather doubted that the elaborate little dress would suit—or fit—anyone else.

"Oh, keep the dratted thing." The dainty old woman swatted the air with an annoyed gesture before she turned back to speak to Viola. "Florence Simpson called to console me. She thinks Roland will likely run off to Atlantic City with that young vamp I caught him kissing."

Viola's mouth tightened to prevent a smile. "Somehow I don't see Roland driving that far."

"Why should he, when he's got her and her fancy yellow convertible? I saw it parked in his car port." Edna shook her head. "Vulgar, flashy thing, just like her. They'll probably get married in their street clothes, in some tawdry little overnight chapel. They have ones now that you can drive through and get married, did you know that? I saw it on the television.

Never even take off your seatbelt, from the 'Dearly Beloved' all the way through to the 'You may kiss the bride.' Like exchanging vows of holy matrimony was the same thing as ordering a hamburger and fries."

"You don't know that he'll go off and marry this other woman, Edna," Viola said, gently sympathetic.

"Don't I? What else can he do? Live in sin with her?" Edna caught her breath at her own suggestion and pressed a gnarled hand to her hollow cheek. "Lord in heaven, you don't think he'd do that, do you? I'd never be able to show my face in church again. Not if he'd be sitting right next to that horrid little gold digger. I'd be mortified."

"Now, Edna—"

"I'd likely drop dead," the elderly woman insisted with morbid satisfaction. "Dead right on the spot, first time I laid eyes on them. My heart's not so good. The doctor said I needed to slow down. But there you have it. I'd see him with that wicked girl, fall in the aisle and that'd be all she wrote."

"Edna, please," Viola groaned.

But the elderly woman was on a roll. "Everyone will pass my grave side and say, 'There's poor Edna Grassnickle, who died of a broken heart.'" She gave Viola a hopeful look. "Would they put that on my gravestone? Would they put that it was Roland who broke it by living in sin with a floozy young enough to be his great-granddaughter?" Her forehead furrowed. "Could they fit all that on, I wonder. I might talk to my mortician. I've got my plot all picked out and paid for. Might as well splurge on a bigger stone and buy the extra lettering, so it sets the record straight."

Louise met Viola's exasperated gaze and decided to try her hand at soothing down the overly dramatic, elderly woman. "Edna, you are letting your imagination run away with you."

"Am I? Roland keeps coming to my place, you know. Shouts outside the door that he doesn't understand why *I* jilted *him*. As if I'd be fooled. *Pshaw!* Florence thought that my idea of buying a BB rifle was a good one. I used to shoot skeet with my brothers when I was a girl, you know. Crack shot, I was. Next time Roland steps a foot on my property, I could zing him proper. Right in the seat of his pants. Then we'd see if he'd come calling again where he wasn't wanted."

"For heaven's sake, this is Roland we're talking about, not a skunk," Viola said.

"I see no difference," Edna said sharply, "although I won't compare Roland to a skunk."

"No, you should not," Louise said.

The elderly woman sniffed. "It's an insult to the good Lord's skunks."

As Viola expressed her scathing opinion of Florence's imprudent advice and the dangers of Edna's handling any sort of firearms, Louise moved away to browse one of the shelves.

Will there never be an end to this silly affair?

It seemed decidedly ridiculous to take Edna seriously, or to expend any worry over her threats against Roland, when a young boy like Conor faced a far grimmer fate. Doubtless Edna's wrath would run its course in short order. The elderly woman's vehemence was disturbing in one regard, however. Such denunciation of Roland, a man she was supposed to have loved enough to wish to marry, seemed so out of character for the normally sweet-natured Edna.

Louise noticed a slim volume of Keats, the poet who had so deeply affected Conor. As she took the book from the shelf to examine it, she saw that it was an unusual edition that contained a collection of Keats's letters instead of his poetry. She opened the book and went unconsciously to the end, where the poet's final letters were printed. Idly she began to read one that he had written to his friend Charles Brown after arriving in Italy in the last weeks of his life.

> The fresh air revived me a little, and I hope I am well enough this morning to write to you a short calm letter;—if that can be called one, in which I am afraid to speak of what I would the fainest dwell upon. As I have gone thus far into it, I must go on a little;—perhaps it may relieve the load of WRETCHEDNESS which presses upon me.

Louise read the rest of the sad, angry letter, in which John Keats expressed his rage and agony over being seriously ill and separated from the woman he loved. At the end, the poet made a particularly poignant statement.

> My dear Brown, what am I to do? Where can I look for consolation or ease? If I had any chance of recovery, this passion would kill me.

Keats had suffered unfairly, to be sure, but the tone of the letter made Louise think that toward the end of his life, the poet had almost hated the woman he had loved and lost.

Something her husband had said to her once, after she tried to apologize for her part in one of their rare but passionate arguments, came back to her. *"Of course you were angry with me, darling. No one annoys or inflames us quite as consummately as the one we love."* He had given her an affectionate kiss and held her close, she remembered, before adding, *"I take every heated look, every snapped-out word as a treasured compliment."*

Louise peeked around the bookcase and examined Edna's lined features. Although she put on a brave, even defiant façade, there was sorrow in the old woman's eyes, and a dullness in her voice that Louise could not remember hearing before. She was miserable. Perhaps as much as Keats had been, forever denied the one he loved. Or Conor, facing what he had thought was a terrible answer to his pitiful prayer.

Edna's ill feeling toward Roland wasn't so inexplicable after all. *She likely feels as devastated as any other woman who has been disappointed does,* Louise thought. *Losing Roland is as hurtful to her as Conor's prospects are to him.*

Louise placed the book back on the shelf and walked to the front of the store, where Edna had finally lapsed into silence and Viola was bagging the books she was buying. Outside the shop, Edna's grandniece had parked her car at the curb and was apparently waiting to drive the old lady home.

"I'm going, I'm going," Edna said when she caught Louise's gaze. "Just give me another minute, and then you two girls can natter on about whatever you like." She sounded defeated, and not at all as she had when she was speaking of Roland.

Love knows no age boundaries. She misses him. She is lonely for him. I can hear it in her voice, see it in her eyes. I wonder if Roland would too.

"Something just occurred to me, Edna," Louise said casually. "If Roland does marry or reside with this young woman, I should pay a visit to them and be introduced."

"What?" Edna looked outraged and stricken at the same time. "You surely can't want to be friends with that . . . that—"

"Oh no, but she will likely take over his finances," Louise went on smoothly, "and we do depend on Mr. Jones's annual contribution to the church fund. He is getting up there in years, as well."

"Roland is not that old," Edna snapped.

"I think you should go and meet her, Louise," Viola said sadly, picking up on Louise's intent. "You know what they say about those June-December relationships. All those demands a young woman makes . . ." she trailed off delicately.

"Let's go." Edna snatched up her bag of books. "I have to talk some sense into him." She hurried out of the store to her grandniece's car.

"I thought as much." Louise regarded Viola. "We are quite shameless, you and I."

"We're women." The bookseller grinned. "We're allowed."

Louise decided to buy the book of Keats's letters and went to retrieve it, not for Conor, although she suspected she might lend it to him when he was in better spirits, but for herself. *It may remind me that no one has the right to judge the depth or validity of another's pain.*

∞

Viola promised to be at the inn by four, and by three-thirty Ms. Renda had not called to cancel, so Louise went into the kitchen to visit with Jane and Ethel, and to help her sister with the preparations for tea. She set the tray with one of the lovely antique tea sets collected by their mother, Madeleine. The one she chose was a stately celadon blue accented with filigree gilt.

"I have Earl Grey, oolong or green tea, if you'd like something exotic to sip," Jane offered as she neatly stacked the crumpets she had baked. "Or our good old reliable blend."

"The daily blend, I think." Louise said. "Or perhaps I should make a pot of coffee."

"I'll set up the coffeemaker, and if it turns out that she'd rather have that, you can just switch it on." Jane set a pot of strawberry jam on the serving tray. "The Jensens are supposed to be checking in by four, and Alice won't be home until six, so I'll man the front desk."

"I'd stay to lend a hand if I could, Jane." Ethel Buckley had stopped over to borrow some baking powder, and had stayed to chat with her nieces. "But I have to go over and check on poor Edna. Florence Simpson called me and told me something you won't believe."

"Roland and Edna are running away to Acapulco," Jane joked, "where they'll live in a grass hut, work as lifeguards, and drink from pineapples with little umbrellas in them. That's one of my favorite fantasies, anyway."

"You'd be bored senseless in a week." Ethel snorted. "No, Florence told me that Edna is talking of buying a shotgun."

"What?" Jane nearly dropped the teapot. "A *shotgun*?"

"Florence is wrong. I saw Edna while I was in town, and it was a BB rifle, not a shotgun," Louise said firmly. "You should call before you go to visit, Aunt. I think Edna may have gone to see Roland."

It was Ethel's turn to gape. "She didn't go over there to shoot him, did she?"

"No. She has not yet had the opportunity to purchase the BB rifle." Louise struggled to keep a straight face. "I believe she went to persuade him not to marry her, ah, rival."

"Good heavens. I had better get to the bottom of this before someone starts firing something. See you later, girls." Ethel hurried out of the kitchen.

"Wait a minute." Jane looked confused. "Roland is proposing to someone *else*?"

Louise filled a diminutive pitcher with cream. "Edna now believes that he might."

"Oh, does she?" Jane's tone changed from bewilderment to irony. "And who, may I ask, gave her that idea?"

"Someone who would like this affair to be settled and over with before it drives her batty," Louise advised her.

Viola arrived at five minutes to four, and Louise took her friend into the parlor to chat. Ten minutes passed, and then twenty, and still there was no sign of Ms. Renda.

"Punctuality appears to be a lost art," Viola announced as she tugged at a fold of her gray scarf. "Like making the courtesy of calling when you expect to be late."

"She is a very busy woman. She may have forgotten about the invitation," Louise said, trying to be practical. "We can still enjoy the afternoon. Have a crumpet."

"Is that so I can pay a compliment on your sister's superior baking?" Viola held out her cup for a refill.

"I never fish for compliments, although I will say these are extraordinarily good."

"There's no celery," Viola said, giving the tea tray a grumpy look. "An English high tea always includes celery."

"Too noisy. 'Celery, raw, develops the jaw / But celery, stewed, is more quietly chewed,'" Louise quoted Ogden Nash.

"And terrible puns will drive me out the door," Viola warned.

"Now, Viola, where is your sense of —" She broke off as Jane opened the parlor door, and Ms. Renda came into the room. "Ah, here she is."

The Franklin phys ed coach had also chosen to wear a suit, although hers was a bright rose-red with a stylish pleated skirt and a plain ivory shell under the jacket.

"Hi, Mrs. Smith, Ms. Reed." Ms. Renda edged into the room before crossing to sit down in one of the armchairs. "I apologize for making you wait. I always seem to be doing that."

"We were a little worried about you. Did you have any trouble finding the inn?" Louise asked as she prepared a cup of tea for the teacher.

"No, I've driven past it several times since we moved here." She looked around the room in the same way a prisoner who wanted to escape would inspect a jailhouse. "It's a lovely old house."

"It is. My sisters and I grew up here, though, so I count myself biased." Louise indicated the tray. "Do you take milk, sugar?"

"Just plain, thank you." Gingerly she accepted the cup and stared down into the amber tea.

Louise gave Viola a significant look.

"Have you been to see Conor, Ms. Renda?" Viola asked in her blunt fashion.

The teacher shook her head and quickly sipped from the teacup.

Louise considered reaching over and giving her friend a slap on the arm, but reminded herself that she was the hostess. She could thump Viola later. "Would you like a crumpet, Eleanor? My sister Jane baked them this morning, and they are very good."

"No, thanks." She crossed her slim legs at the ankle, uncrossed them, and then fussed with the hem of her skirt. "I'm on a low-carb diet."

"Everyone is on that crazy diet." Viola helped herself to a crumpet, to prove she was not party to the madness.

"It's only become a fad recently," Ms. Renda said. "Most

athletes have been following low-carbohydrate diets for years. It's part of routine conditioning in most sports."

Viola frowned. "Do you still have to train like an athlete? You're a teacher."

"I like to keep fit. I feel better when I'm in shape, and it provides a positive example for the kids." The younger woman shrugged. "It's a way of thinking, a way of life."

"A very healthy one," Louise commented.

Abruptly Ms. Renda set down her cup on the low table between them. "Look, ladies, I have a good idea as to why you asked me to meet with you. I can't be moderator of the poetry club *and* supervise the track team. The principal will find someone more suitable, and"—she glanced at Viola—"I think *everyone* involved will be a lot happier."

"I wish you would reconsider, Eleanor," Louise said. "You do know that Conor's medical condition is not your fault."

Ms. Renda shook her head. "I should have known something was wrong. I should have noticed, and listened to him. That's my job."

Viola didn't comment, but her expression changed from detachment to sympathy.

"Conor told me that he was hiding his condition from his parents, so that he would not disappoint them," Louise said. "To do that successfully, he also had to hide it from you. I expect that when he did complain, he did not say enough to make you think he was in real trouble."

"It's not just what he said." Ms. Renda turned almost as red as her jacket. "Conor is . . . was . . . one of the best, naturally gifted athletes I've coached. I never had to correct his form or pace, and running seemed to be effortless for him. I depended heavily on him to lead the team. I also took him for granted, basically ignoring him so that I could work with the other, less gifted kids and raise their performance levels."

Her confession made Viola's eyes narrow. "You shouldn't have neglected him, and when he quit the team, you shouldn't have harassed him about it."

"Viola." Louise knew a confrontation between the two women had been brewing for some time, but this was not the time or place to have it.

Ms. Renda lost her embarrassment and gave Viola an unfriendly look. "*Some* kids," she said as she set her teacup aside, "don't have the kind of grades to earn academic scholarships. Some kids have to depend on *sports* scholarships to get to college. Conor's quitting meant that I had to put more pressure on the other team members to fill in the gap. Their performances suffered. That isn't going to help them snag the few scholarships out there for track stars."

"Maybe your team members should have run around less and hit the books more often," Viola suggested. "Studying for a change wouldn't kill them."

"Some kids can study what's in those dreary textbooks night and day and still not make good grades." The teacher's expression turned bitter. "But you wouldn't know about that."

Viola lifted her chin. "No, I wouldn't. I didn't think they were dreary."

"We should discuss when to hold the next meeting of the poetry club," Louise suggested, feeling alarmed by the escalating tension between the two women.

Ms. Renda ignored her. "You probably never had to study, did you, Ms. Reed? I'll bet you were still at the top of your class without even trying."

"Straight A's until I graduated." Viola gave her an

unpleasant smile. "How were your grades in high school, Ms. Renda?"

"I maintained a low C average," the coach said, her teeth gritted. "I had to fight for every point. I wouldn't have made it to Penn State if I hadn't been a track star."

Viola huffed. "You wouldn't be teaching, either."

"I am a good teacher and I work very hard to help my students." Ms. Renda rose from her chair with a jerky movement. "I don't have to listen to this."

Viola also got to her feet. "Yes, why ruin your perfect record?"

Louise felt dismayed, but she was determined to have things work out. "Ladies, may I remind you that we are here to talk about the poetry club, which we have yet to discuss. Sit down, please. *Please*." When both women reluctantly resumed their seats, she continued. "I would ask that you each set aside your differences and concentrate on the children. They need our help."

"They don't need mine," Ms. Renda said, matching Viola's frankness. "I've always hated books and poetry. I hate snotty kids who think that reading all that fine literature makes them better than everyone else."

Which makes you the worst possible choice to advise the poetry club, Louise thought, feeling defeated. Now doubtless Viola would shred her to ribbons.

"Reading literature and poetry enlightens the mind and enriches life," Viola said, but she didn't sound angry. She sounded bewildered. "Enjoying it does not make a person superior to another. Why on earth would you think that?"

"I don't know, maybe it was the way smart girls like you in school made fun of me for running track," Ms. Renda snapped.

"Intelligent people do not ridicule those who are less fortunate than they are," Viola objected. "They try to help them."

"Those girls helped me, all right." The younger woman gave her an indignant look. "Helped me make a fool out of myself. They smirked every time I was called on in class. Half the mistakes I made were because I knew they were laughing at me behind my back before I could even answer."

"I can assure you that I personally never ridiculed anyone for their academic performance, or anything else, for that matter," Viola stated. "But I did endure a great deal of grief from athletic girls like you for being unable to play sports."

"I'm sure that was a terrible thing for you, seeing how much you *love* sports," Ms. Renda said, her tone sweetly sarcastic.

"Maybe I would have liked sports more if I'd been given a chance to play them." Viola sniffed. "Girls like *you* never chose me for a team until I was the last person left. Quite often the coach made me sit on the sidelines."

"It is a shame the two of you were not in high school together," Louise said. "I think you might have been friends."

Viola glared. "What are you talking about, Louise Smith?"

"Friends? With her?" Ms. Renda laughed. "Go ahead and admit it, Ms. Reed. If we'd gone to school together, you'd have looked down your nose at me or made jokes about me."

"You would have pretended I was invisible," Viola countered, "or hated me for being so clumsy."

"You are both wrong. I know you to be a kind and generous person, Viola Reed. You love your books, and you're willing to share your love for them with others," Louise told her friend. She looked at Ms. Renda. "I can safely say the exact same thing about you, and your love of sports. Like it or not, ladies, you are two peas in a pod. You might have been the best of friends."

"I don't know about that." Viola gave Ms. Renda a reluctant look. "I do know I would never have ridiculed you in class."

"There were some girls at my school who didn't like sports," Ms. Renda said slowly. "I still picked them for my team, because I thought everyone should have a chance to play. I certainly never would have made fun of you for being clumsy."

"Perhaps we can agree," Louise said, very gently, "that there is nothing to prevent you from being friends now."

The two women stared at each other as if seeing each other clearly for the first time.

"What did the smart girls do to you?" Viola asked softly.

"They called me names. You?"

"Their favorite nickname for me was Bumble. Bumble Reed."

"Mine was Ignorenda."

A helpless chuckle escaped Louise, and the two women stared at her. "I am sorry, but those names are so ... so ... so inappropriate."

A smile played around Viola's lips. "Oh, I don't know. I did more than my fair share of bumbling. I think it was a take-off on bumblebee. I did walk directly into a nest of them once, out on the playing field."

"I got mine because I didn't know that Bolivia is land-locked," Ms. Renda admitted. "When my teacher called on me to tell her something about Bolivia, I told her that it was a popular place for surfing."

Louise stared hard at the ceiling, willing herself not to laugh again.

"The only time I ever hit a softball—purely by accident, as I had my eyes closed when I swung at it—I broke the bat," Viola said, having a harder time with her mirth. "In three pieces."

"The only time I ever got an A on a test is when I gave up trying to figure out the answers. Instead I filled in the circles to form a stairway on the test card." Ms. Renda giggled like a young girl. "I only missed one question on that test."

Both women dissolved into laughter, freeing Louise to do the same.

"We are a pair, aren't we?" Viola took out a handkerchief and dabbed at her eyes. "I can't remember the last time I laughed at myself like that. Years, at least."

"I could never laugh at myself when I was a kid. Too serious about everything." Ms. Renda sighed and dragged a hand through her short hair. "I feel much better, though, Viola. Thank you."

Viola smiled at her. "So do I, Eleanor."

As the tea continued on far friendlier terms, Viola surprised Ms. Renda and Louise by revealing that she had recruited several local merchants who were willing to buy advertising space in the poetry club's debut issue, which the students were busy preparing to go to the printer's.

"June Carter would like to put in a coupon page, and the Holzmanns have a booth at an antique show in August that they'd like to advertise. And I'd also like to feature an ad for Nine Lives."

"The two main problems are that Conor's in the hospital, and I have regional competitions next week," Ms. Renda said. "There is no one else to help the kids with the editing and layout until the principal assigns another teacher, and heaven only knows when that might be."

"I believe Louise and I could fill in," Viola suggested. "I'd be willing to take over supervising the production of the copy and advertising. Louise, would you mind overseeing the proofreading and editing?"

Louise nodded. "I would be delighted."

"Then we don't need another teacher," Viola said firmly.

"You've already been so generous with your time, and meeting with the kids." Ms. Renda seemed overwhelmed. "I don't know what to say."

"You can thank us by staying on as moderator," Viola suggested.

The teacher's jaw sagged. "I've already resigned. I don't know anything about poetry or publishing a magazine."

"I know you will be busy with the track team, but a show of support from you will mean a lot to the kids," Viola told her. "Give them your approval, Eleanor, whenever and however you can. They can do the work, and do it well, but they need motivation."

"I know how to motivate athletes," Ms. Renda said slowly. "But how do I motivate kids who are probably ten times smarter than I am?"

"Exactly the same way," Louise assured her. "Encourage them, and show you have faith in them."

Viola pretended to shake pom-poms. "Cheer them on."

"Now that I think I can do." Ms. Renda thought for a minute. "Viola, you mentioned recruiting some of the local merchants to put advertising in the magazine. What if I talked to some of the sports equipment suppliers over in Riverton?"

Chapter  Fifteen

I t was a marvelous thing," Louise told Alice and Jane later that night while they made their rounds to tidy the inn's front rooms. "They sat and talked for over an hour about the magazine, and came up with some new, creative ideas for fund-raising. Best of all, they're friends now."

"How long do the kids have to raise the rest of the money they need?" Alice asked as she picked up a brochure left on a side table.

"The printer has accepted a deposit, but he will not run copies until he receives the balance." Louise checked the desk calendar that they kept on the front desk. "About two weeks."

Jane went in and came out of the library with an armful of newspapers. "This is a poetry magazine, right? Why don't the students have a poetry reading?"

"How would that raise money?" Alice asked.

"You could use it to raise awareness rather than money," Jane suggested, setting down the stack of newspapers. "It could be a kick-off event, to generate some excitement among the parents. Maybe some preorders too. I know if I had a kid who was having a poem published, I'd want twenty copies."

"That is an interesting idea, Jane," Louise said, "but where would we have it? Wendy told me there are more than forty students whose poems are to be published in this magazine. If each student's parents came to a reading—"

"Yikes," Alice said. "That's about one hundred and twenty people when you count the kids. Where would you put everyone?"

"I don't think everyone would show up, but I guess you're right. That rules out having it here too." Jane mulled that over. "I don't know. The school auditorium, maybe?"

"June is a busy month for Franklin. The senior class is holding their Prom Night and commencement there," Louise said. "I rather doubt that it will be available for any other function."

"We could fit that many people in Grace Chapel," Jane said. "Easily."

"I'll check with the members of the church board in the morning," Alice volunteered, "but seeing as it will benefit the school, I'm sure they'll have no objection." The phone rang, and she excused herself to answer it.

"I will speak with Viola," Louise told Jane. "We can coordinate it with the students at the Saturday meeting."

"Sounds like a plan." A bell dinging in the kitchen made Jane gather up her newspapers. "Whoops, my croissants are done, and I need to pop in some Danish. Can you handle tidying the parlor?" When Louise nodded, Jane headed off to finish her baking.

Louise went to straighten the parlor. The Jensens, their new guests, had spent an hour playing cards on the coffee table before retiring for the evening. Louise was glad to see they had not disturbed the tidiness of the room, although she thought the sofa's pillows could use some fluffing.

"Are you going with the pastor to the hospital tomorrow?" Alice asked, startling her as she came into the parlor.

Louise straightened a magazine on a corner of the coffee table. "Yes, I wanted to see Conor as well as the other patients we plan to visit. Why?"

"Nancy, one of my friends who works on the surgical ward, just called me—this can go no further than us, Louise," her sister said. "I asked her to keep an eye on Conor for me. She said the biopsy test on his tumor came back, and it has to be repeated."

Louise looked over at her. Alice had wandered over to Louise's piano, and was straightening the ivory-and-violet shawl she kept draped over the case. The shawl did not need straightening. "Why does the test have to be repeated?"

"The pathologist repeats a test to obtain another tissue sample." Alice looked strained and unhappy. "Sometimes because the first sample was contaminated or accidentally destroyed, but usually it's to confirm a finding."

The pillow that Louise had picked up to fluff almost dropped from her fingers. She clutched it against her like a shield. "What are you saying, my dear? What did he find?"

"I don't know how else to tell you this." Alice released a long breath, then went to her sister and drew her down to sit on the sofa. She held Louise's hands in hers. "Tests like the one Conor had are sometimes repeated to make sure that there is not a false-positive. When the pathologist finds something that merits drastic measures for treatment, he sometimes orders a repeat test to be absolutely certain of the diagnosis."

"Drastic measures being . . . ?"

"Procedures that can be life-threatening, like radiation treatment, or life-altering, like an amputation."

All the air went out of her lungs. "Oh!"

"I'm sorry, Louise. Of course I can't say for sure why the pathologist ordered the repeat," Alice rushed to add. "It could be that he wants to confirm a negative result instead. I'll call in the morning and see if I can get more details."

Louise wanted to clutch that hope as hard as she was holding her sister's hands. "But these second tests are usually for positive results, you said."

"Yes, usually they are." Her sister sounded despondent. "I only wanted you to be prepared, Louise, in the event that it is . . . bad news."

All the happiness from the success of the day dwindled away, leaving behind a hollow feeling. "How long will the second test take?"

"Not long. They're given special priority. A day or two at the most." Alice squeezed her hands. "Conor will not go through this alone. God is with him, Louise. So are his parents, and his family and friends. I've volunteered to take some extra shifts so I can be on hand too. The doctors will do their best for him, whatever the results may be."

"Thank you for telling me, dear." Louise gave Alice a careful hug before she rose. "I think I will go to bed now, so that I can be rested for tomorrow."

Yet when Louise had turned out the light in her room and slipped under the covers, sleep seemed as far away as the stars twinkling outside her window. She turned onto her side and stared out at them, feeling small and insignificant, and not at all brave. She wanted to stay home from the hospital the next day. She did not want to face Conor, not after what Alice had told her. How could she offer words of hope, when everything seemed so hopeless?

Conor may be sitting by his window in his hospital room,

looking at these same stars, Louise thought. *Does he feel alone, frightened, hopeless? What will I say to him? What can I do to comfort him?*

"God is with him," Alice said.

Louise had to believe that. There was no other way to get through the days ahead. She recalled what her father had told her countless times. *"When things become too much for your head, you must use your heart. Pray, and in your prayer turn it over to God. Let His will be done."*

Louise prayed. Just before she fell asleep, she felt a soothing warmth spread inside her, as if someone had wrapped a quilt around her chilled soul. It was the warmth of faith, the faith that had never abandoned her. Just as she knew the Lord never had.

God is with Conor, and with me. He will watch over us. He will help us to carry our burdens, and to face our fears. He will hear our prayers.

When Rev. Thompson and Louise arrived at the hospital to visit Conor the next afternoon, Louise was prepared to find the boy depressed and worried about the second biopsy. She would not have been surprised if Conor had begun questioning his faith again.

The sound of laughter coming from Conor's room made Louise hesitate outside the open door. Inside, members of the track team and the poetry club surrounded the hospital bed. Jason Gerber was perched on the end, and from what Louise overheard it was apparent that he was trying his best to embarrass Conor.

"So Byrne takes the outside lane, and as he passes me he says, 'I'm gonna catch Macy,'" Jason said, gesturing to indicate the movement. "Macy's breathing through his mouth, slowing down 'cause he kicked off too early, and I watch Con close the gap. We all know he'll catch him and take first, like always. Then I look down and see a shoelace flapping." The boy grinned. "Byrne was in such a hurry to snag first place that he forgot to knot his laces. Another few yards and they were flapping all over the place."

"That's the only reason Macy won that heat," Conor shot back as the other kids laughed again. "He deliberately stepped on them and tripped me."

"He's the same way when he edits," Wendy said, a big smile lighting up her dark face. "He's in such a hurry to get through the submission stack he forgets how to spell the really hard words like *sunrise* and *forever*."

"Can't run, can't spell, can't dress, either." Hadley shook his head. "Sherrilyn probably does all his homework for him. Sad, really."

"Oh, come on, I'm not *that* bad off." Conor turned his head to look at his sister. "How many times have I asked you to do my homework?"

"This semester?" Sherrilyn asked innocently.

Rev. Thompson exchanged an amused look with Louise. "Here I was, ready for the worst."

"So was I."

By that time a few of the kids had noticed them, and Conor urged them to come in. After introducing the pastor and Louise to those of his friends who had not already met them, he sat back against his pillows, feigning exhaustion. "It was easier when everyone hated me."

"Who says we've stopped?" Jason asked, touching off another round of laughter.

A nurse walking past the room stopped and looked in, a

frown on her pleasant, careworn face. "Kids, keep the noise to a minimum, please."

The group chorused suitably low *sorry*'s.

Wendy glanced at the wall clock. "I've got a ride to catch, Con. See you tomorrow?"

Conor's easy smile wavered for an instant. "You don't have to make the trip, Wendy. I'll be fine."

"Hey, I like hanging out here. I'm hearing all kinds of dirt on you I never knew." She bent over and rubbed her hand over his hair, mussing it as an indulgent aunt might. "Behave."

Wendy's departure seemed to move the rest of the group to leave also, and in a few minutes most of the visitors had departed. Jason Gerber lingered, listening silently as his friends bid Conor good-bye and good luck. Many others besides Wendy, Louise was happy to see, promised to pay a return visit.

"Would you and your friend like a few minutes?" Rev. Thompson asked, sensing as Louise did that the boys wanted to talk.

"No, Pastor Thompson, that's okay," Jason said. He turned to Conor. "I just wanted to apologize for being such a creep. If I'd known you were ..." he looked at Conor's knee, which was encased in a light dressing. "I want you to know that me and the guys, we'll do what we can to get your magazine out there. Whatever it takes."

"You don't have to do that," Conor said, clearly touched.

"Yeah, well, it's the least I can do. You know, for acting like a jerk before."

Conor snorted. "You're a natural jerk, Gerber. I think it's a birth defect."

Rather than taking offense, the insult made Jason grin with delight. "You'd know, Byrne."

The boys shook hands with the self-consciousness of young men who didn't often express affection toward their peers, and Jason nodded to the pastor and Louise before slipping out of the room.

"You are fortunate in your friends, Conor," the pastor said as he sat in a vacated visitor's chair. "They are a great blessing."

"Yeah, they are. Don't tell them that, though, or I'll never hear the end of it." Conor's expression grew somber. "I guess you and Mrs. Smith heard about my test being repeated."

Louise nodded. "We thought we would stop in and see how you were."

"I'm okay. Disappointed, because I was hoping to find out whether I have to . . . stay here." The boy looked down at the sheet that lay crumpled and pushed down at the edge of the hospital bed. "My dad took my mom home earlier than usual this morning. She was pretty wiped out. I'm glad my friends from school stopped by, though. They kept me from thinking about it too much."

"It's a difficult and frightening thing to deal with, Conor," the pastor said, "but you won't have to face it alone."

"I'm not scared so much as I'm angry. I hate it, not because it's happening to me, but because I feel so . . ." He made an uncertain gesture.

"You feel powerless." At Conor's surprised look, she gestured toward the windows. "After my sister told me about your test last night, I could not sleep. I felt powerless, too, until I remembered that I am not."

"I just want it to be over. To know, one way or the other.

It's so hard, waiting and not knowing, and not just on me."
Conor's chin dropped. "I know my mom and Sherrilyn are
worried about me, but my dad looks like he hasn't slept in
days."

"Your father loves you very much, Conor," the pastor
told him.

"He blames himself, for pushing me. For a while I did,
too, but not anymore. The doctor said that it doesn't work
like that, that I could have gotten the tumor anytime. It
didn't come from running track or playing sports." Conor
sighed. "If anyone is to blame, it's me. I should have told
Coach Renda or my parents how much my knee really hurt,
instead of covering it up. Maybe I wouldn't be in such bad
shape if I had."

"Hindsight gives us such amazing clarity," Rev.
Thompson said. "Luckily it also helps us to learn from our
mistakes, if we allow it."

The boy's shoulders hunched. "I know I messed up, big
time."

"Conor, if you can forgive your father," Louise said gently, "you should also be able to forgive yourself."

He gave her a pained look. "That's the hardest part,
isn't it?"

She nodded.

"My dad must feel the same way." Suddenly inspired,
Conor turned to Rev. Thompson. "Pastor, I know my dad's
been seeing you. Could you get him to speak with me one on
one when the time is right for him?"

"I'll speak to your father this evening," Rev. Thompson
said. "I think you both have a great deal to say to each other."

"If he and I could, you know, talk it out, maybe he won't

take it so hard if I have to have the surgery," Conor said. "I want that. For both of us."

"There is no greater gift you could give your father now," Rev. Thompson assured him.

As the pastor and the boy talked, Louise quietly left the room. The fervent hope that had shrunk the night before grew again inside her, but not for the same reason. Whether Conor had cancer or not, he had God's love, and through that love had found a way back to his faith. Now he was reaching out with love, not for his own needs, but out of concern for his father.

God is with him. God is with us. She had never been more certain of anything in her life.

∽

"I have one more stop to make," Rev. Thompson told Louise as they left the hospital. "I would appreciate your company, if you don't mind, and if you have the time for another visit."

"Of course, Kenneth, and I have plenty of time. May I ask whom we are going to visit?"

"I promised Roland Jones I would look in on him," Rev. Thompson said. "He has been in low spirits since Edna broke off their engagement. Since he lives alone, I like to stop by occasionally."

Louise had not seen Roland since the breakup, and there was the matter of what she had said to Edna at the bookshop. What had seemed like a clever, subtle way to push the old couple back together now seemed rather foolish. *I only hope I did not make things worse.*

Roland lived in a modest, sturdy home that he had built himself after moving to Acorn Hill. He had spent his life

working as a bricklayer, and the house displayed his profi-
cient skills in its simplicity. Louise loved Grace Chapel Inn,
and she had been very happy in the home in Philadelphia
where she had lived with Eliot; but seeing the mellow, rosy
brick of Roland's house made her wonder how it felt to live
in a home one had personally constructed, brick by brick,
from the ground up.

An old, silver Chevrolet sedan occupied the carport, and
Rev. Thompson parked behind it before he climbed out and
opened Louise's door. "I think he's home. I can hear the
radio."

The pastor knocked twice at the side door, heard an invitation to enter called out, and went in with Louise. They
found Roland sitting by the radio in the living room, listening to one of his favorite talk shows. He turned off the radio
and smiled at them.

"Good afternoon, Roland. You remember Mrs. Smith."

"Pastor Thompson." Roland fumbled for his cane before
rising. He still had much of the raw-boned strength that had
served him for better than sixty years in the construction
business Louise judged from the firmness of his handshake.
"Didn't expect *you* to come calling, Louise. Let's all sit down
and take a load off. I've just been listening to some politicians
making speeches and fools out of themselves."

"Mrs. Smith and I were visiting over at the hospital," the
pastor said. "We thought we'd stop in to see how you are."

"Well, I'm a mite confused," Roland admitted. "Edna
called me yesterday and babbled on about getting married in
a drive-through. I told her I don't like fast food at a wedding
reception, and she told me someone was going to kill me.
Then she hung up." He glanced at Louise. "She didn't go
and buy that gun she was talking about, did she?"

"I do not think so, Roland."

"Well, there you have it. She was in a real snit." He sat back and sighed. "I love her more than clover honey on hot buttered biscuits, but the woman hardly makes an inch of sense anymore." He frowned. "You don't think she's gone senile, do you?"

Louise shook her head. "No, Roland, although she is . . . easily excitable. She's also very lonely."

Roland's expression darkened. "She doesn't have to be. I've done gone over to her place to re-propose about three or four times now. She keeps threatening to call the sheriff. She might be lonesome, but she doesn't want me to step foot on her property."

Through the front windows, Louise saw another car pulled up behind Rev. Thompson's. It belonged to Edna Grassnickle's grandniece, who got out and helped Edna out of the car.

"Edna is here," she told Roland.

Rather than coming up to the house, Edna walked to the center of the lawn and called out in a querulous voice, "Roland Jones, you left your phone off the hook."

The tips of Roland's big droopy ears turned red as he gave Louise a guilty glance. "I don't deal right well with females in a snit."

Edna wasn't finished. "You come on out of there before I come in after you."

Roland sighed as he eased out of his chair. "You sure she didn't buy that gun?"

Rev. Thompson rose and looked through the windows. "She's not armed. We'll go with you."

Edna's grandniece was holding the old lady's arm, and was instantly apologetic. "I tried to talk her into staying home, but she insisted on coming here. She hardly slept a wink last night."

Edna made a shaky but angry gesture. "How am I supposed to when this fool for love is about to ruin his life?"

"The only love I've ever been a fool for," Roland informed her stiffly, "is you, Edna."

The old lady straightened. "Oh?" she said softly. "What about this flirt you're running away with? What do you call her?"

Roland's silver eyebrows knitted. "What flirt?"

"That girl with the yellow convertible. I saw you kiss her the day I came over to show you our wedding invitations," Edna shot back. A moment later she seemed to collapse against her niece. "Oh, take me home, Martha. My heart's broken, God will do the rest. Just take me home."

"You hold on there, Edna Grassnickle." Roland marched over to her, his gait jerky but surprisingly swift. "You saw me kiss Melissa?"

"I don't want to know her name," Edna cried out.

Martha cringed.

Roland glared. "Well, you need to, because she's my only granddaughter, and she and her husband are moving to Potterston to be closer to me."

"Your granddaughter?" Edna seemed to shrivel for an instant, then threw an accusing glance at her beau. "She can't be. You're a bachelor."

Roland sighed. "Edna, honey, I wasn't always. I was married for a bit when I was a young man. Melissa's grandmother is my ex-wife. She remarried right after our divorce and wanted her new husband to be a father to our baby son. I was still in love with her at the time, but I thought it best not to confuse the boy, so I moved down here."

Louise felt oddly touched. No wonder Roland had never remarried.

The old man went on with his story. "Melissa's grandmother decided not to tell me, and only after she died did her son—our son—Melissa's father, find out the truth from his stepfather. It was then that my son began trying to find me. We met about twenty years ago, when Melissa was still a little 'un. We haven't made a big fuss about it, but I keep in touch."

Edna sighed. "Oh, Roland, I'm sorry."

He looked perplexed. "Why should you be? I've got a son who's a fine man and a pretty granddaughter. Melissa and her husband want to raise a family, so more than likely I'll have some great-grandchildren coming along soon."

"But why didn't you tell me about any of this?" Edna demanded, angry again.

"I thought it might scandalize you to know I'd been divorced, but I've wanted to tell you. I just never found the right occasion."

"Maybe it was for the best." Edna leaned against her grandniece. "Perhaps you should take me home now, Martha."

"Oh, I see now." Roland folded his arms. "You saw me kiss Melissa hello when she came to see me, and decided I was carousing with her behind your back." He smiled and walked toward Edna. "You *do* love me."

"I do not." She tried to dodge him. "I'm a stupid blind old woman who needs to go home now. Get out of my way. Martha."

"Oh, I'm staying out of this," Martha said, clapping her hand to her forehead.

Roland laughed and caught Edna in his arms and gave

her a kiss. Martha covered her mouth with her hands. Rev. Thompson chuckled, and Louise let out a breath she had been holding.

Roland's voice dropped low, but his words were still audible. "I love you, you silly, blind old woman. This is your home now. Yours and mine."

"Are you sure?" Edna asked, as unsure as any young girl was when she stood on the brink of something unknown but wonderful.

Roland looked over the top of Edna's head. "Pastor, can we still have the church, end of June?"

∞

After congratulating the elderly couple, Rev. Thompson suggested that Edna and Roland have a private talk. Martha promised to return for her grandaunt on the way back from shopping, and Rev. Thompson drove Louise home to Grace Chapel Inn.

"Imagine Roland Jones keeping a secret like that all these years," Louise said along the way. "When my aunt hears about this, she will be fit to be tied."

"I'm glad Roland told Edna the truth. He hadn't planned to, you know. He didn't want to shock her."

Louise smiled. "I think he knows now that Edna is made of sterner stuff."

Rev. Thompson bid her farewell at the inn, where Louise found Jane at the front desk filling in for Alice.

"Alice is in Father's study," Jane told her in between answering calls on the inn's busy phone. She flipped her long, dark hair off her shoulder as she stooped to retrieve a pencil from the desk supply drawer. "Sitting in there brooding about Tess."

"Bad news?" She had wanted to share the story of Edna and Roland's reunion.

The phone rang and Jane answered it before she gave Louise a direct look, nodded, and waved toward the study. It was sisterly sign language, a wordless version of "Go and talk to Alice." "When would you like to reserve a room, ma'am?" she asked the caller, and checked the calendar. "Oh yes, we have that week available. How many will be in your party?"

Louise tapped on the door of the study before entering. Alice was sitting in Daniel Howard's favorite chair, curled up like a little girl, reading the Bible. Knowing her sister as she did, Louise suspected that she might be reading something from Galatians. Alice often turned to that book when she was troubled.

Alice looked up. "Did Jane tell you?"

Louise sat across from her. "You have heard some bad news about Tess, I gather."

Alice nodded. "Sylvia called me earlier. Jack O'Hara's office got a call from town. Apparently someone taking a short cut between two buildings ran into Tess. I don't know who the man was, but he told Jack that she clawed him hard enough to draw blood."

"He must have provoked it," Louise said. Certainly, she believed, the little stray would not have attacked unless cornered. She was terrified of people.

"Whether or not he did, Jack is back in town and hunting her. Tess has hurt someone, which makes her dangerous to others." Alice closed the Bible and set it aside. "Someone has to tell Viola. Sylvia offered to go over to the bookshop, but I thought you and I might. You know how stubborn Viola can be."

"I do." Louise could well envision her friend running out

to try to prevent the animal control officer from catching the little calico. "He will deal with her in a humane manner, Alice."

Her sister sighed. "I know he will. He's a nice man and I respect the work that he does."

"We might help by letting Officer O'Hara know about the Tess Watch," Louise advised. "We can ask the merchants to alert him as to her whereabouts the next time she is spotted."

"That would be the right thing to do now." Alice sat straighter. "Sometimes I really, really hate doing the right thing."

Louise bent down to kiss her sister on the top of her head. "God loves you for it, however, Alice. So do I."

Chapter  Sixteen

S ometimes I wish I had a car like this," Alice said wistfully as Louise drove to town. Her own little car was back at the garage, this time for a replacement fuel pump. "Cadillacs are so elegant."

Louise rarely associated people with their vehicles, but she could not imagine Alice driving anything that was not small and gas-efficient. Alice's peripheral vision was not suited to a larger car, either; she often complained of having a difficult time parallel-parking. "Are you thinking of selling your car?"

"No, I like it well enough when it's running. I was just daydreaming a little." She sighed again. "To keep from thinking about Tess, I suppose. I feel so . . . guilty. She's just a little cat. Why couldn't we catch her?"

"We did everything we possibly could for her, Alice," Louise reminded her as she parked. "Do not blame yourself for this."

The door to the bookshop was unlocked, but there was no sign of Viola. Louise paused inside and turned to her sister. "Let me tell her. You watch the door."

Alice's eyes widened. "Do you think she'll try to stop Officer O'Hara?"

Louise hoped not, but the bookseller was so unpredictable and so devoted to her beloved felines that she could not be sure. "I do not think that it will come to that." In a louder voice, she called, "Viola? Are you here?"

"Just a minute."

It was several minutes before Viola emerged from the store's back room. "Louise, what are you doing here?" Her gaze moved to Alice's face, and she paled. "Is it about Conor?"

"No, Viola," Louise said quickly. "I went to see Conor earlier, and he is doing very well." She would explain about the repeat test later. "We do bring some unhappy news, however."

Viola looked perplexed. "Edna didn't buy that BB rifle, I hope."

"No. Edna and Roland have mended things, and the wedding is back on. But that is another story. This is about Tess." Before Viola could say a word, Louise held up one hand. "I know how much you wanted to catch her and care for her, but you cannot save every stray animal, my dear."

"I know that," Viola said.

"It isn't as if we haven't tried, either," Alice said, echoing Louise's earlier reassurance. "If Tess could have been caught, we definitely would have gotten her. Everyone in town tried to help too. Which was really wonderful of them."

Viola frowned. "But we—"

"Viola, this is very hard to say, but Tess has hurt someone," Louise said as gently as she could. "That person called Officer O'Hara and he is out looking for her."

"Oh, that." Comprehension showed on Viola's face. "I know about that, but—"

"She's probably gone and turned feral, Viola," Alice said miserably. "Even if you had been able to catch her and bring her home, she might have attacked your other cats. Don't take it too hard."

"Do not overreact, either," Louise felt she had to say. "Officer O'Hara must do his job."

Viola folded her arms. "Am I going to be able to get a word in here edgewise, or aren't you two done fussing over me yet?"

Louise glanced at Alice, who shrugged. "Of course. Say whatever is on your mind."

Viola gave them each a measuring look, and then broke into a chuckle. "Come into the back room, both of you." She turned and walked away.

"That's what I was afraid of," Alice whispered as they hurried after Viola. "She's in denial."

"I do not think so." Louise was beginning to sense something fishy.

An unexpected figure stepped out of the back room—Officer Jack O'Hara, looking large and fierce. Both sisters were startled, knowing that the man had likely heard every word that they had said to Viola.

"Ladies." His imposing mustache twitched, as if he were fighting a smile. "You'll want to have a look at this."

Louise expected to see chaos, one of Viola's pets wounded from a tussle with the ferocious Tess, or disorder from the stray tearing through Viola's back room. She did not expect to see Viola crouching next to a large box, half-filled with paperback books, one small, scraggly-looking calico cat, and four tiny newborn kittens.

"Oh thank goodness. You found her," Alice murmured, entranced by the sight.

Tess raised her head, inspected Louise and Alice, and then turned her attention back to her little ones, who were frantically squirming for the best position next to their mother's warm belly. After heaving what sounded like a sigh of relief, she began licking the one closest to her head, her pink tongue rasping over the newborn's delicate pelt, cleaning it and helping to improve the tiny creature's circulation at the same time.

"Tess found me, or rather what she wanted for her nest. That goes to show you how smart she is." Viola tapped the side of the box.

Louise read the lettering and chuckled. "Oh dear."

Alice read it as well. "Isn't that the title of the latest military thriller?"

"Yes. I ordered fifteen copies of it." Viola sounded complacent. "Tess shredded them up a bit before she delivered the kittens, and they make a fine nest. Fred and some other folks"—she eyed Alice—"will just have to read something else until I put in a replacement order."

"Too bad she didn't pick Ms. Songer's storeroom." The glint from Jack O'Hara's uniform badge winked as the big man shifted his position. "My wife could do without adding to her fabric stash for a few weeks."

Louise turned to address him directly. "I know you received a call about Tess, Officer O'Hara, but you can see that she is no threat. Please, would you let Viola take care of her?"

"We'll help find homes for all the kittens, once they're weaned," Alice promised.

"I reckon you'll have time now that you're not on the Tess Watch," Jack said with a bit of a smirk.

"Yes, well . . ." Alice gazed helplessly at the new mother

cat. "I suppose we should have told you about that before now."

"No need. I already knew about it. Ms. Reed was the one who called me out in the first place." The animal control officer picked up his clipboard and made a note on it. "You ladies take care now. Good luck, Ms. Reed, and let me know if you need anything." With that, Jack O'Hara departed.

Louise stared at her friend. "*You* called Jack O'Hara and asked him to look for Tess?"

"Of course I did," her friend said. "Jack drives around all day looking for stray animals. Who else would I call?"

"But he would have taken her to the pound," Alice said.

"No, he would not have." Viola looked amused. "I've worked with Jack O'Hara to collect strays countless times over the years. He often gives me a call if he finds one when he's off duty, too, so that I can find a home for it. As long as they're healthy and not dangerous, he has no objection to my taking them in or helping to see that they're adopted."

Feeling a little weak in the knees, Louise found a chair and sat down. "You should have said something, Viola. When we saw Officer O'Hara, we thought the worst."

"I thought you knew." Viola looked at both women. "Just what have you two been up to that you'd be afraid of Jack?"

"It's a long story," Alice said, saving Louise's dignity. "But what about the report Sylvia told me about, that Tess had clawed someone in town? Wouldn't that make her dangerous?"

"It wasn't Tess," Viola said. "Jack told me that there was another stray—a big, black-and-white spotted tomcat—lurking around the Coffee Shop. He's the one who clawed the man—who got what he deserved, if you ask me. June saw him kicking the cat away from his car. When he cornered the poor thing and bent down to grab him, the cat naturally defended himself."

"That was the same cat who chased Tess off that day," Alice said. To Viola, she added, "Part of the long story."

"You'll have to tell it to me someday. In any case, Jack has given me permission to keep Tess. She'll have to see my vet, of course, to be dewormed and have her shots. Once the kittens are old enough, I'll find homes for them." Viola gazed fondly at the calico and her kittens.

"What about that other stray?" Louise asked.

"He was hurt by that man, so Jack was able to catch him fairly easily." Viola reached down and carefully stroked Tess's head. Rather than cringing or trying to run, the calico rubbed against her palm. "He's a tough customer, though. Jack says his behavior is consistent with abuse by a former owner, the same kind of situation that I've feared Tess must have endured."

"Poor thing." Alice looked distressed. "Will Jack put him down?"

"Probably not. He has a real soft spot for abused animals, and he knows a vet in Potterston who rehabilitates them. He called him, and the vet is willing to take in the stray." Viola grimaced. "It's not guaranteed, but at least he has a chance now."

"As does Tess," Louise said, "thanks to you."

"I had very little to do with it in the end," Viola admitted. "I opened up this morning and found she'd come through the cat door sometime during the night and made herself at home. I barely had time to call Jack before the kittens started coming." She gave the calico an exasperated look. "Took her long enough, although I have no idea what made her come here."

"It must have been the smell of the books," Alice teased. "I'll bet Tess loves literature as much as you do."

Louise regarded the box of shredded paperbacks. It was sitting next to another, open carton of expensive collector's editions of Henry James's novels. "Thank the good Lord that she prefers popular fiction."

∞

Louise drove Alice to work an extra shift at the hospital on Saturday afternoon, and decided to stop in to see Conor before she went to the library for the poetry club meeting.

"Just to see if he needs anything," she told her sister. "I brought some magazines, too, in the event he would like something new to read."

Alice gave her a shrewd look. "He's going to be fine, you know. He's a strong kid with a good heart, and everyone is behind him."

Louise nodded. "Let me worry a little anyway. It does my heart good."

When she arrived at Conor's room, however, the boy seemed to be sleeping, and she decided to sit in the visitor's chair and wait for him to wake.

"You didn't have to come today," Conor said as soon as she sat down. His voice sounded drowsy.

"I wanted to bring you something to read, and I was in the neighborhood." Louise looked over as the door opened and Conor's father came into the room. "Here's another visitor for you."

Like Conor, William Byrne was tall and had the same light brown hair, but was much heavier, with a slight paunch in his midsection. He stood very straight, the same way that a soldier at attention would.

Of course he does, Louise thought. She recalled that William Byrne had spent some years in the military before he had to take a medical discharge for—-of all things—a serious knee injury. That might be another reason he had driven his son to compete—because *he* no longer could.

After William had exchanged greetings with Louise, he said to Conor, "Your mother was so tired I let her sleep in, so now she's catching up on her housework. Your sister has that poetry club meeting to attend, but she'll stop by tonight to see you."

"You don't have to come every day, Dad," Conor said.

William Byrne shrugged. "It makes your mother happy."

Louise heard the grief behind the seemingly matter-of-fact response, and hoped that Conor had too.

"I'm glad you came alone this time," Conor went on. "We need to talk about this thing with my leg."

"I should leave you two alone," Louise said, and started for the door.

"No, please, stay, Mrs. Smith," Conor said. "I might need some help with this."

Louise felt uncomfortable but nodded and sat down again.

"There is nothing to talk about, Conor." William paced over to the window and looked out at the parking lot. His hands folded behind his back, his arms and elbows at the precise angle required for military parade rest. "We'll do whatever the doctors say to do."

"I don't mean what they're going to do to my leg, Dad. I mean the cause."

Louise watched William's shoulders stiffen. "If you want an apology, then I am sorry. I only wanted the best for you, and I never meant for you to end up like this."

Conor's hands twisted against the bed linens. "Dad, I don't blame you for what's happened to me."

"You don't have to." A ragged note entered William's voice. "I blame myself, every day. If I hadn't pushed you, harped at you to succeed where I had failed—"

"I pushed myself, and you've never failed."

"I've talked to Rev. Thompson, Conor, and he has urged me to be open with you. I am quite willing to admit that I failed." William's voice turned flinty again. "I should have respected what you wanted to do with your time instead of forcing you to relive my youth. There is no excuse for it. I simply couldn't accept that my son would prefer poetry over sports."

"And now?" Conor asked.

William turned to face his son. "All this time you have been growing up, I would have given my right arm to trade places with you. To be able to run and jump and compete without pain from my knee. Now I would give my leg to trade places so that I could endure this situation for you."

Conor stared at his father thoughtfully. "Can I have the one with the good knee?"

A spasm of pain crossed William's expression. "Don't joke about this, son. I'm the one who put you here. I know you'll never forgive me for it, but I am sorry. More than you can know."

"You didn't put me here." Awkwardly Conor climbed off the bed. He was as tall as his father, Louise saw, and just as proud. "It just happened. I'll get through it, but I need you now, Dad. I need to lean on you."

"Do you want to?" The idea seemed to stagger William Byrne.

"Nobody understands what I'm going through better

than you do." Conor balanced on one leg and spread his arms. "Nobody is as strong as you are, and I'm pretty sure besides Mom and Sherrilyn, that no one loves me as much."

"Conor." William pulled his son into his arms and held him close.

Louise used a hanky to blot tears from her eyes.

Conor was rubbing his father's shoulder. "We'll get through it, Dad. You and me, together. Everything's going to be okay."

Since they had completely lost track of her presence, Louise tiptoed out of the room, and left word for Alice to call her at the nurses' station.

"Need a tissue?" one of the nurses working at the ward station asked in a sympathetic voice.

"No, my dear." Louise smiled at her with relief and joy dancing inside her. "Everything is going to be okay."

∽

Jason Gerber had not been exaggerating when he made the promise to help as much as possible with the production and publication of the poetry club's magazine. That Saturday he was the first student to show up at the library for the meeting. With him he carried a number of books, which Louise was amused to see were mostly mentor and study guides on how to read and interpret poetry, as well as two weighty biographies on Wordsworth and Keats.

"Holy cow!" Jason sat the books down with a small thump. "No wonder Con is in such excellent shape. Lugging these around gives you a better workout than bench pressing free weights."

"Why do you think I joined?" Hadley said as he came in, similarly laden but with proof copies of the magazine.

Jason gave him a curious glance. "Why *did* you join this club, Gustafson? I don't have a poetic bone in my bod, but I don't think there's one in your entire family."

"For Sherrilyn," Hadley mumbled.

Jason frowned. "What?"

"For Con's sister, okay?" The boy jerked his head around to check the door and then lowered his voice to an angry murmur. "She was writing a poem in homeroom, and the teacher caught her and made her read it out loud. The other kids laughed at her, but it was really a good poem. She writes about growing up and making the right choices. So I thought, I'd join the club, you know, and help her get stuff like that printed."

Jason sat back in his chair with an expression of immense satisfaction. "You've got a crush on Sherrilyn Byrne."

"I do not." Hadley turned an amazing shade of pink.

Jason snickered. "Wait 'til Con hears this. Hadley Gustafson, in love with his sister. Man oh man."

"Will you shut *up*." Hadley gave the door another horrified look before glowering at Jason. "If you say one word to her or Con, Gerber, I swear I will beat you into the ground."

"Oh yeah?" Jason seemed tickled rather than threatened by the prospect.

"Until your mother has to run the mower over your head just to get your ears clean," Hadley promised.

Louise cleared her throat. "Boys."

"Don't worry, Mrs. Smith, Hadley's not going to do anything." Jason produced a devilish grin. "Except be my personal slave for the rest of high school, maybe."

"If you live that long," Hadley growled.

Now used to the casual insults and threats teenagers exchanged on a regular basis, Louise decided not to comment.

Both boys quieted down by the time the other members of the club arrived, and Hadley settled for shooting dire looks at Jason, who returned the favor with a few smirks.

"What is up with Jason and Hadley today?" Viola asked as she noticed the mute volley between the two boys.

Before Louise could answer, three members of the track team and Ms. Renda came in. The quartet were dressed in training uniforms and looked somewhat flushed from their reinstated practice session.

"I hope we're not late this time," Ms. Renda said, giving Viola a smile.

"I was just about to begin." Viola gave the three athletes a puzzled glance. "Did you need to talk to Jason and your students first? We can wait."

"No, John, Carl and Derek are here to join in." Ms. Renda waved the boys to some empty seats. "They all have excellent voices, so I asked them if they'd help with the poetry reading."

"We just have to read them," one boy said, "not write them, right?" When the coach nodded, he blew out a nervous breath. "I'm in."

"Some of the other guys want to help too," Jason added. "They aren't into reading poetry, but they'll spread the word, get pledges from parents and sell ad space. Whatever you need done."

"You track guys want to help us?" Wendy seemed shocked.

"Anything you need to get this thing to print," Jason assured her. "We're a part of this now too."

"I also have a contribution for the printer's fees," Ms. Renda said, and handed an envelope over to Sherrilyn, who acted as the club's treasurer.

Conor's sister opened the envelope and gasped. "There's almost a hundred dollars in here."

"That comes from the teachers at Franklin with their best wishes for a successful debut issue," Ms. Renda told her.

"You're not going to use it for the track team's shoes or hurdles or whatever?" Rob asked, clearly still suspicious of the coach.

"Nah, we don't need it. But if you don't want it for the magazine"—Jason clapped Rob on the shoulder——"we'll use it to get you a nose job, Dierdorf."

"Before or after your brain surgery, Gerber?" Rob retorted.

The word *surgery* echoed around the room, and smiles disappeared quickly.

Almost at once Rob seemed to realize his gaffe and gave Sherrilyn a penitent look. "Geez, Sher, I didn't mean . . . I was just . . ."

Everyone tried not to stare at Conor's sister.

"You might need it for that foot-ectomy," Sherrilyn said in a very serious way.

"A foot-ectomy?" Rob blinked, unsure.

"You know." She tapped her lips with one finger. "That procedure where they open this up so they can remove your foot."

Embarrassment turned to relief, and Rob grinned. "Would a hundred bucks cover two feet?"

∞

A week later, Ms. Renda and Viola Reed met Louise and Jane at Grace Chapel. One third of the little church's pews were already filled with parents who had come for the Franklin High School Poetry Club's first poetry reading.

Eleanor Renda wore an unusual dress with a delicately feminine, floral pattern. She had also curled her wavy hair so that it made a bubbly frame around her face, softening her features.

"I thought this was better than my sweats," was the coach's explanation when Louise complimented her. She cast a wry glance at herself. "There's not much opportunity to put on a dress when you spend half your life on a track. It feels nice."

"I feel like an expectant mother," Viola confessed as she paced back and forth in the hallway outside the chapel. She wore an evening dress of navy blue with a jacket of matching lace. The snowy white silk scarf around her neck was, she said, in honor of Franklin's school colors.

Ms. Renda busied herself with inspecting the students who, also dressed in their best clothes, were going over for a final time the poems they were to read. She straightened ties, adjusted sleeves and sent one member of the track team to the restroom to wash the shiny glaze of perspiration from his forehead.

"He asked me if he could run a couple of laps around the church before we came in," she confided to Louise.

"Does he need to practice?" The regional championships were to be held on the following day.

Ms. Renda grinned. "Nope. He's just scared to death, as I am."

Louise noticed that Jason Gerber, who was acting as master of ceremonies, grew quiet as he watched the audience grow.

"You okay, Jase?" Wendy asked as she joined him.

"Yeah." He looked over at Sherrilyn, who was patiently listening to Hadley rehearse his reading, and lowered his voice. "I just wish Con could be here. He'd have loved this better than running at the state finals."

Louise felt very proud of the teenagers. Thanks to their cooperative fund-raising efforts, enough parent and advertising pledges had been received to cover the last payment to the printer. The first run of *Promises* magazine was to be delivered on schedule.

The poetry club's membership had also more than tripled over the last week, thanks largely to the very public endorsement provided by Conor's former teammates on the track team, who had worked as hard as the club members to raise the needed pledges. Rob had told her that suddenly poetry was "the thing" at Franklin High, and that if the club grew any bigger, *two* moderators might be needed during the next school year.

"How are Tess and the kittens?" she asked Viola as the last of the parents arrived and were taking their seats.

"The little ones have opened their eyes," her friend told her, "and Tess has finally made peace with Gatsby. He patrols the downstairs, she patrols the upstairs."

After receiving a clean bill of health for Tess from the vet, Viola had brought the little calico home, although not without some adjustments to be made on both sides. Still trusting no one but Viola, Tess had been very defensive of her kittens. Gatsby, the most aggressive and possessive of Viola's cats, had not immediately welcomed the new arrivals. After a near-brawl between the two felines, Viola decided to keep Tess and her kittens in an upstairs room until the little ones were better able to look after themselves. Separating the two cats and giving them their own territory had been just the thing, and now both were much happier.

"I am glad it is working out," Louise told her. There was

only one shadow over the evening, Conor's absence, but she refused to feel depressed about it.

"Mrs. Smith, there's a lady in the church looking for you," one of the kids told her, and Louise excused herself to go out to see who needed her.

"Louise." Alice waved from the back of the church to catch her attention. Earlier she had gone over to the hospital to check on Conor.

Using one of the side aisles, Louise went to the back of the church as quickly as she could. "Do you have some news?"

"Yes, that's why I came straight here. Conor made it through the surgery without any complications." Alice hugged her. "It was benign. He's going to be fine, Louise."

.Louise closed her eyes. *Thank You, dear Lord, for hearing my prayers.*

Jane appeared. "Did you hear? Alice, did you tell her?"

"Yes, she did. Oh, we have to tell Sherrilyn. She has been carrying a cell phone with her all night, waiting for the call from her parents . . ." Tears had welled up in Louise's eyes, making it difficult for her to see. "I should make some kind of announcement. Everyone will want to know. I cannot see straight." She dabbed at her eyes.

"Let me do it, sweetheart," Jane said, and left the shaken Louise with Alice. She walked to the front of the church, took the microphone from the stand provided for the reading and turned it on. "May I have your attention for a moment, please? Would the poetry club and the athletes come out here too?"

Louise and Alice found seats together, and Louise leaned toward her sister. "I thought that the surgery was supposed to take much longer."

"The surgeon had better luck removing it than he had

thought," Alice told her. "Conor's being in excellent physical shape also helped a great deal. We should mention that to Ms. Renda."

By now everyone had directed attention to the slim, dark-haired Jane, who was surrounded by the poetry club and what appeared to be the entire track team.

"You all probably knew that Conor Byrne was having surgery today," Jane said, "and I am very happy to announce that his operation was a complete success."

Cheers broke out as well as applause. Sherrilyn sagged against Hadley, who held her tenderly. Jason Gerber put two fingers in his mouth and whistled.

Jane spoke over the noise. "According to my sister Alice, who has been at the hospital all day, Conor's tumor was successfully removed by his surgeon. The test results for the tumor showed that it was benign, and he'll be coming home as soon as he recovers. The prognosis is that he'll be walking again in a few weeks."

More cheers and shouts of triumph resounded through the church.

Jane held up her hand, and everyone slowly quieted. "I know not all of you are members of this church, but I'd still like to ask everyone to share now in a short prayer." She put an arm around Sherrilyn, who had come to hug her, and closed her eyes. "Heavenly Father, You give us blessings each and every day, but today You have given us a very special one. We thank You for bringing our friend, Conor Byrne, through his surgery without complications. We rejoice in Your healing love, for it takes away the pain of the world. Please accept our humble gratitude and bless all the ones we love with the gifts of health, happiness and faith. Amen."

∽

The news of Conor's successful surgery seemed to bestow its own special blessing on the evening. It proceeded to be one of the more memorable events of the year in Acorn Hill, beginning with readings of poems to be printed in the club's magazine.

Sherrilyn stepped up to the microphone to read "Competition," the poem Wendy had liked so much. But before she read, she made an announcement of her own. "Conor and someone else are probably not going to thank me for giving away a secret tonight," she warned, "but what else are bratty little sisters supposed to do?" After the subsequent laughter died away, she added, "This poem is titled 'Competition,' and although it was handed in anonymously, I know for a fact that it was written by my brother's good friend, Jason Gerber."

Jason, who was standing to one side, blushed as everyone gaped at him. He kept his head up, however, and didn't blush again until after Sherrilyn finished reading his poem and the audience applauded with genuine enthusiasm.

The readings continued. Some of the track team members surprised their own parents with their individual readings, and Louise counted a number of astonished but proud faces among the audience. After tonight, no one at Franklin would ever say that sports were more important than poetry. Louise hoped some of the parents might even encourage their athletic children to read more verse.

In addition to serving as master of ceremonies, Jason Gerber was the final student to read. He stepped up to the microphone and took a folded piece of notebook paper from his pocket.

"I was supposed to read something by Wordsworth," he warned the audience, "but I thought I might read something

written by a member of the poetry club. It may not be in
Wordsworth's league, but I know it comes from the heart."
He unfolded the paper, and after a moment, began to read.

"I never had a brother,
My parents stopped with me,
I like my older sister
Even when she yells at me.
I never wrote a poem before
And man, it's really tough.
To think up all these rhyming words
Is really kinda rough.
I never told you just how much
Of a friend you've been to me;
I've said a lot of stupid stuff
I'm not too smart, you see.
I never knew you were hurting,
I never had a clue,
I only hated arguing
And didn't think of you.
I never had a friend
Who might be fighting cancer;
It scares me to my wit's end
But I'm looking for an answer.
I never prayed for anyone
To keep them in one piece,
But God's supposed to listen
When you get down on your knees.
This poem could be lots better
And I'll try again sometime;
I never had a brother
But I wish that you were mine."

238 * Rebecca Kelly

The applause was just as enthusiastic as it had been for Jason's poem. Maybe more so, Louise thought as she clapped, because the awkward poem sounded exactly like what it was—a labor of love.

Sherrilyn looked at the faces of her friends, and then held out her hand to Hadley. With a little tug, she brought him up with her to the microphone.

Hadley looked out at the audience, gulped, and then sighed. His expression was that of a condemned man, but one willing to see it through to the end. "Okay, I wrote it. Thank you very much."

The applause only grew louder. Hadley looked pleasantly dazed, but never more so than when a delighted Sherrilyn hugged him and kissed his cheek.

Epilogue

F ree blackberry pie a la mode with any meal order?'"
Louise read from the neatly hand-lettered placard on the
table after she and Alice had each enjoyed a BLT.

"Yes, ma'am," Hope Collins, holding a pencil poised
above her order pad, said. "It's a lunch special that June's
running this week, to honor our championship team."

Ms. Renda and the Franklin High School track team had
gone to the regional championships and brought home the
coveted first-place trophy. This not only had them written up
in nearly every paper in eastern Pennsylvania—Franklin had
been an underdog—but it also guaranteed them a position in
the state finals. Merchants in Acorn Hill, Potterston and
Riverton were proudly celebrating the accomplishment by
displaying the school's colors in every possible way.

Trust June to serve *the school colors.* "Blackberry pie is
actually rather purplish, you know," Louise said, handing
Hope her menu card.

"I know, but we ran out of blueberry," Hope said in a
stage whisper. "Besides, almost everyone likes blackberry
better."

Alice smiled. "Why don't we have a slice of pie, Louise?"

Jane had yet to arrive, and there was still time to indulge themselves before going over to the Nine Lives Bookstore, so Louise nodded. "Alice will have the blackberry pie special, and I will have an order of apple. Please add a slice of cheddar cheese to mine, Hope."

"Got it. It'll be just a minute, ladies." Hope finished scribbling down the order and went to the counter.

"You never ate cheese on your apple pie when we were girls," Alice said.

"I never had to worry about my calcium intake when we were girls," Louise informed her. "Besides, Eliot always liked his apple pie with cheese. It reminds me of him." She looked up as the door to the restaurant opened. "Here comes Jane."

Jane spotted them and hurried over. Both of her arms were laden with small plastic grocery bags. "You'll never guess what the manager over at the General Store has brought in now."

Alice froze.

After eating authentic but somewhat experimental Chinese recipes, not all of which Jane's sisters had found to be completely agreeable to their tender palates, Louise was almost afraid to guess.

"Would this be a cuisine originating from within the continental United States?" Louise asked.

"Sure." Jane peered in the bags and recited a quick inventory. "Chilies, refried beans, avocado, *posole*, blue corn and piñon nuts."

"Posole," Louise repeated, trying out the word. She had never heard it before in her life. It sounded a bit like possum. *Dear Lord, please, do not let it be any manner or variety of possum.*

"Uh-huh." Jane rummaged through her purchases.

"Piñon nuts." *What is a piñon? Is it a palm tree? A pine tree?* As far as she knew, only squirrels coveted the nuts produced by pine trees. "In what part of the United States do these ingredients originate?" Louise asked.

"The Southwest. He has also stocked some great little, pre-made, white-flour tortillas. They're about the size of a teacup saucer." Jane tucked the bags to one side of the booth and looked up to find her sisters staring at her. "What, you don't like Tex-Mex?"

Alice rested her face against her hands and made a sound vaguely like restrained sobbing.

"Dearest," Louise said, "We love you. We love your cooking."

"I know." Jane smiled proudly. "I'm a chef. You're supposed to."

"Of course. But, dearest, if you do not feed us something with at least two recognizable ingredients in each recipe, I will . . ." She tried to think of an appropriate threat.

Jane sat back. "You'll what?"

"Why, I will have to repay your kindness and make my famous corn chowder." Louise took a sip from her coffee cup. "And stand over it the entire time that it is cooking, just to be sure no extra herbs or spices *accidentally* fall into it."

Jane made a sound like a choked-back sob. "You wouldn't."

"I have had to eat bok choy and purple cabbage for four nights sitting," Louise countered, giving her sister a steely look. "There is *much* I would do at this juncture. Such as have *Alice* prepare my corn chowder."

Alice was acknowledged—even by herself—to be a less-than-gifted cook.

"I haven't had a turn in the kitchen for a while," Alice added for good measure. "Not since I made those pancakes. You remember. You ate all but the mostly black ones."

"Oh, all right." Jane leaned forward on her elbows, ready to bargain. "Tex-Mex three nights this week, good old Pennsylvania home cooking the other four."

Louise shook her head. "One night of Tex-Mex, and you will restrain yourself while using the chilies."

"Two nights, and you have to try the *posoles. Really* try them, not just one nibble."

"Done." Louise thought better of it the moment the word left her lips, but compromise among the Howard sisters was what kept Grace Chapel Inn running smoothly. "What are *posoles?* That is not Spanish for sheep's brains, is it?"

"No, it's like hominy. Sheep's brains are used to grease the skillet when you make *piki* bread, but that's Hopi Indian cuisine."

Alice dropped her hands, seemingly outraged. "Absolutely no *piki* bread."

"Okay, okay." Jane turned to Hope, who had been listening to the entire exchange as if mesmerized. "May I have a coffee, please?"

"Coming right up." Hope raced into the kitchen, where the Howards heard her ask, "June, want to know what the Hopi Indians use to grease their skillets?"

"Why?" June's robust voice carried even better than her waitress's. "Has one applied to be our short order cook?"

∞

After stowing Jane's exotic purchases in the trunk of Louise's car, the three Howard sisters walked over to Viola Reed's bookstore. Swags of ribbons in Franklin's school colors decorated the storefront, and all of Viola's cats had blue-and-white striped bows tied to their collars.

All except Ahab, who had untied his and was dragging it like a snapped leash as he stalked back and forth in the window. Bookcases had been moved temporarily to the sides of the store, and the cleared area was filled with teenagers and teachers.

"It looks as if everyone is here," Louise said as they approached the beveled glass door. On it was posted a sign that read "CLOSED SAT. FOR PRVT. PARTY."

Viola and Eleanor were in the center of the crowd, talking with five of the six original members of the poetry club. Jason Gerber and all the other members of the track team were also present and wearing the regional-championship T-shirts a local merchant had made up as a gift for their performance. Tall stacks of a long, blue-and-white, glossy magazine sat on every available flat surface, and nearly everyone had a copy of the same magazine in his hands.

"Oh, it's here," Jane squealed, and snitched a copy from the nearest pile. "Wow! Look at the cover design."

Hadley Gustafson and Rob had worked together with a student photographer. The latter had taken hundreds of candid shots of youngsters during different classes and activities at Franklin during the school year, and the three students selected the best of them and made a collage for the magazine's cover. The faces of those pictured showed a range of young emotions, from serious to comical.

Louise noted that in the center of the collage was a photo of Conor Byrne, not playing a sport or running, as he had been photographed doing a hundred times before, but sitting in the school library and reading a book.

"Didn't it come out great?" Wendy asked after she had

made her way through the crowd to greet the Howards. "Had and Rob did such a great job."

Louise looked over at Hadley, who was standing beside Sherrilyn. The teenagers were holding hands and talking to Jason and Millicent, who also had their hands entwined. *There is nothing like young love*, she thought, *and no way to predict where it will spring*. After the poetry reading at Grace Chapel, no one had been surprised when Hadley and Sherrilyn had started dating. That Jason and Millicent did the same, however, had completely shocked their respective friends.

Viola said something to Jason, who gave one of his infamous two-fingered whistles to quiet the room. Rather than becoming upset, she patted his shoulder fondly before she addressed the crowd.

"Thank you all for coming out to celebrate the first issue of *Promises* magazine with us. Ms. Renda, the poetry club moderator, has a few words she'd like to say before we bring out the refreshments and start selling copies."

Since the track team had won the regional championships, Eleanor Renda had undergone a subtle transformation. Instead of her usual coach's uniform, she had begun wearing more feminine dresses and skirt sets. Her hair, now expertly permed, bounced with bright, sun-streaked curls.

"We'd like to thank Ms. Reed for graciously hosting this party," Ms. Renda said, "but we're going to put her to work first. We're going to make her read." She produced a magazine, and many of the kids cheered.

"That will be no hardship," the bookseller assured them. "I will read to you all afternoon, as long as I pick the books."

After the laughter had died down, Ms. Renda continued. "Viola, the Franklin High School Poetry Club would like to present you with this, the very first copy of the magazine." She placed the copy into the bookseller's hands. "Would you be so kind as to read the third page out loud."

Viola put on her bifocals and opened the magazine. "Let me see here, this is the dedication, and what a nice job you did with this layout, Wendy. The page looks as if it came from an old, illuminated manuscript." She tilted her head to look through the bottom half of her glasses and began to read. "'This magazine is dedicated to our guiding light, who helped us bring it to life, who made promises to us and kept them, and who inspired us with her professionalism, her passion, and her own love of poetry." Viola paused and blinked rapidly. "We thank Ms. Viola Reed. With love, the Franklin High School Poetry Club."

Louise smiled at her friend. It was the perfect dedication.

Viola looked around at the students smiling at her. "I suppose this sort of emotional blackmail is to insure that I'll maintain contact with the poetry club."

"Actually, Viola, we would like to ask you to do just that," Ms. Renda said. "I'll be on the road with the track team quite frequently next year, and I can't think of anyone I'd rather call upon for help while I'm out of town than you."

The bookseller looked at the faces of the students, who were all smiling at her.

"I'd make you read twice as much poetry as you did this year," Viola warned gruffly. "Maybe three times."

"Excellent," Hadley said. "I'll get extra credit for it from my World Lit teacher."

"Hadley *wanting* to read poetry." Rob clapped a hand to his chest. "I think that jolt might have stopped my heart."

"Do you want to smack him, Sherrilyn, or should I?" Wendy asked casually.

Sherrilyn grinned at Rob. "Make him size all the fonts this year. That only takes about a week, give or take a few days."

Rob gave her a mock-wounded look. "Don't be so sweet, Sher."

She tucked her arm through Hadley's, more confident now than Louise had ever seen her before. "Then don't make fun of my boyfriend, Rob."

"I would like to add something," Viola said, and the voices around her fell silent. "The greatest joy in my life has always been reading. When you open your mind to literature, to poetry, you begin a marvelous journey that never really ends, to places that are a bit off the beaten track. In the words of Robert Frost:

"The woods are lovely, dark and deep.
But I have promises to keep,
And miles to go before I sleep."

Viola looked around the room. "In that manner, I've traveled all over the world, through time and back again. I've treasured some books so much that I have read them over and over. All those pages, all those wonderful stories, and yet now I can honestly say that nothing has ever meant as much to me as this. This is truly a promise kept." She looked down at the magazine in her hands, and then at the students who had worked so hard on it. "Thank you so much."

The students applauded, and those nearest to Viola shook her hand or hugged her.

The door to the shop opened, and a familiar voice called out, "Hey, is there room for one more at this party?"

Everyone turned and began to cheer as Conor Byrne came in balanced between two crutches, one knee and lower leg in a soft cast.

As Louise watched Conor making slow but steady progress over to greet Viola and Eleanor Renda, she took her sisters by the hands.

"Now there walks a prayer that God truly answered," she murmured, "and is there anything more beautiful than that?"

Jane slipped an arm around her waist. "*Piki* bread is really pretty," she said with a note of mischief in her voice. "It comes out yellow, red and blue, depending on what type of corn you use, and how many sheep's—ow, Alice, that was my *foot*!"

"Nothing more beautiful, Louise," Alice said firmly. "Nothing at all."

Snickerdoodles

YIELD FIVE DOZEN

1 cup butter (softened)
1½ cups sugar
2 eggs
2¾ cups all-purpose flour
1½ teaspoon cream of tartar
1 teaspoon baking soda
¼ teaspoon salt

Topping:
3 teaspoons sugar
1 teaspoon cinnamon

Beat together butter and sugar until creamy. Beat in eggs. In another bowl, mix together flour, cream of tartar, baking soda and salt. Add dry mixture to creamed mixture. Mix well. Shape into one-inch balls. Chill for one hour. Meanwhile mix together topping ingredients and grease baking sheets.

Preheat oven to 350 degrees. Coat chilled balls well with topping. Place on baking sheets two inches apart. Bake until golden brown (about ten minutes). Cool on wire racks.

About the Author

Rebecca Kelly wrote her first book at age thirteen and hasn't stopped writing since. When she's not writing or being a mom, Rebecca volunteers weekly at an animal shelter, creates comfort quilts that are distributed to children hospitalized for cancer treatment and teaches creative writing to local public school students. Rebecca was recently honored by the United States Air Force for her efforts over the last six years in sending books and other reading materials every month to American soldiers serving in Iraq.

A Note from the Editors

We hope you enjoy Tales from Grace Chapel Inn, created by the Books and Inspirational Media Division of Guideposts, a nonprofit organization that touches millions of lives every day through products and services that inspire, encourage, help you grow in your faith, and celebrate God's love in every aspect of your daily life.

Thank you for making a difference with your purchase of this book, which helps fund our many outreach programs to military personnel, prisons, hospitals, nursing homes, and educational institutions. To learn more, visit GuidepostsFoundation.org.

We also maintain many useful and uplifting online resources. Visit Guideposts.org to read true stories of hope and inspiration, access OurPrayer network, sign up for free newsletters, download free e-books, join our Facebook community, and follow our stimulating blogs.

To learn about other Guideposts publications, including the best-selling devotional *Daily Guideposts*, go to ShopGuideposts.org, call (800) 932-2145, or write to Guideposts, PO Box 5815, Harlan, Iowa 51593.